SWIMMING MAN
BURNING

SWIMMING
MAN
BURNING

*A Rip-roaring Novel of
the American West*

Terrence Kilpatrick

DOUBLEDAY & COMPANY, INC.
GARDEN CITY, NEW YORK
1977

ISBN: 0-385-12610-7
Library of Congress Catalog Card Number: 76-45264

For: MARILYN
TERESA
KELLY
AND
CONNIE

And for my mother, who as a girl and young
woman on the plains of central Oregon was forever afraid of the Indian—may this assuage her
fear.

And for my father, who was never much afraid
of anything.

Prologue

Above, the father had separated, the sun arching vast across the mesa to the east, hot and golden, tasting of mule and smelling green, the air grainy with crushed sage and burnt wheat, the Thunder People to the west striking flint against the building black mounds, buffalo heads, broken-horned and shagged, beards threading down to the land, webbing the sky with rain, a cayuse wind running the rim, picking at the heads of the bullgrass.

To the north the Great White One waited, Grandfather moiling where He clashed with the blue, mottled, the gods undecided. Was it to Him Gray Owl looked; for Him Gray Owl watched; to Him Gray Owl prayed, searching for the sign?

Over the southern rim glinted Manuel's totem, the grizzly and spotted eagle flashing defiance to the lords of sun and death, from the shaft whang-leather laces, a scalp and eagle feathers fluttering, Light Hands crown scoring the slate sky, beseeching the earth mother and the evening star, the two-leggeds and four-leggeds and all the winged of the earth, the braves never taking their eyes off Gray Owl.

This the final *find-out*.

And when Gray Owl finished his prayer and the totem scored down the vault of the bowl into the valley, they would charge.

BOOK ONE

The Barricade

I

....

A Horse Sneezed into the Sun

We were nine, six skinners, a swamper, me and the Frenchman gunners, with three wagons of hides, a summer's kill, when they caught us. Kiowas. Just south of the Brazos. Twenty of them, bucks, so the last mile and a half we had to run for it across open desert, the mules drawn to a lather, foaming and farting and stumbling in the traces, east to Bloody Walls, cliffs of red clay and rock, backed up in a gorge against the central shelf where at the base of a scoop of tailings we dug in.

Wagons upended in a half circle, butts out, hides over the frames so they couldn't fire us, we waited. Mules tethered in the back. The overhang too shallow for cover, so the first thing they did was circle and bunch. Arrows pointing straight up. Looping them in behind like hail so quick I got the skinners and the Frenchman got his dolly boy, the swamper, a thirteen-year-old kid you couldn't tell nothing to, all under the wagons.

By the second release they had the range; by the third they had us scraping belly, and by the fifth arrows came plummeting down out of the sky like hawks, killing all the mules and pinning the swamper, who I'd warned and who the Frenchman had twice pulled back under the wagons, but that boy, all beans and back-jaw and stiff-spined as a blue mule, had got to have himself a look-see and snailed out in the open while no one was paying him any mind to get himself doweled to the wagon tongue through the right cheek of his rump—a real oily one that boy, blaspheming without using the same word twice since he'd been hit. Everyone starting now to talk self-kill and saving up the last round for one another. Pairing off. Which sure don't make for no fighting force, and I lined into them:

We had water for two days and grub for six. We had clean shooting, them coming straight on through loose sand, the sun across us, the cliff at our backs and more powder and shot than they had braves, who, 'spite all their warrior societies and deeming it a great honor to die young, yelling at one another it was a fine day to greet the Great Spirit, I never found no more eager to cut picket from this globe than the next man, and the next man talks pairing off, I said, I'd oblige him personal.

Two skinners I stuck on the flanks, four abreast full on. Me and the Frenchman, the best guns, at the center, and we hunkered down to wait.

"Wot you theenk?" said the Frenchman after a while, a fine marksman and shrewd hunter, but hanging back now, making coffee, whether because of them out there or the young swamper I couldn't tell, the way his eyes kept cutting from one to the other.

From up around the Great Lakes, the Frenchman hadn't my plains-people sabe and it made him skittish and I looked away from his fear.

They wouldn't come today, I knew. And tonight they'd celebrate. Preparing—feasting and speeching and drumming and dancing and maybe waiting for reinforcements or a vision. Which is why you never know with a savage, unable ever to do a thing just for the thing. Like the Frenchman making coffee. To the Frenchman, just coffee. But to a savage that pot it's boiling in, because it's round, without beginning or end, like life, is wacan, *holy*; the water, from a raincloud, is mahpiya, *the sky*; the fire wi, *the sun*, His living breath which goes back to mahpiya completing the sacred circle. A holy act. Or maybe it's like they say, the white man has but one eye, he sees so little. An Indian's life one big parfleche of omens and signs. The spirits and magic all around him . . . in the air, in rocks, trees, brush, clouds, animals, water. And how he reckons those signs, that's how he'll do—so I remembered Major Forsythe socked in with forty men of the Fifth by the Cheyenne on Beecher's Island, in the middle of the Arickaree River. The major wounded, his lieutenant dying, men dropping all around him from arrows and thirst, when come the fourth day and the Fifth finished, a leaf fell wrong or a horse sneezed into the sun and the Cheyenne were gone.

So they might come at dawn or the next day or the day after, or if someone had a bad dream—never.

Just before dark we rolled the dead mules, already starting to bloat and nose high, out in front of the wagons, making a kind of first line of defense.

The Frenchman I put in charge of the grub. The water pouches and canteens I took to myself. One sip now, another tomorrow noon. The young swamper, on his belly, was starting to moan and beg for drink.

The Frenchman pulled down the boy's pants, the swamper's whole right cheek a dirty scarlet and beginning to belly. Tears started in the Frenchman's eyes.

"Geeve heem a dreenk," the Frenchman said.

"No," I said and the Frenchman began to get mean, him and the boy special together the whole hunt, pitching camp away from us nights, bedding in the same roost. Ring-tailing, we all knew. Which more than a few wintered in lone cabins or caught up in the high solitaries have did, but the Frenchman's dolly boy was out of it now. He couldn't fight, and if the time came, he couldn't run. The skinners moving in behind me, so the Frenchman backed off, cradling the boy's head in his lap, crooning to him.

To the west the mesa lowered black and sullen as a bruised beast where the night began to gnaw at its flanks, lightning skittering crazy as ghost dancers along the horizon. Always a sign. The Indian doesn't like to fight in the rain. It wets the bowstring, tightens the gut, throws him off bead; mucks up the footing for the horses, but, above all, violates the thunderbills, sacred bird of thunder and lightning. The mesa as empty as morning and as still.

"They've gone," a voice—it sounded like the pock-faced skinner's—said from behind. (From outside Llano, the pock-faced skinner had just joined on.)

"The fort's due south of that peak," I said without looking around. "You wanta try fer it?"

Pock Face swore.

Then I heard it, low, a hum, like a swarm of locusts threshing to settle. The drums starting to pick in behind, and then the surge of sound shimmering down the walls of the night, the voices beginning to swell. Chanting. Two thousand of them. Mingling with the Thunder People to the west, the squaw's high tremolo over, so I knew: that war party, they hadn't been chasing us; they'd been *herding* us. *Into the center of a Kiowa camp.*

::

2

Belly, Balls and Bowels

They didn't come at dawn or the next day or the day after. Instead, each afternoon they'd string out along the top of the opposite ridge, not howling or gesturing or riding up and down, but just sitting. Waiting. Coffin quiet and waiting.

The sun boiled across the mesa in wormy swells, a white sore in a sand-yellow sky, warping the land, blowing up the mules so we had to slit them craw to crotch to see over their bellies. Wrapping our faces. The stench drawing every hungry thing on the desert. Vultures leaning lazy on the wind and squatting on the sand. Swarms of flies during the day driving us crazy. At night coyotes and wild dogs fighting. Slobbering and crunching. Eating the mules and each other. Keeping us awake till dawn of the second day we looked like a meat rack and smelled like a slaughter shed.

By the afternoon of the third day our water was gone, along with the Thunder People to the west and our rain, lips starting to crack and tongues to thicken. So now the waiting worked against us. The young swamper dying, the Frenchman tender with his dolly boy as a woman:

"Please, *vous* look at heem."

Since the day before, the boy had been unconscious.

"Nothin' I c'n do," I said.

"*Vous* look."

The Frenchman had rigged up a small tent of hides over the boy to keep off the sun and flies. The smell inside was choking.

The boy lay naked on his stomach. Not only his rear but all the way around him swole, so turning him on his side didn't help, because he had no side, the skin so tight it glistened. That arrow had been dipped in something. Like the mules, he needed to be slit.

If I'd cut the boy the first day, he'd maybe have had a chance. But Lordy! I'd helped cut off a foot and once a thumb and two fingers, but how would you go about carving into a man's behind?

I took out my bowie knife and pointed to a spot just below where the arrow had gone in. The Frenchman bleached but nodded.

Outside I burned the point to a gray red, then inside I handed it to him. He pushed it back at me. "It's all I know to do," I said. The Frenchman nodded and I stuck it in the swamper's behind. Like puncturing a balloon. The boy's behind exploded, the stuff geysering out, green and ropy, hitting the Frenchman up alongside the head, spattering the top of the tent. The reek like a chop to the stomach, so I had to stick my head outside. I never saw nothing like it.

As it drained, the swamper's eyes fluttered open, and the Frenchman bent down and kissed his dolly, the boy straining up sideways to look at him, but I don't think he could see anything; then the boy sucked in and died and the Frenchman started to bawl and I left.

Outside, up along the ridge, they were still sitting. Senseless, because, though a Wasichu (white man) with this hand would have had you belly, balls and bowels, an Indian's no siege fighter. War a game to him. Deadly. All the same a game. Less honor in killing an enemy than being the first to touch his dead body—*count coup* —an even greater honor touching an armed enemy and getting away. Battle to him a hell-for-leather riding, howling, shooting glory hunt and damn little glory in starving a man to death, but there they waited.

For what?

We couldn't hold out another twenty-four or sixteen or even six hours, and I climbed out over the barricade through what was left of the mules, the skinners behind thinking I was deserting, hollering what did I think I was doing, and to come back.

I walked out in the sand about a dozen yards beyond the mules and stopped, looked up along the line of the ridge to their chief, the Blade, held out my arms from my sides to let them see I was unarmed—to show my contempt—and spit. The young bucks coming up over their mounts' necks.

I began by calling them every filthy name, Lordy! I knew in Sioux, Kiowa, Comanche, Mexican and English: they were seducers of children and copulaters with their horses; they were eaters of dog droppings and swillers of urine; befoulers of their mothers and suckers of young boys; they were—

A bubble of sand erupted at my feet.

I whirled around. It was the pock-faced skinner waving me in, eyes glazed, so I knew the next shot could be right up my spine.

Back inside, Pock Face and the others were wild: What was the matter with me? What'd I think I was doing? Fanning them like that! Trying to get them all killed? They'd charge for sure now.

I looked around. In the ten or so minutes I'd been gone, Pock Face had taken command.

Through the flap of the tent of hides, I could see the Frenchman dressing the young swamper's corpse.

Two reasons I reckoned they weren't attacking: their medicine man had told them the signs were bad, or someone'd had a bad vision. Only, they weren't sure. *We had to make them sure.* And to do that we had to get some hothead to make a run at us.

Pock Face screwed up his mouth. "What's to keep the whole tribe from makin' that run?"

"The Blade."

"How you know?"

"They woulda done it before."

"You're guessin', old man."

"Hee ees right." It was the Frenchman. "Eenytime, they could take us, overrun us, burn us, starve us. When they theenk of eet, roll beeg rocks down on us from above. Wee are out of water. Wee are feenish now." He brushed at the wetness under his eyes. "Wot else?"

"Start pairin' off," I said.

Pock Face hesitated and in that moment lost his command.

"Go on," the Frenchman said wearily, jockeying in behind Pock Face so both Pock Face and I knew I was covered, pointing up to the Blade on the ridge, "talk to heem."

Seeing me coming out through the mules, the braves again came up stiff over their mounts, squirming, fingering bows and spears. I'd burned them that last time.

Again unarmed to show my contempt, I spit at the Blade: they tongued my anus and licked my genitals; I urinated on their women's breasts and made dung in their father's mouths; their spirits were tellers of lies, their medicine from the bowels of carrion. . . .

I was burning them good now, the braves having trouble with their ponies. And yet they knew exactly what I was doing. They'd done it too many times themselves. The Blade impassive. Then I dropped my pants, cupped my genital in both hands and shook it at them, daring them: their men were flat between the legs like woman, and their warriors suckled the newborn; then I turned around, bent over, spread the cheeks of my bare bum and waved my hole at them. Above the barricade I could see the white faces of the skinners suddenly contort, mouths making yelling sounds, arms waving at me when I heard it. The howl. A high KI-YIing and without turning to look I jerked up my pants, tripping on the bottoms, falling, rolling over, and there he was, coming for me. Barebacked. Splashed with paint. Naked except for a breech clout and leggings. Little Rabbit. An Arapaho. There were *two* tribes up there—*Kiowa* and *Arapaho!* Little Rabbit streaking out from behind an outcropping of rock. Whooping. Fitting an arrow to his bow.

3

―――――――――――――――――――――――――

Desecrate the Holy

Yanking at my pants, I part ran, part crawled, part fell into the mules. Burrowing into one of the half-eaten bellies. Trying to pull the flaps of flesh about me. Seeing Little Rabbit draw his bow and release. At the same time hearing the sharp cough of Pock Face's scattergun. The arrow chunked in above me, just behind the mule's shoulder, Little Rabbit jackknifed back into the air, gut-shot, and I started out the mule's belly when another—I couldn't tell who—came whirling out from the other side of the outcropping. Screaming. Spear raised, so I ducked back pulling the flaps of meat about me, thinking all the while how that spear could cleave me and the mule like suet, when I heard the skinner's guns. Like a war. Three, five, six shots. All at the same time. Just what they wanted. Coming at us one at a time to draw all our fire, then charge whilst we reloaded. The shots blowing the second Indian back off his pony like cotton.

I didn't duck out again, but jerked back around, and, head down, bulled, hacking and tearing with the bowie at ribs and meat, out through the opposite side of the mule's belly and over the wagons into the barricade, where, like I'd reckoned, they were all bent over reloading, ramming home. Like quail in a cage. I scrambled back up on top of the wagons. Nothing except the flies resetting on the mules. Under the shimmering light, the mesa as empty and still as Little Rabbit and the second one out there on the sand.

The Frenchman knew better, and I began to give him hell for not checking the skinner's fire; but griefing over his dolly boy, the Frenchman didn't hear a word I said. He sat in the dirt staring at his knees. So I thought of taking away the Frenchman's gun, a Markham, a beautiful handcrafted weapon I could sure make more use of than him. I decided also not to waste any more water on the Frenchman.

Up along the ridge the bucks were starting to churn, but still the Blade, unmoving, held them.

If they were to come, it was now. Right now. The tension stretching out and out, when the Frenchman gave a yell and ran back at the tent of skins he'd built over the corpse of his dolly boy, a buzzard inside picking at the boy's face, the Frenchman trapping the bird, hacking it up so I thought how it'ud be something for tonight; then, still yelling, the Frenchman went out over the tops of the wagons, running out through the mules to stand over the second Indian. Then he bent down, rolled the second Indian over on his back and sliced him neck to navel, reaching in, ripping out a handful of insides like you'd gut a buck; then he began to cut: first, the privates, sawing and chopping; then jamming down on the lower jaw, pulling out the tongue, hacking it off at the root; slitting the nostrils to the forehead, lopping off both ears, and, like oysters on the halfshell, scooping out the eyes, throwing the lot onto the intestines. Stark howling *loco*, I thought; because of his dolly boy, I thought, until he stood up and, holding the bloody knife out in front of him at arm's length over his head, gestured first to the Thunder People west; north to the Great White One; east to the place of all knowledge; south to the bed of creation; then to Mother Earth and Father Sky.

Immediately the squaws' high tremolo shivered out across the gorge.

The Frenchman might not know Plains Indians, but he knew Indians.

Griefing and the buzzard at his dolly boy had fused him, but that last, the holy sign of desecration, that had taken real sabe, and something more than I had.

It's why in battle an Indian carries off his dead: to keep them from being mutilated for the afterlife, because, when the Great Spirit took up that butchered brave to the great green hunting lands teeming with buffalo and antelope, of streams heavy with fish and trees dragging with fruit, he'd not only not be able to make love to the beautiful maidens there but he'd be unable to eat or swallow or digest or even smell his paradise, and when they came to welcome him, his mother and father and father's father and forebears back to the beginning of light, all the great ones gathered, chiefs and warriors and holy ones, he'd be unable either to see or talk to or even hear them. And before they'd risk that, they'd look again at the Frenchman's little collection out there on the sand.

Again the Frenchman, holding the knife out before him, made the holy sign of desecration, then started toward Little Rabbit, gutshot, when a third Indian came streaking out from behind the outcropping with the same mad abandon, screaming through dissolving breakers of heat.

Only, this time our fat was in the fire for certain, because this one—this one was *Manuel*, Chief Blade's only son, the cone of conscience in me like a horn:

These—Little Rabbit, the second one and now Manuel—their best.

Hair streaming, bodies glistening, flat out over their ponies' necks, melding with the flow of flesh beneath them, the way an eagle dives, they came.

"World's greatest cavalrymen," General Sherman called them, and once, in the mountains during rendezvous, I heard an old silvertip argue that if the Indian'ud had the horse twenty years afore he did, we'd never have got west of the Mississippi.

But if he was a great cavalryman, he was a poor soldier. Too scattered to army and too arrogant to command.

Like now. Angry children. Exposed. Defenseless. Open. Like picking apples.

The Frenchman drew an old handgun, a hogleg, from down his pant leg and stood waiting. As calm as a man in chapel.

If we took Manuel, nothing could stop them.

I drew a bead on the back of the Frenchman's neck.

4

The Unforgiving Ones

But Manuel, unlike the others, came at an angle, cutting his pony from side to side so it was hard to line him up. The skinners paying me no mind, spraying the gorge. The Frenchman, the dripping knife out in front of him like an avenging angel of the Lord, continued on up to the gutshot little Arapaho, Little Rabbit, motionless, standing over Little Rabbit, setting himself with the old hogleg. Waiting.

I sucked in, drawing the bead fine just above the back of the Frenchman's neck.

Manuel, leveling a long gun with a cutoff barrel, straightened out his pony the last dozen yards. Manuel and the Frenchman so close now you didn't see how either could miss.

I squeezed off my shot the same time as Manuel, both shots followed by the explosion of the Frenchman's hogleg. And all three of us missed!—Manuel at six yards when his pony shied at something in the sand; the Frenchman, solid as a bear, at three yards when Little Rabbit, at his feet, kicked the Frenchman sideways so I, too, missed, but Pock Face, with the same thought as me, didn't, taking off the back of the Frenchman's head the same time as Manuel, slashing down with his ax as he went by, halved the Frenchman's skull to the chin, the Frenchman, dead, still half raising the hogleg to fire the second barrel before he went down.

Lordy! . . .

We'd stopped them, yes, but for how long? A meager choice at best: We'd just lost our best gun, but, worse, the Frenchman's death could've changed their medicine. Grit down to his socks, that Frenchman.

I looked up along the ridge for the totem. It was still upright, scalp and feathers fluttering from the shank, the Blade turning to one of his lieutenants, who rode down to where the main force strung out.

Pock Face had the same thought. "What's he doin'?" said Pock Face when from behind us one of the skinners fired, the smoke pungent on the air. I looked between the wagons.

They came in a wedge toward Little Rabbit, now up on his knees, arms out from his sides like a rooster preening to yawp, two of them, Manuel and one other. A Comanche, from the markings on his pony. Lordy, how many tribes were up there! What was going on? Their timing a marvel of horsemanship. Manuel and the Comanche catching Little Rabbit, one under each arm, carrying him between them, when there was a second shot, the Comanche coming up twisting then back down over his horse's rump. Manuel now trying to hold Little Rabbit by one arm, dragging Little Rabbit, bouncing and flopping feebly against his pony's side. A dead weight. Slipping finally from Manuel's grasp, the little Arapaho tumbleweeding along the sand into a still mound.

The feathers in the Blade's hair wagged. He was shaking his head. Then he brought his free arm up across his chest and flung it out. Maybe. Just maybe. Then he reined his horse about, pony heads all along the rim swinging up and to the side, mounts turning, following the Blade down the ridge.

For a moment we stared, stunned; then a hand slapped me lightly between the shoulder blades.

"You done it. You did! We done it!"

Their faces began to twist with the pain of grinning through their thirst with split lips, trying to cheer with puffed tongues, touching each other weakly with congratulations, some crying, saying over and over: "We done it, we drove 'em, we licked 'em," when there hadn't never really been a fight. Nor was it over. Them aware of it about fifteen seconds after me. Quiet now and staring out over the wagons.

They sat in a half circle. Just out of range, like the coyotes and

wild things at twilight waiting for the night. Ringing us. Silent.
Watching. Manuel and a dozen others, the steady, unforgiving
ones. Fighting now as they should have from the first Wasichu.
These the ones who knew. Something in them shifted. You could
feel it. For weeks now. When you traded with them in the mountains, along the streams and cool places.

They'd got brittle as dry grass. Wire-edged as young bulls. Even
the old ones, brooding, looking east across the grama grass down
into the hollows. In the young ones, desperation.

The dawn-early massacres—mostly of children and women—the
way at Sand Creek they'd killed Fleet Fawn, my wife, still in the
light doeskin she slept in nights, the center of her blown away, my
skinning knife still in her hand where she'd rushed the soldier.
And after Sand Creek, Two Rocks and Broken Hump and Little
Hill and all the lies and forked pledges. But the unforgiving ones
out there—*they'd learned*.

They'd heard from the Sioux north. From the wandering lone-
somes east. From the little dark ones south. *But now they listened.* "First a nibble, then a bite, and then they gobble."

It began with the trails . . . like knives carving. The Oregon
and the Bozeman and splinter trails off to the coast diggings. First
frightening then splitting the great buffalo herds. Driving them to
seek far feed.

Learning at last from the Wasichu that it wasn't cut, dash,
howl, fire and fall back—it was *his* way, *this* way, or be extermi-
nated.

Around the edges the light burned in yellow streamers, the desert sweating wrinkled oceans that turned the mouth to dust, the
body to sand; in the dazzle the mesquite writhing, head feathers
snaking about umber faces.

"Old man. . . ." It was Pock Face. "We can't make her, old
man."

I reached down for my gun.

"Not another day," Pock Face said. He dropped his hand over
mine on the gun.

I shook my head, no.

"You got any ideas, then?" he said.

"Not after what I just done to 'em," I said.

"Old man, we ain't got options." He held his hand tight over mine on the gun. "You was married to one of 'em onc't," he said.

"Only makes it worse."

"You can parley with 'em."

"About what, the relatives I've just killed—no!"

"Yes!—squawman," and Pock Face, back in command, brought the muzzle of his gun up to my mouth.

The only white flag they could find was the fancy lace shirt the Frenchman had dressed the dead body of his dolly boy in. They stripped the shirt off the boy's corpse, tied it to an arrow, waved it back and forth a dozen times, then handed it to me.

"This walk's only one way, old man," Pock Face said, "so if you can't do nothin', don't come back," and, gun barrel in the small of my back, Pock Face shoved me out of the barricade.

BOOK TWO

The Chosen

5

I Will Take Him Your Tongue

Gen'l Sheridan called the turn:

"The buffalo hunters have done more in the last two years to settle the vexed Indian question," the Gen'l said, "than the entire regular army in the last thirty years.

"They are destroying the Indian's commissary," the Gen'l said, and he was right.

The buffalo—the cause of all this ruckus now—that had always been the key.

It was the buffalo had turned the Indian into a nomad, so in time he'd all but forgot how to plant or cast pottery or live off growing things, the buffalo giving it all to him, his shelter, his fuel, his clothing and most of the utensils he needed, nothing wasted: from the hide, his tipi, robes, beds, blankets, caps, moccasins, leggings and bull boats for river crossings; from the skin at the neck, dried and hardened, a warrior's shield—a good one could turn an arrow and even a musket ball; from a patch of rawhide stretched over a hoop, a drum; from thongs, lassos and bridles; a wet rawhide lashed to a stone, a war club; from the tender underbelly, parfleches and saddlebags; from the sinews, thread for sewing; from the stomach, a cook-pot; from the bladder, a water bag; from the horns, spoons and cups; from the skull, painted with red dots, the center of the sun-dance altar; from the ribs, sleds for the kids; from the shoulder blades, hoes; from the leg bones, fleshers, scrapers, knives, awls; from the small bones, needles; from the brains, a tanning acid; from the hoofs, mallets, hammers, glue; from the dung, fuel; even the tail, a flyswatter; the buffalo the holiest of their animals, the White Cow Buffalo Woman the greatest of their saints. Whereas us, we slaughtered the buff for their tongues or hump—finest eating anywhere—or for just plain sport, the old Kansas Pacific selling round-trip tickets from Leavenworth to the shooting grounds, where hunters could kill the buff from a moving railroad coach.

But it really started back—two thousand miles back—in Vermont, where a young fella, John Moar, got a new tanning process going where a buffalo hide, up to now near worthless for commercial purposes, could be used for shoes, saddles, upholstery, anything a cowhide could be used for, and suddenly buffalo is three dollars and fifty cents a hide, and everyone is out to make a killing: the hunters killing the Indians to get to the buffalo; the Indians, the hunters, 'cause they're starving. Over six million of the brutes we killed in two year.

Lordy!

A new way of tanning leather. Progress. And out of it, all that burning and looting, greed and grief. A whole civilization cut down—for $3.50.

No one's apologizing nor proud of it, only with the beaver gone, a mountain man hadn't a lot of choices: some soldiering maybe, like Carson, or train guiding, like Bridger and Meek. Which don't exactly give a man a stake. Or slaughtering the buffalo, like me. And my not doing it wouldn't change or slow it down one whit.

Outside the barricade, I stopped only once. Over the Frenchman. The hogleg, one barrel unfired at his feet, the knife still in his hand. Only, carrying a white flag, you don't go armed.

The black mounds hunkered down on the sand in their blankets, cross-legged, Manuel farthest off, by the rock outcropping, so I had to pass through the mounds. Letting me pass. Their eyes in me like augers. The first time I ever felt my back, the rounds along the tops of my shoulders, the sheer drop of my spine down to my buttocks.

Hunched over folded arms, Manuel sat looking past my legs at the barricade. I waited. He must speak first. And soon. Because, from the heat and dehydration, I wasn't sure my tongue would work.

The sun seethed like malice out of an alkali sky, the sweat pooling in my brows, sliding down along the channels of my nose over my upper lip into my mouth, bitter with salt and gunpowder.

Behind Manuel, his pony, with four white stockings, switched flies. Up along the rim where the Blade had been, some children sat, one drinking from a buckskin pouch, the water spilling down over his chin and chest. I looked away. A breeze lifted a braid of Manuel's hair, a catch of horse and sage on it. I wanted to push back my hat, the sun starting now to shadow the east. To the west, at either end of the half circle, the mounds began to inch forward.

Unless I negotiated something and soon, the mounds would have them by morning.

Without looking at me, Manuel spoke in Kiowa. "What would you?" he said.

"To—to—" I started, the words fumbling my mouth, "to speak to your father."

"I will take him your tongue."

I kept silent.

"What would you?" he said again. His eyes came up at me, hot, the whites red from the sun. Twice more he repeated the question.

Whatever was to be done, I knew it wasn't with Manuel.

I looked away from him, and Manuel exploded to his feet, hitting me three times in the V at the neck and shoulder with his coup stick.

"I do not talk to children," I shouted.

Again he started to hit me with the coup stick but caught himself. He shoved his face into mine: "You speak boldly for a dead one."

Inside, I squeezed down, everything beginning to waver. "That is why I should be heard," I said. I stared back into his flat, agate eyes.

"Later," he said, "later I shall do for you."

Of that, I thought, I could be most certain.

Manuel crooked his thumb across his tongue and whistled to

the children up on the rim, and the little boy who'd spilled water over his chin jumped up and ran.

I hoped the boy would hurry with the horse. Inside, I was beginning to lose hold.

To pass out before I'd talked to the Blade could finish us all.

I let my arms hang loose and punched down, making all inside taut.

6

Face on Water, Evil

We sat, Chief Blade and I, across from one another, outside his medicine lodge, the wavering inside gone now so I hadn't to strain down any more, the Blade unspeaking, unseeing—listening.

From the firing in the gorge, I reckoned three to still be alive: Pock Face with his scattergun; the other two on Hawkins, one a .50-caliber, the other a .30.

The rest, like I'd omened earlier, had gotten it on that first rush, all letting loose at the same time, with no backup fire and so overrun.

Since then they'd done some better, jump-shooting still, but spacing their shots—through it all the Blade's old, pitted, worm-wood face as blank as bark on a tree, in his lap his hands gnarled, the knuckles awl-edged, the Chief in a froth at their going against him down there in the gorge. 'Specially his son. And 'specially this son. Manuel. Youngest and sole remaining of the Blade's three sons. The expectation of the tribe. Unpromising promise of the future. Last of the litter. Least of the litter. The oldest, Black Horse, the old man's favorite—tall, heavy, bull-chested, an elk even as a boy, an athlete who by fourteen could outrun, outwres-tle any brave in the tribe, a fine hunter and trapper and bold war-rior, Black Horse, one of the rare ones: gentle with the old, play-ful with the young, generous to all, a recognized chief while still a young man, who, when he was slain—*murdered*, the tribe said, at Fort Grange by a fur trader who claimed he'd caught Black Horse

with his wife—the Blade's oldest had been lamented for months, a
measure of tribal disbelief in the charge and their love of Black
Horse—though there were those who doubted, because Black
Horse's mother, Light Hands, had been so fair. Light Hands part
Wasichu, they whispered. Which was why, they said, Black Horse
had taken to the fur trader's wife. It was in the blood. I didn't believe any of it, but, rather, that Black Horse had been murdered
because, as most said, the Wasichus could see the great one the
Blade's oldest was to become. Nits make lice. The Blade these
many, many years still mourning the loss of this oldest son.

But Manuel was no Black Horse, no, nor no White Eagle neither, the Blade's middle boy—White Eagle already a speechmaker
of power, heard and deferred to by the elders in Tribal Council
for his shrewdness and wisdom, and near enough in age to Manuel that the brothers were also friends. "Say-do-hahas," the tribe
called them, *Pair Alikes,* they were so close—Manuel idolizing his
middle brother—though they weren't really alike a-tall, for Manuel was the family craftsman. Kay-veer-nay, he was called by, *the
carver:* Manuel's arrows the straightest, his lances the truest, the
work on his bridle, on his trappings and bows the most intricate,
the ornamentation on the hides of most of the lodges, much of
the bead, blanket, jewelry and pottery designs after drafts of
Manuel's. But when Manuel's middle brother, White Eagle, too,
was murdered—shot through the lungs while bent over a map during a peace parley with Captain Schoon—all that changed, Manuel so stricken with grief everyone thought he'd surely die until he
went on a blood feud that carried all over the north, south and
central plains, killing a lieutenant, a sergeant, and two aides, everyone who'd been in that peace tent when his middle brother,
White Eagle, had been assassinated, all except Captain Schoon,
who'd died of the grippe the winter before at Fort Phil Kearney,
Manuel digging up the captain's corpse to shoot it through the
lungs.

Still, that's what the tribe expected of Manuel, a Black Horse-
White Eagle Manuel. Because now that's what they needed . . .
not Manuel the carver (squaw's play), *not* from the Blade's only
son. And because Manuel hadn't the chiefry of his oldest brother,
Black Horse, nor the wisdom of his middle brother, White Eagle,
they took it ill of him . . . like a cold-jawed horse.

They understood neither his differences nor his excesses—like now down there in the gorge where suddenly it had gotten quiet, quiet, until the gnarls at the end of the Blade's wrists began to unravel, the old man coming up tall over his knees: he was back in command, again the Chief, but, in the continuing silence, again slumping old. He'd been old when I'd first come to the plains, gray and old, but like an old bull salmon yet able to fight upstream. Only, now he was old, old, his chest muscles hanging like dried breasts, his arms and hams twig thin, his left hand palsied; only his eyes remained unchanged, the rage in them still young.

For a long while the Blade went on listening, and when there was still no sound from the gorge, he turned to me of a sudden and said in Kiowa, "Copperheart." Like Manuel, not looking at me, crevasse carved features aged to the bone so his nose hooked out at me sharp and ferocious. "Face on Water, traitor."

Face on Water—I looked off toward where the hills turned ocher then raisin down near the plain. *Face on Water*—a long way since I'd heard that, the name Fleet Fawn had given me when, bathing, she'd first seen me, my face in the still pool. August 19 on the Republican River. My birthday. The first time I saw her. I was twenty. Trapping the south bank when I heard a beaver slap and crawled out onto a shelf over a hook of the Republican and there she was . . . glossy as a cat's eye, naked as a cockajay, breasts glistening up at me, between her legs the pelt dripping, looking down at my reflection in the water, *Face on Water*; then she looked up and smiled that slow, squawgirl smile so I went hollow all the way to my knees, and, long gun, powder, traps, clothes and all, I went feet first off the shelf into the water with her.

Two weeks we stayed on that bank swimming and hunting, eating plums and antelope. Some birthday! That girl pretty as feathers, soft as a blush; eyes large as a doe's; hair to her hips, glass-black and thick as beaver; skin fine as bee powder and always smelling of meal and sage.

Twice Fleet Fawn's daddy and brothers came through, hunting her. A virgin—if they'd found us, they'd've built a slow dung fire in my lap.

At the end of the second week, she went back to camp, and a week later I rode in and married her, her brothers and daddy looking sideways at me the whole time. We had two years together before the Sand Creek massacre.

The Blade's head started up. They were shooting again in the gorge, and again, this time in sign, the Blade called me *traitor*.

"You are a traitor," I said back.

"Face on Water fire on his own."

"You, too, fire on your own."

"I fire at Wasichus."

"Am I not of you by wife?" I said.

He drew his right forefinger across his forehead for *white man*. "You are nothing," he said. And yet I knew the way I'd gotten them to come at us, the old man admired me for that. The same as I'd felt his son Manuel's shame. But if there was admiration, there was no forgiveness. Which was part of why they were still down there in the gorge.

"We talk like young boys," I said.

He was silent, then: "What would you do?" he said.

"I cannot kill my people," I said. "It is a waste. Stop the fighting."

"*You* bring the fighting."

"I will give you all I have."

"Do you think for that we die!"

"Stop the fighting."

Right hand up, he made the gesture of helplessness. "It has gone past," he said.

"The Blade is Chief," I said.

"I am not he of the vision."

"Who does the vision?"

"Buffalo Who Runs."

"What does he see?"

"Two rattlesnakes entwined, one red, one gray. The red swallows the gray."

"The rattlesnake was not white?"

He made the sign, *no*.

"Then it was not us," I said.

"It was gray."

"Could not the red be poisoned in the gray's stomach and both die!" I brought my hand away from my heart, palm up. "It is an evil vision."

The Blade made the same gesture: "Face on Water, evil."

"Like the snakes," I said, "we destroy one another."

A brave—neck-shot from the sound of him—began to gurgle out the Blade's name, and the Blade got up and went over to where the women wove in and out among the wounded, sucking, bandaging with mud and moss, soothing, softly wailing and moaning, chanting prayers and incantations.

While he was gone, an old squaw handed me a gourd of water. I gulped at it and gagged. It was urine. I started to spit it out—the squaws were watching—I swallowed it and set the gourd down in the sand.

The Blade, seeing what the squaw had done, started back, when Manuel and four others rode in, wounded over their ponies' necks, one maybe dead the way his head flopped; another was the little Arapaho, Little Rabbit, who told how Pock Face's bullet had hit the center bone holding up his loincloth, driving it back into his middle, knocking him off his pony, so I thought how Little Rabbit was one gritty little Indian to have lain out there like that, watching the Frenchman carve up his friend then start toward him, the Rabbit lying motionless, waiting through all that to do what he'd done—the squaws all the time unloading more wounded. Manuel started to rein about when his daddy caught his pony by the bit.

"No," the Blade said, "no more fighting."

"See," Manuel pointed to me, "the white face carries the white flag."

The Blade threw his right hand out in a wide half circle: "No!"

"They thirst," Manuel said. "Their food is going. Soon their bullets."

"Each bullet is of life."

"They are beaten." Manuel tried to back his pony away.

The Blade held the horse's bit. "Buffalo Who Runs is dead." The Blade pointed. "The vision is done."

The medicine man came out from behind the Blade. "This dawn I hear the night owl make day sounds. The medicine is bad," he said.

Manuel shook his rifle at them. "This is my medicine!"

"It is finished," the Blade said and walked away. Manuel jumped from his horse to stand glaring after his daddy. But with

Buffalo Who Runs, he of the vision, dead, there was little Manuel could do.

I didn't see the Blade the rest of that night. Later they gave me water and jerky, and hobbled me with the horses, the squaws and children spitting and throwing dung on me. But I wasn't beaten or tortured.

The Blade, I was sure, hadn't believed anything I'd said. So, what was he saving me for? The strappado? Crucifixion? They'd been using both of those little Spanish novelties a lot lately, I'd heard, to show the weakness of the Wasichu and so build up the courage of the young braves. Big doings, for a fact! Already in camp I'd made out Sioux, Kiowa, Arapaho and Comanche. My fear tasted of Confederate nickels.

Sometime that night, around the eleventh hour, an orange glow lit up the eastern sky, so I knew they'd built a fire on the ridge above the barricade. Something even the Frenchman hadn't thought of. Then, later, with all the KI-YIing, I knew they'd started to push the fire down over the rim on them, the screams of Pock Face and the others going on for some time but not as long as might have been if—like me—they'd been took.

7

::

Sun Dance

After that first day of spitting and dung throwing, they treated me like I wasn't there, already dead—to make me think on it—even the children, the Blade forcing the old squaw who'd given me the urine to drink to look after me, morning and evening bringing me water, checking to see were the hobbles on my ankles secure, and, once a day, a handful of pemmican to eat. A good sign. She was being punished. She'd insulted an enemy of worth.

The second day, they stuck me in a square, the circle too sacred. The universe is a circle, the sky, the sun, the base of the tipi, the burrows of animals, all circles. Whereas, the Blade said, the white man's symbol is the square. His home, his buildings with walls to separate people, his dollar bills, his doors to keep strangers out, his jails, windows, wagons, weapons, all with corners and sharp edges, boxes upon boxes, all squares. My square ten feet to a side, inside which I could wander at will, outside which I would be killed.

It wasn't as large a camp as I'd thought, but, for the hunting and feed this time of year, bigger than most.

There were also some Wasichus in camp, a white man I'd seen the braves tormenting and who I seemed to remember from somewhere, and a little boy, the man's son, I guessed, playing with the other children. Jed the boy's name. Asking me over and over, before they run him off, when he could go home.

Then it began—whatever it was—toward the end of the third week during the Moon of Making Fat, when they commenced to come in, walking, mounted, on travoises, families, clans, tribes. For two weeks they came—Comanche, Arapaho, Sioux, until it was one of the biggest convocations of Indians that I—or few red men, for that matter—had ever seen. The Blade had plans, all right.

The best part was that the hunt had been plentiful, so even I ate good. The old squaw throwing my meat in the dirt to watch me fight the dogs for it.

The first few days went speeching, drumming, dancing and exchanging gifts, then the squaws started to mark off postholes in a circle, twenty-eight of them, and a scouting party was formed. Four young girls to go along, so now I had a pretty good idea: the burning of sweet grass and sage, the women gathering holy herbs and cutting out sacred symbols, the braves purifying themselves in the sweat lodges, the kids excited. It was also coming on the Moon of the Red Cherries, when it's usually celebrated. For a fact, the Blade was making medicine, big, big. Their most religious rite, the sacred sun dance.

I'd taken part in it—though I hadn't understood it all—once, with Fleet Fawn, up on the Platte River.

The preparations for the sun dance are the same as for going into battle. The center of the dance is the cottonwood, the waguchun, the rattling tree, one of the Standing People, sacred because it stretches from earth to heaven. It was the cottonwood had taught them how to make their lodges, the leaf of the tree the exact shape of a moccasin or, curled, a tipi, and if you cut an upper limb crosswise, in the grain you'll find a perfect five-pointed star, the sacred evening star, which stands between the darkness of ignorance and the light of truth, the symbol of Him, in the gentlest breeze the voice of the cottonwood praying to the Great Spirit, for in different ways all things pray to Him.

"Tree," the lead scout would say, "you are about to go to the center of the sacred hoop. You are a kind and good-looking tree. Upon you the winged peoples have raised their families. For all, you are a support. You always look to Heaven. I have chosen you. Be proud. I could have chosen another." Then a warrior who'd just distinguished himself by some brave deed—Manuel, by my guess—would be selected to count coup on the tree. A great honor. After which the four young girls, chosen for their virtue,

would chop it down, not allowing the tree to touch the ground
but being caught by the men.

Midday, the procession came up out of an arroyo carrying the
tree, stopping four times—4 and 7 the sacred numbers: 4 for the
four seasons, the four directions, the four ages of man, the four di-
visions of time, the four parts to all that grows, four kinds of
things that breathe, four fingers to each hand, four toes to each
foot, the thumbs and big toes making four; 7 for the seven sacred
rites—all circling the camp sunways, howling like coyotes the way
warriors do returning from the kill, when from the opposite direc-
tion a throng of mounted warriors appeared. The top young bucks
from each tribe. Strutting. Preening over their ponies. Howling
back. Then the Blade came out of his medicine lodge holding a
long, black-tipped eagle feather which, when dropped, was the signal for the warriors to race their mounts to be the first to touch
the holy spot where the sacred tree would stand. Much honor in
this. The four tribes gathered at the four corners.

For a moment even the dogs were silent. Then the Blade
dropped the feather and Lordy!—it sounded like a stampede and
looked like a war.

They came racing, wheeling and screeching, jostling, shoving,
bumping and butting mounts, crossing and blocking one another
off to keep each other from being first to touch the holy spot. Ripping and tearing, they punched and kicked and jumped on one
another, wrestling one another off their ponies. The nearest to
making a touch, a Kiowa riding under the neck of his horse, when
the little Arapaho, Little Rabbit, punched him loose. Horses rearing and pawing and squealing now, the dust so thick you could
hardly make out what was happening when, out of the melee, like
a mad bear, howling and smashing through on a big bay, straight
up on his mount, swinging arms like tree trunks, came this big,
flat-faced, one-eyed Comanche, Noisy Walking, a bullsnake thong
covering his blind eye, charging until about ten feet away, when
he went sidewinding off the bay, sailing through the air like a tree
squirrel, landing full on his chest—like hitting a hollow log, the
sound that came out of him—flush on the holy spot, the Comanche tribe doing their best to keep from screeching in triumph
and so insulting their hosts. Noisy Walking standing, the eyepatch gone, the hole where his eye had been a black smudge, the

big Comanche strutting, knowing he'd brought not only great honor to his people but much luck to himself in battle.

Then, four days later, the tree was set up and the chanting began:

O Grandfather, Wakan Tanka, You are the maker of all things. You have always been and always will be. Help us to walk the two red and two blue days.

The medicine man attached the images of a buffalo and a man to the sacred cottonwood, praying:

It is from the buffalo person our people live. He is the chief of all the four-leggeds upon our sacred Mother Earth.
Behold this two-legged. These are the two chiefs upon this great island. Bestow upon them all Your favors, O Wakan Tanka.

And now they built the sun-dance lodge, a circle around the sacred tree of twenty-eight forked posts, from each of which a pole was placed reaching the cottonwood at the center; this the universe, each of the posts an object of creation, at the center the cottonwood, He, the Great Spirit. Everything comes to Him and goes to Him. Twenty-eight posts because the moon lives twenty-eight days; the buffalo has twenty-eight ribs; in their war bonnets twenty-eight feathers; 4 and 7 the sacred numbers so if you add them up, the four sevens make twenty-eight.

After that, more prayers and purifying in the sweat lodges. And then the sun dance. Each man painted and wearing his symbols. Many with rabbit skins on arms and legs, for the rabbit person is quiet and soft and not self-asserting, a quality one must possess when going to the center of the world:

I hear Him coming; I see His face.
Your day is sacred! I offer it to You.
I hear Him coming; I see His face.
This sacred day You made the buffalo run.
You made a happy day for the world;
I offer all to You.

Without food and water they danced—four days—to the drum, which, like the universe, is round, its steady, strong beat the pulse, the heart throbbing at the center, blowing on eagle-bone whistles, the voice of Spotted Eagle, His voice, a wreath of sage on their heads and around their wrists, this the crown of heaven and the stars, mighty mysteries of life, swaying, weaving and rocking, staring at the sun, collapsing and getting up and collapsing again until the fourth day's climax, when those who'd vowed to have themselves pierced were brought together.

They were four: Noisy Walking, the big, one-eyed Comanche who'd hurled himself from his horse onto the sacred spot; Little Rabbit, the Arapaho who'd lain there and kicked the Frenchman sideways; Gray Owl, a tall, lordly Sioux; and Chief Blade's son, Manuel.

Again, for the Four, the purification lodge and prayers, the dance ground purified with incense, a burning braid of grass. Four flags marked out the sacred circle, a line which only these Four were allowed to cross.

A buffalo skull—to remind all of the shortness of life and man's end—was set up as an altar. All of the dogs were chased away, and the ceremony of the piercing began.

First the procession, led by a beautiful young girl, Sweet Sage, carrying the peace pipe—Sweet Sage now the Holy White Buffalo Cow Calf.

Then the Four danced, all the time blowing on plumed eagle-bone whistles, bodies glinting with sweat, one by one going to the buffalo altar to lay down a piece of wood clenched between their teeth, the sign of their holy brother; the priest praying:

"When we go to the center of the hoop, we shall all cry, for we should know that anything born into this world must suffer. We are now going to suffer at the center of the sacred hoop, and by doing this we may take upon ourselves the suffering of our people."

The cutting of the bodies, an Indian believes, is fulfillment:

All that truly belongs to a man is his flesh. **1955477**

If a man gives things, a horse, tobacco, a blanket, he gives only what Wakan Tanka already owns, and perhaps the man keeps what is best for himself.

So one must give what one values highest, and to show that one's whole being goes with the lesser gifts, one promises one's body.

And now the vows, the first one forward Little Rabbit, who chose *Gazing at the Sun Leaning*: "I will attach my body to the thongs of the Great Spirit, Who came down to this earth to save and teach us," Little Rabbit said, a rawhide thong running from the top of the sacred cottonwood to an eagle claw hooked into the flesh of Little Rabbit's chest, about a hand's width above the nipple.

Little Rabbit was followed by Manuel—*Gazing at the Buffalo*: "I will bear eight of my closest relatives," Manuel said. By this Manuel meant that into his back would be tied four thongs attached to eight buffalo skulls, these four bonds the pull of ignorance which should always be behind us as we face the light of the truth before us.

Then the stately Gray Owl—*Standing Enduring*: In this, Gray Owl is actually at the center of the universe—for, standing at the center of the four posts, rawhide thongs from the posts are tied into the flesh of his shoulders, his breast, and back, and in this manner he dances until he tears the thongs out of his flesh.

And last, Noisy Walking—*Gazing at the Sun Suspended*, thongs tied to skewers in his chest and back, by which he is pulled up into the air above the ground. This the most severe of all, Noisy Walking unable, like the others, to end his ordeal by pulling or jerking but, rather, hanging until his own weight tears the flesh free.

And now the chanters:

"O Wakan Tanka, be merciful to me!

I do this that my people live."

And Little Rabbit went to the medicine man, who in two places bit the flesh over Little Rabbit's heart until it was white, where he pierced Little Rabbit's skin with his knife, inserting an eagle claw in each wound, tying one end of a rawhide thong to each, the other end to the top of the sacred cottonwood—like a Maypole—the flesh is ignorance; the thong running from the top of the tree into the flesh over the heart is the light from Wakan Tanka: *For in the beginning we are like young colts.*

Next came Manuel, with the eight buffalo skulls dangling at the ends of thongs hooked into his back, the buffalo horns gouging and cutting his back and hips, his thighs and the calves of his legs: *At first a halter is necessary, but later, when we are broken, we no longer need the rope.*

Then Gray Owl was fastened between the four posts, from each of which thongs led to skewers in his shoulders and breast and back: *The bonds of flesh severed, we submit to Him.*

And last came Noisy Walking, hoisted into the air by the thongs in his chest and back, left suspended, dangling: *And now we are one with the Great Spirit.*

Then, at a sign from the medicine man, himself one of the dancers, pierced like the others, eagle feathers embedded in his flesh, forty pieces of skin cut from each of his arms as a sacrifice to the spirits, the medicine man and the holy Four began to dance— Little Rabbit dancing forward to the pole and back trying to tear himself loose; Manuel dancing up and down and whirling in such a way that the weight of the eight skulls would rip the thongs free; Gray Owl skewered so tightly front and back between the four posts he could barely move; Noisy Walking hanging motionless above the others; all disregarding the blood and pain at this great honor. Enduring with joy.

They danced and wiggled and jiggled and hung, friends encouraging, cleaning the long, jagged tears in the flesh, wiping away the cold sweat with bundles of sage leaves (these leaves a powerful love charm prized by the women, the sagewood skewers also greatly sought after, the dancers later presenting them to a friend to tamp down the tobacco in their pipes), all staring up into the sun snailing slowly up the canyons of morning to its midday fire, where it hung in the sky like a great red wound before slipping back down into the valleys of dusk, before the first ripped free, Little Rabbit, his girl, Sweet Sage, giving him a drink, then Manuel tore loose, and a short time after, Gray Owl, to stand quivering, muscles spavined, all floundering, stumbling and falling down, lurching to numb feet only to go reeling off into one another, drooling prayers and gibberish, eyes sliddery, fumbling at themselves with thick hands, at the sweat and blood, trying not to hold where it hurt, the skin hanging in ragged explosions from their several stigmata—all now free except Noisy Walking, his single eye glaring out at the setting sun, hanging and hanging, like a side of beef on a meathook, his muscles too thick and heavy to tear, his family glowering at the medicine man, who they thought had skewered him too deeply, Noisy Walking passing out and out until his uncle grabbed Noisy Walking's left shoulder and opposite hip and yanked down, tearing him loose, after which, reviving Noisy Walking, all continued to dance, the blood mixing with their sweat, veining their bodies like rain, jiggling numbly, jerking with pain and an emptiness beyond thought, beyond bone and tendon, until the medicine man called a halt.

Powerful, powerful medicine!

There's more I don't understand, all pretty strange, but I'm from a pretty strange sect myself, where we eat the body and drink the blood of our Great Spirit, Who was born of a virgin, got killed, rose up from the dead three days later for all to see, then went up into the clouds; yet not that different either. My Great Spirit also pierced. To a cross for the sake of His people. The real difference, I think, in the redeeming power of pain, the Indian refusing to lay this burden on his god, believing that he must himself come face to face with his suffering, that in his pain he helps all, pain no abstract to be suffered by somebody two thousand years ago, but, rather, the immediate means by which man most nearly enters the soul of the Great Spirit and so experiences sudden insight, for insight is never come by cheaply, as with angels and saints at second hand.

That night, for the first time in a month, the hobbles were cut off me. I was to be taken, the old squaw said cackling, before the four nations assembled.

The Blade had been saving me, all right!

Four young bucks threw me to the ground, first jerking off my boots and all my clothes, so I felt with shame the wetness leaking from my center down my thighs as they dragged me before the Grand Council.

8

::

The Four Chosen

They stood me naked before the four nations in front of a fire so hot it burned my face and eyes so I began to sweat, facing me east —from whence came the evil—on the lip of a pit, two feet deep, six across. Coiled against the far rim, a rattlesnake. A diamond-back. Enormous. As thick as your arm and a good five and a half feet in length. Rattles cracking dryly as it tucked in, not yet having seen me.

"Pennacook, Wabanaki, Agawam, Montagnais, Nahaton, Snapat, Hassanasit, Pocumtuc, Nanticoke, Narraganset . . ." for the last half hour the Blade had been speeching, calling out the names of those tribes the Wasichus had pushed off the edge of the earth and were no more.

Starting to shed, a flap of skin hung down over the snake's eyes, so, partially blinded, the diamondback, already crossgrained and testy with discomfort, now with fear, was ready to strike at anything.

The Trial of Defilement, they called it.

Lordy!

"Cheraw, Catawba, Waccamaw, Oconee, Ocheso . . ." the Blade continuing to call out the names of those tribes the white man had cast down and were now forever departed, the white man a mad soul who thought that by putting up fences he could own the grass. Which surely was mad. But worse, the Blade said, the Wasichu took unto himself all God's works and creatures.

But a trial meant someone was defending me. Who? Why? Why bother? They'd all heard and seen what I'd done back at the barricade.

The Blade started to circle the fire.

"When we kill, we eat all," the Blade said; "when we dig, we make small holes. When we build homes, we dig little burrows. When we burn grass for grasshoppers, we don't destroy all. We shake the tree persons for acorns and pine nuts. We don't chop them down."

Justice in the snake pit: If I died of the bite, I was dishonest of heart and of all guilt.

The Blade stopped in front of me, his back to me: "The tree says, 'Don't, I am sore. Don't hurt me.' They blast rocks and scatter them on the ground. The rock says, 'Don't, I am sore. You are hurting me.' But the Wasichu pays no attention. When the Indians use rocks, they take the little round ones for cooking. How can the spirit of the earth like the Wasichu? Everywhere he touches is sore."

And if I survived the snake? Like a bad run of cards. It seemed to go on and on.

The Blade turned and came over to the pit to stand looking down at the snake: "They ask us to plow the ground. Shall I take a knife and tear my mother's breast? Then, when I die she will not take me to her bosom to rest."

Though coiled, head up, tongue flicking, a single half-covered eye flat on me, the rattler was sluggish. The heat of the fire was drugging him. And when the fire went out?

But, then, not to be bitten was just as unthinkable. For to be rejected by the earth crawlers was itself proof of guilt. *I must force the snake to bite me.*

The Blade kicked dirt on the snake to wake and anger it: "They ask us to dig for the yellow metal. Shall I dig under my mother's skin for her bones? Then, when I die I cannot enter her body to be reborn again."

I stepped down into the pit, the snake recoiling, rattles starting to sing, and stood and waited, all pretending not to watch, watching.

Not once had the Blade looked at me.

"They ask us to cut grass to make hay and grow rich. But how dare I cut my mother's hair!"

I looked away from the snake, up at the speeching Blade.

"Still, the Wasichu medicine is strong. So unless our medicine is equal to theirs, we, too, shall be pushed by the mad one into the everlasting void."

At this, Manuel started to his feet. There was a gasp, the Blade staring in disbelief at his son.

A real breach of etiquette, cutting in on his daddy thataway.

The rattlesnake's head shrank back stiff against the rim.

"Here about me I see warriors, a number greater than anyone can remember." Manuel was starting to gesture. "With such a host we could sweep them before us like quail."

"Have we not tried?" the Blade said, reining in his anger at his son's disrespect, spacing his words carefully: "At Prairie Wells? At Haystack? At Valley Run?"

"Never with such a force."

"Do you not think they could make such numbers?" The Blade brought his left hand down on his chest, right palm up to his face in the sign of *suffering*. "Is there not now enough weeping in the tipis? Soon there will be only the children and very old."

"Soon there will be no one! Never have we been greater."

"It is not our strength, but *their mystery* we seek. Not our courage, but *their medicine*."

"You would steal from them?" Manuel shouted.

"Have they not from us!"

"You would become that against which you fight."

"Who has not?"

"I speak of the infinite."

"Just so," the Blade said softly.

"No," said Manuel, "the essence cannot be stolen."

"*It must be.*"

"They cannot be us," shouted Manuel, "*nor we, them!*"

The Blade looked down. "Then do we perish."

"You would put feathers on a dog," taunted Manuel.

"I do not ask the dog to fly."

"And if you asked?" called Manuel, starting forward, when the old man brought his palms together like a pistol shot in the sign for *enough!* And in that moment the old and young bull locked wills.

Manuel stepped forward, head up as though sniffing the wind, arrogant, waiting for encouragement, followers, help. This was the challenge. But there was no help, and, though showing disdain before his daddy, you could sense the boy's falling away, the old man silent, knowing he'd won, letting the boy strut, to salvage his pride, back to his place at the council fire.

The snake lay coiled. But content. It was almost long enough to hit me from where it lay. The sand under my feet squished where the sweat had run down my nakedness. I must make him strike. But I couldn't move.

After the Blade, the Chief of the Comanches spoke, then the Chiefs of the Sioux and the Arapaho and once more the Blade.

By now the fire had gone down, the snake cold, getting nervous, seeking a way out, starting to slither along the rim.

"The elders have decided," the Blade said. "From each of our four tribes has been chosen one brave, our straightest spear, our swiftest arrow, fleet like the antelope, a bison in strength, a grizzly so fearless; in the ways of man, a coyote.

"These Four, the heartroot of our four nations, will we send among the Wasichus to ravel out the secret of their medicine."

Which only shows how little they knew, I thought. Rather than their stoutest, most fearless, send their shrewdest, most devious.

The Chosen Four were brought forward to stand before the four nations. Much honor in this, much. The sacred sun dancers: Noisy Walking, the big, one-eyed Comanche; the gritty little Arapaho Little Rabbit; Gray Owl, the lordly Sioux; and the Blade's son, Manuel. The Blade telling of their greatness as hunters and warriors, all with many coups, all with many scalps hanging from their lodgepoles.

The Four, even after all they'd been through these last four days, pierced, torn, the flesh still hanging in strips from their bodies, yet straight as lances, tall, lithe. The best of this or any nation, I thought.

The snake commenced to lift up over the rim. I stepped forward, the rattles upleaping to a whine.

I concentrated on the Chosen Four. If I looked down—

I'd watched them grow, made thoughts with them on the hunt, traded with them in the mountains and at the forts:

The biggest, most powerful was the Comanche, Noisy Walking. He'd lost his eye as a child in a plains skirmish against a Pawnee raiding party. Still, one-eyed and maybe not the brightest, he was one mean dog in a fight. Give him a hold, he'd gnaw the heart out of a blue wolf. The little Arapaho, Little Rabbit, his dead opposite. Not that Little Rabbit, like the others, wasn't a warrior bred, but without all that bragging, swaggering glory look to him most braves worked at, Little Rabbit one of the solitaries, self-effacing, the smallest of them, yes, but with more coups than any two braves in the four tribes, a killer, absolutely fearless, a member of the wildest, most reckless of all the warrior societies, the Dog Soldiers, the dog rope, *ho tam tsit*, over Little Rabbit's right shoulder and under his left arm, at the end a red-painted wooden pin, a picket pin which, during a hard battle, was stuck into the ground and from which the Dog Soldier's only retreat was death.

Twice against the enemy Little Rabbit had picketed himself to the ground against great odds, shaming the tribe into standing with him and fighting—and winning. Yet, remarkable to tell, Little Rabbit was also the peacemaker, a ghost voice having told Little Rabbit during his vision at manhood—a blood arrow bitten in half by a black eagle—that he must forever protect his people, the combination of which, the vision and the voice, meaning he must eschew the lance for the law, whenever possible, for peace. A heavy injunction on a brave. It did strange things to Little Rabbit. Still, if to the others it made him appear just a mite too soft, he wasn't weak; and if unassertive, he wasn't fallow; if too patient, never passive. Whay-kay-na-set, his people called Little Rabbit, *Seeker After the Day*, and the most dangerous of the lot, because the Rabbit really believed there was an answer to all this.

You can just reckon what'd happen if he ever truly found it.

Far as that goes, I wouldn't have given a lick for any of their chances if it hadn't been for Gray Owl, the Sioux, the oldest of them, the only one with a family, and something of a medicine man with a great beaked nose like the Blade's and a dignity that took in everything around him, the only one capable of holding them all together, even Manuel, who just at that moment, without warning, broke away from the other three to stalk off—the Blade nubbing him up short.

"Day-ha-kay-nah!" the Blade called.

"I am red," the boy shouted back at his father. "I do not live with the no-colors."

"You do as is wished upon you by the people."

Again the boy started to stalk off, when, as one, the nations rose up around him, a solid wall of flesh blocking him off.

"You will kill your pride," the Blade said, "or your pride will do as much for you."

Manuel understood the threat right enough and returned to the other three.

The Blade brought both hands up to his chest and threw them out, palms down: *It is finished.* Then the medicine man came out to dance around the Chosen Four.

It was cold now, the fire down to coals, so only eyes and teeth shone, the night vast, the stars like fires, so I felt alone, a breeze, the damp sweet smell of grama grass on it, starting to pick across the mesa caking what I'd done earlier between my legs. Then the medicine man took a little run and jumped barefoot into the center of the burning coals, stamping on them, arms up to the night fires, praying, the four nations breaking into a howl, and, frightened, the snake struck.

Like a pair of spikes, he slammed into me. Halfway between my left knee and foot, on the inside, in the fat part of my calf.

I must not cry out or make the face of pain or look down or may-dah-quin—*try to shake him loose.*

9

·······································

Trial of Defilement

I stepped up out of the pit so that, not seeing, seeing, all could see the diamondback, unable to pull loose, embedded in my calf. The scaly, cold rope of him whipping against my leg. And, turning to the four powers, I made obeisance and stood still, willing the poisonblood to stop flowing, waiting for the dizziness, the sweating and cramps, the foaming and jerking like the falling-down disease.

The diamondback coiled down around my leg to my ankle, the length of him pulsing against my pulse, rattles rasping across my instep, body snapping up and back to tear loose, pulling away, then sinking his fangs deeper, milking himself into me. Like being punctured by a pair of Mexican dowels, the pain making me want to retch.

And still they ignored me, watching the medicine man chanting and churning barefoot among the coals, walking now out of the fire across to a small lodge set up earlier by the elders. And then it began, the ringing in front of my ears, the dizziness gathering behind my eyes.

The medicine man danced around the lodge four times, then pulled up the flap, and the white man I'd seen the braves tormenting earlier and who I seemed vaguely to remember came out, followed by the little tow-headed boy and a girl, maybe twelve, and a woman. The McMurtys.

They'd been taken over a year ago by the Kiowas at the confluence of the Cimarron and Arkansas.

The poison was taking hold, the nausea welling up from below my throat.

The McMurtys stood huddled together, clothes in shreds, so filthy that, except that the boy and girl were blond, you wouldn't have known they were white.

Four times the medicine man circled them counterclockwise, making a long speech of purification, and then, almost before it started, the nausea began to leave, the dizziness clearing up behind my eyes. The diamondback was working loose. I steeled myself for the contractions, the gut spasms and convulsions.

After the medicine man, the Blade made a long speech about how the Wasichu asked for peace and built forts; asked for justice and stole their land; asked for equality and prepared to divide the earth with the steel snakes (railroads) splintering the great buffalo herds, driving away the game, bringing more Wasichus into the land. But this one time, just as the Wasichus had used the Indian, so now would the Indian use the Wasichu.

The diamondback jackknifed, then ricocheted off my leg. I bit down on the inside of my mouth. He tore free. I glanced down. Rattles singing, he flopped back into the pit.

But no more cramps, no nausea, no dizziness, the ringing gone. Except for a throbbing where he'd jerked loose, nothing. I felt— fine.

At the diamondback's yanking free, the Blade's eyes cut across at me—waiting for me to fall foaming, I thought—afraid I wouldn't die, I thought—the first time he'd let on I was even there, whereas the McMurtys had never taken their eyes off me, and for just a beat, across the glow of the coals, I thought I saw Tom McMurty nod, the corner of his mouth lift.

I didn't know it then and they sure didn't look it, but this was the happiest the McMurtys had been since they'd been took, Tom McMurty having just made a deal with the Blade that for Tom's teaching the Chosen Four the tongue and ways of the Wasichus, the Blade would stop Tom's wife and daughter being passed around among the braves or being loaned out to other tribes, a pimping learned them by the whites with Indian girls.

And still, since the nausea and dizziness, I hadn't felt a thing. Over twenty minutes now since I'd been hit by the snake.

They made the McMurtys abase themselves on their bellies

while the Blade sprinkled red powder over them, at the end of which the Blade glanced once more at me so fleetingly that for just that second I wasn't sure, but then abruptly I understood, if not *why* at least *what* I should do, and I began to weave and stagger and fell down.

I lay there for maybe ten seconds before I began to twitch, first my feet the way I'd seen the rabbits do, then my legs and arms and head, arching my back and jerking all over, trying to foam, spitting on myself until they came and took and lay me in the McMurtys' lodge.

For almost eighteen hours I lay there. The old squaw looking in on me every two or three hours, the first six hours motionless. Then I began to mumble, and the next morning I opened my eyes.

The elders came that afternoon to declare me alive and so undefiled and so not guilty.

That night, the Blade came alone. For a long while we sat and smoked.

"How do you, Face on Water?"

"Wakan Tanka has been good," I said.

"Then has He need of you."

"Indeed am I full of grace."

"A thing of great wonder, Face on Water."

We smoked.

"The Chosen Four go to the land of the Wasichu," the Blade said after a while, "to seek their medicine."

I waited.

"I wish you, Face on Water, to go before to prepare a place for them."

It *had* been the Blade, then.

"Where is that?" I said.

"Where the Great Father resides."

"Washington?"

"There."

"It is long, long," I said.

"You have been to this place, Face on Water?"

Pap had been to Washington back in '14. "One o' them dead little southern towns," Pap said of it. "Not much more 'n' a wart on the nation's ass," Pap said.

"No," I said to the Blade, "I do not know it. I have only heard."

"You will speak to the Great White Father, Face on Water."

"President Grant!"

"Him."

Twice more the Blade went to the pipe; then he began to speak of the buffalo, of his ancestors and Wakan Tanka, the railroad and sodbusters and what was the future, but what it all came down to was a little righteous coercion—I was to go to Washington to tell President Grant that, for stopping the buffalo hunters and the forts, the Blade would allow the Kansas Pacific Railroad as much land as would fit between the steel snake's coils and safe passage for all headed to the land of the Thunder Persons (West Coast). Otherwise there wouldn't be a rail, a cabin, a string of wire or a fence post standing from the Missouri to the Great Salt Lake Basin, from the Rio Grande to the Black Hills.

Even now, said the Blade, there was a subchief to the Great White Father in Dodge City. (Senator Mathew Devlin. I'd heard of him all spring and summer. Another one of those sent out by Washington to investigate Indian affairs.) I was to start with this subchief, the Blade said, then on to the place of the sun rising.

I held back. "One does not speak so easily to the Washington Great One," I said.

The Blade shook his head in wonder. "He is your sachem."

I brought my palms up from my sides to show doubt.

The old eyes studied me out of the bark of his face. "Do you not know the Great Washington Chief?"

I followed a plume of smoke up to Grandfather Sky. . . . Hiram Ulysses Grant, Ulysses Simpson Grant, ol' red-white-and-blue, ol' U.S., Unconditional Surrender, Grant—I knew him, all right. Not the cigar-crawnching, gristle-chinned old grouser you saw in the papers. But Sam Grant. Then Lieutenant Grant of the 4th Infantry at Vancouver Barracks. Slim, young like the others, but not like the others. Boots forever needing a cloth, his uniform puckered all the way around—brooding, with that little stoop, over an old meershaum pipe—that was long before the cigars—on something the rest of us couldn't see, with a face near as pretty as a girl's, skin white as a gull's wing, eyes steady as a forest pool, beard just starting to yield gentle along the rimjaw, bloodstone where the sun hit it. Yes, I knew Sam Grant for a fact. In a manner of speaking, you might even say we was partners. Anyway, broke together. And that's an adhesive as binding of men as ever you'll find.

I was sixteen then, younger than Sam by twelve, fourteen years. Still, by then I'd been down "to look at the crossing" as they say. With Pap you looked or went blind. Pap a four-square stud with a whipstitch spine: three wives and two grass widows. Of Pap's ten boys and eight girls, I was fifth from the top. But then, out there in the scrub where twenty-five hours wasn't enough for a day, a litter paid, Pap reckoning to work all eighteen of us for room and not much board till we all died of the shivers, and I run off. I was twelve. Teamstering, then trapping. Mostly in the mountains. Finally taking off for the gold fields, not coming up with much except down with pneumonia, tracking back home that spring to see how the family was cutting it, and met Sam—the Columbia River, where Sam was stationed, coming off the mouth of the Snake, where Pap had his farm.

We was all shot short. I'd just tapped out a month earlier in a mine up on the Yellow while Sam and the other officers, because of the inflated prices of the gold rush in California, would have starved if the government hadn't allowed them to buy food from the commissary at East Coast wholesale prices; not that Sam was a greedy one, but he wanted to bring his wife and children out from Ohio, which was the cause of his brooding, which drove us into the potato business—food prices in California so high a man could make a fortune if he could just get a crop to market.

I had the wagons, and Sam with some others rented land along the Columbia, bought horses, farm equipment and seed and planted a field. But the Columbia overflowed her banks come spring and wiped us out—which was no great loss because everyone else on the Coast had planted potatoes and the price fell so low it didn't pay to dig the crop.

Then it developed ice was as scarce as hens' teeth in San Francisco, and Sam and some others had a hundred tons of the stuff cut up on the Columbia. I hauled it to the schooner and lumped it on board, but the schooner met heavy head winds, took six weeks to make the trip and arrived to find shiploads of ice just in from Alaska and the market bust.

Later, I helped Sam and some of his friends ship hogs to San Francisco, but once more we ran into falling prices, our last deal together when we bought up all the chickens we could find, chartered another schooner and watched them all die en route. Lordy! Sam's ideas were good enough, but he was a man snake-bit and I threw in my hand and went back to the mountains.

Later, I heard they shipped Sam out to Humboldt Bay, in California, where he'd got in some sort of jam drinking, quit the army, and went home.

I didn't see Sam till near three years later, in St. Louis. He was peddling wood out of a wagon—a little more stooped, stubble-bearded in a battered hat and a faded army greatcoat, seedy.

I was flush from selling a year's catch of beaver, and though Sam wouldn't take no money, he let me buy him dinner.

He'd been farming sixty acres his father-in-law had give him, but I could see things hadn't gone too good.

He'd just voted for James Buchanan, the Democrat, for President, he said, and he spent most of the evening telling me how he feared a Republican victory would goad the South into secession, which worried him a great deal, and that was the last time I saw Sam Grant.

I lay my right palm over my chest and pushed away to show the Blade I knew the President and *his heart was good.*

The Blade nodded his approval and said a sachem should know each of his braves.

I reminded him that they were beyond count, which made him frown.

"You will go?" he said.

I looked away.

I had him cold.

"That was not my word," I said.

"What, then, would you, Face on Water?"

"I have many snows on my back," I said.

"Far fewer than I."

"I am tired."

"You are not old, Face on Water."

"I would stay with your people."

It's not often you catch an old coyote.

His head, with the long, ferocious nose, came up at me, pointing.

I placed the first two fingers of my right hand at my mouth for *brother*.

"Your people are honest," I said, "you are brave."

His black, old agate eyes studied me narrowly.

"Then, Face on Water will do as he is requested."

"No. I would pitch my lodge in your hoop. I would marry, have children."

He flared. "For that you were not saved!"

"Oh? Saved? How? Who has done this for me? Let me know that I may thank him."

He'd tipped his hand and it infuriated him. "You will go!" he hissed.

"You would drive me out?"

"I would as I would."

I brought up my hands and to the side in the sign for *virtue*. "I am now of much honor, O Chief."

"I—*I!*—have given you the honor."

I had him for a fact. Within the camp I could now come and go as I pleased.

He looked away, east, out through the lodge flap. "After you have been to the Washington place, Face on Water, you may return."

"To go an' do in the land of the Wasichu takes much, much. I have nothing."

Not a line in that old, pitted face altered. He now knew where I'd been and where I was going. He hooked his right index finger over his thumb for *peag*, money.

"Ask, Face on Water."

"All the buffalo hides, three wagons to carry them in, an' horses to pull the wagons."

He looked hard at me with—among other things—respect: all the while I'd been bargaining, he'd not suspected. He brought the edge of his right hand down across his left palm: *It is done.* Then he got up, all dignity and anger.

So it hadn't been the death of Buffalo Who Runs, or the night bird making day sounds, or concern for his braves, that's not why the Blade hadn't overrun us. It was also why Manuel and the others hadn't done for us right there on the mesa—at the Blade's orders. The Blade had known: the Chosen Four couldn't possibly make it on their own. Someone had to lead them. The French-man was dead; the skinners, even had they been alive, too young and too ignorant; McMurty, bred to the plains, as wanting as the skinners. That left me. So, if I had played into the Blade's hands, so had he into mine. But I was a traitor. They'd all known and seen. And so the Trial of Defilement. And to make sure I passed, the Blade had milked that diamondback of every last oozing of poison, so that, nailed to me as he'd been, all I'd known was some ringing, a little dizziness and nausea . . . those times the Blade had glanced at me, not in fear I wouldn't die but that I wouldn't *look* like I was dying. So even McMurty had guessed.

One shrewd old man.

The Blade looked hard at me.

"The McMurtys will I keep, Face on Water, until your return."

One shrewd old man.

I held back the tent flap and watched him cross the compound with the bowed-kneed roll of an old riverman. . . .

To search for the Wasichu power.

The Wasichu medicine!

This the big *find-out.*

Foolish people.

Sam Grant—the President—was no fool.

They were searching for the wind.

School and Home for Indian Teachers and Students

We never laughed at it.

Though I guess to some it was funny enough.

School and Home for Indian Teachers and Students, we called ourselves—SHITS, Faith McMurty said one afternoon and spelled it out, "S-H-I-T-S."

"Faith!" Mrs. McMurty said.

"Well," Faith said, "that's what it comes to, Mama."

Which was what it came to, all right.

Faith laughed.

"Now, see here, young lady," Mrs. McMurty began.

"Oh, Mama!" Faith snapped.

And it was—pretty foolish—after what that girl had seen and done and been subjected to this past year!

Barely thirteen, she looked near as old as her mama, and suddenly the girl, most often silent and staring off at pictures inside, began to laugh and laugh, the lost in her eyes turning to a glitter, Mrs. McMurty and Tom trying hard to rein her in.

In the months following (after I'd gone), the girl would bust out more and more like that until the Indians, frightened—they believe the mad to be possessed of the Evil One—would put her out on the plains to starve. The girl, running wild, eating roots and insects until some mountain men found her and built her a sod hut, supplying her with food and cache until, they said, she began to get better, when she was murdered by some Tonkawas. The most detested tribe on the plains. Because not only had the Tonkawas sold out completely to the white man, serving as scouts on campaigns against any and all but, worse, they were the only plains tribe of cannibals. Half-eaten parts of the girl found all around her shanty.

That same year, Mrs. McMurty died of the plague and Tom hung himself, the boy turning Indian. Later, as a young buck, leader of a band torturing and killing all through the Southwest, the boy became one of the most feared, most hated men on the plains. So vicious that at last his own couldn't take him any more and cast him out one winter to freeze to death.

Still, SHITS it stayed, and whether or not we said it out loud, always without humor, that's how we thought. Which didn't mean just us and the Chosen Four, but every day the whole she-she-shebang: squaws, braves, chiefs, the elders, the old, young, sorry and sick. From everywhere and anywhere. Whoever happened to be passing.

For six months, from the Moon When the Plums Turn Scarlet to the Moon of the Red Calf, we were the featured attraction from the Brazos to the Powder, from the Arkansas to the San Pedro, an extravaganza nonpareil, a minstrel-burley house-vaudeville-sideshow complete with clowns and tents, the most successful, the biggest, the only Chautauqua on the central shelf.

"Cl-o-th-es," Mrs. McMurty would say, sounding out each letter, waving her hand over a blanket on which she'd laid out everything a white woman wore, and they'd all repeat after her, "Cl-o-th-es," and she'd reach down and pick up something.

"Pet-ti-coat," she'd say, holding it up to her.

"Pet-ti-coat," they'd all—sometimes two hundred Indians—would yell back at her. "Help keep squaw warm, make dress puff out," and she began to explain how it was worn, when Noisy Walking picked up a bustle, studying it with his one fierce eye.

"What this?"

Of the Four, Manuel was the quickest study; Little Rabbit, the deepest; Gray Owl, the wisest; and Noisy Walking—like his name, you always knew where Noisy Walking was.

Mrs. McMurty corrected him: "What *is* this?"

Noisy Walking grunted.

"This *is* a bustle. It *is* worn like this," and she held it up behind her.

"Make softer ride pony," Little Rabbit said.

"No," Noisy Walking said, "sack, go poop."

"It *is* the style," said Mrs. McMurty.

"Still?"

"Style, sty-ull. Style is what everyone does. It makes women pretty. Like buffalo grease in a girl's hair."

"Big butt make pretty?" Noisy Walking asked.

"It's the style, yes."

And Noisy Walking slapped a fat squaw on the behind. "You much still, big butt," and everyone was off howling.

Little Rabbit whirled a brassiere over his head. "Sling. Throw rock at Pawnee."

"No." Mrs. McMurty held it up to her.

"Breast harness," said Gray Owl.

"Dry up milk," said the Rabbit.

Mrs. McMurty tried to explain how it helped support, "hold woman up."

"Smash tit," said Noisy Walking, "make too small, lose squaw under blanket," and they were off screeching again.

Or—the time Tom McMurty tried to explain money to Manuel: On the ground between them, a silver dollar, two fifty-cent pieces and four quarters.

"Eight bits make one dollar." And Tom picked up the fifty-cent piece. "This is four bits." He picked up the quarter. "This is two bits. Eight bits, one dollar. Two four-bits, one dollar. Savvy?"

Manuel studied the money, then turned to Tom: "What a bit?"

We broke class early that day.

Or—the time the girl Faith tried to teach Noisy Walking his name:

"I am Faith McMurty," the girl said. "Who are you?"

"I am Faith McMurty," Noisy Walking repeated.

"No. *I* am Faith McMurty. *You* are who?"

Noisy Walking pointed to the girl: "You are *who*."

"No, I am Faith McMurty, but you are—"

"I are who."

"No, you are—" she flared, "a big, red—"

Again Noisy Walking pointed to himself: "You are a big, red—"

"One-eyed sonofabitch," the girl blurted.

Noisy Walking jumped to his feet. "I are who, a big, red sonofabitch."

It was funny, I guess, all turning to look at Noisy Walking, chest out, single black eye looking about defiantly, pointing proudly to himself, but nobody laughed, Tom and Mrs. McMurty glancing at one another, then at their daughter, the girl as expressionless, as cold as that diamondback in the pit.

By the Moon of the Red Grass Appearing they knew words and counting and money and clothes and houses and food and forks and tables and something of manners, and the Blade decided it was graduation day—with the Chosen Four at the four sacred corners: to the west, Gray Owl painted red; to the north, Little Rabbit splashed with white; to the east, Sonofabitch (since that day with Faith, that had become Noisy Walking's name) Sonofabitch east, enlimned with a yellow mud, even the bullsnake thong over his eye; and south, Manuel, blue stripes brushed up and down and all around him. Much, much honor. The only way, I think, the Blade could have gotten them to do it.

Distinction, renown, honor—life to a savage. Because none of them, I don't think, wanted to go; these last months all sticking close to their lodges and families: the little Arapaho, Little Rabbit, newly married to a sloe-eyed pretty, Sweet Sage, the one who'd led the sun-dance procession, the Rabbit off with his bride every day, pitching his lodge away from the others; Gray Owl playing daily now with his two small sons—hunting, trapping, fishing with them; Sonofabitch popping his eyepatch at all the girls, chasing the divorced women and widows as if he wouldn't never get to use it again; only Manuel was distant, twice hazarding his daddy's plans on raiding parties which, if his daddy had caught him, would have finished him right there, Manuel sometimes off for days on a hunt—except, Manuel wasn't always hunting.

I fetched up on that one evening just before dusk when, trapping, I heard the chunk-a-chunk of a knife from the bottom of an old dry wash under a heavy overhang of choke brush—not that I'd surprised him—he'd probably known of me for the last half hour; fact is, the last twenty yards he'd called out to me, "She-choo," *over here,* and I'd slid down the bank and ducked in under the choke brush, out of which he'd made a sort of secret workroom, secret because he was back at his secret vice, *carving* (in this time of trouble unseemly squaw's play; the Blade would never have allowed it). What Manuel was carving, I couldn't make out. He sat bent over, a log across his knees.

Manuel didn't look at me. I squatted down next to him and watched. A puzzlement, because Plains Indians, 'most always on the move, don't go in for those. They're too hard to hump along. It looked like a—"Totem?" I asked. Manuel didn't answer until just before the light began to fade. "Lodgepole," Manuel said. For who or what he didn't say, but pulled it out from under the overhang and stood it up on its end so the setting sun bounced off its length. Tall as a lodgepole all right, though thicker, but like no lodgepole I'd ever seen, no, nor no totem neither, figures carved the length of her, not gouged and lump-hunky like most, but fine as willow tips, so detailed and exact I could've sworn I caught movement, the dart of an eye, flutter of a wing. At the base, holding up the world, a buffalo head, an old bull from the look of him, shatter-horned and shagged, forehead butt-blistered from half a thousand fights, teeth missing, from the sink of his muzzle; on top of the buff, a grizzly, upright, hind legs spread, chest barreled, forepaws reaching out, claws unsheathed, ready to fight; above him, a rabbit, hunkered down, head turned shyly, looking up and away from the grizzly, ears forward, wary; and growing out of the rabbit's back, the rattling person, Waguchun, a cottonwood, the tree of life, a serpent entwined in its roots, the branches bare, a winter tree when all things sleep or die.

I glanced over at Manuel. I was confused, flattered, because, hidden off thisaway, I was most probably one of the first, more likely the only one he'd shown it to. But why me? Why? His face was flushed with the doing. I looked back up at the totem. On the topmost branch of the cottonwood, an eagle, eyes fierce and glaring, the sacred seer, couched behind a beak hooking out sharp and ferocious as the Blade's nose, and floating above all, the holy

White Cow Buffalo Woman. I looked again: the holy White Cow Buffalo Woman was Manuel's mother, Light Hands, before the pox had pustuled away first her beauty and later her life (infected by a Wasichu baby she'd lifted out of a burning wagon train—a third of the tribe dead before the pox had run its course). "Light Hands." I pointed. Manuel beamed that I'd recognized her. "See," he said turning the pole to make the light flicker across her face, "she smiles," which was why me—*she*: because Manuel thought it would mean more to me, because I'd always been good to Light Hands, at odd times bringing her some trim, needles, a scraping knife, a swatch of cloth, beads—because she was the Chief's wife and I wanted to keep up my trading rights within the tribe . . . Lord, Lord—the light slanting down across the surfaces, dredging up hollows, softening corners, sharpening edges, the wood in Manuel's hands alive, as if each of the figures had drawn a deep breath and were now about to let it out so that later, eating some pemmican and tiny, hard winter apples of Manuel's and some beef belly and fixings of mine, the totem pulled up to the fire where we could look at it—I've never seen a man prouder.

He'd been at it for weeks, you could see. He showed me how for hours he'd sketched and resketched the design in the sand until he'd got exactly what he wanted, then how he'd transferred it to doeskin. He'd even invented special tools for the fine work: a punch out of a sharpened beaver pizzle and a sort of chisel from the hipbone of an antelope. He'd even made a kind of burning needle from an old firing pin. A marvel, that boy. He lay back, eyes shining, looking at what he'd done. "Mad Dog," the troopers called him. One of the most vicious manslayers on the plains they called him.

Eating, I thought of how a man got made into something else, of how Pap, hardscrabble mean, had scattered us, my brothers and sisters and me, all over the country and of Little Rabbit's bride and of Gray Owl's family and what would happen to the Four out there, because I'd seen what happened to the rah-tons-bah, *the comebacks*, the returned ones from the white towns, corrupt, lazing around the forts, dragging along without pride or place after the Wasichus, grinning after handouts. And suddenly I wanted to take it all back. Call it off. I could. The tribe had cleared me. I could do it. Refuse to go. Tell the Blade. Refuse to lead them. All bets off. It hadn't been all bluff, my telling the Blade I wanted to marry, raise a family and make a house in his hoop . . . but even as I made the vow to myself on Manuel's totem, I knew!—I hadn't the sticking for it.

It was snug down in the creek bed, out of the wind, under the choke brush, and for a long while we sat and smoked and looked at the totem, when a coyote coughed and Manuel looked up and nodded at hanhipi-wi, *the night sun,* the fingernail moon rising shy as a young girl up over the scrub, and "Mad Dog" stood up to say his prayers, the same as now, praying, the Blade dusted each of the Chosen Four with red powder, rubbing sacred sage over their chests and eyelids, for they must never forget, the Blade said, that they were Maha tahan wicasa wan, *men of the earth,* Ikce Wicasa, *the natural human beings,* the free, wild common people, and there were more prayers, after which the Blade got down to it:

First off, the Blade said, the Chosen Four must seek out the Great White Grant Father—one of the many little confusions bolstering the Blade's blind faith in this whole *loco* lashup— *Grant Father,* so much like *Grandfather,* the good, the kind, the generous, all-merciful God of their heavens, that the Blade couldn't conceive of Sam Grant's turning down their request to stop the forts and the buffalo hunters.

Second, the Blade said, the Chosen Four must seek everywhere for the Wasichu medicine: in his earth and beneath his waters, without his air and within his people, for the source of his sticks of fire and dirt of flame, for the power of his engines and the wells of his wealth; above all, to learn the signs in his cages (I think he meant books) and the drawings on his temples.

So, you see, the Blade had it all figured, for a fact. Simple and direct. But if the Blade's grand scheme sounds, to those who don't know him quite that well, just a mite simple, the man wasn't.

The Blade was a child of his people. He believed in his gods, in himself and his destiny. He'd read tomorrow in today's tracings of yesterday's sacrificial blood in the timeless sands, and it was plain, plain: the Indian was doomed unless the white man could be stopped.

What the Blade had in mind, I think, was nothing less than

driving the Wasichu, all Wasichus, all the way back across the Mississippi, and to do it the Blade was buying time.

I think he figured if he could get the President to stop the whites long enough for him to build up not only his own but all the plains tribes, then, together with the secret of the Wasichu medicine rooted out by the Chosen Four—this was the true *find-out*—they'd be primed, erupting one blue day over the red land like a flash fire to sweep the white man forever off the plains in one great, glorious rout.

The Blade's last act was to give the Chosen Four their final affirmation, the blood oath, slicing their right palms with a bone awl from thumb to little finger, pressing the cuts palm to palm, intermingling their lives as Brothers of the Body, meaning that in battle they'd die together as one, after which the Blade signaled the Four to gather around him, calling the medicine man, who, with much ceremony, approached with a great basket of rock and gravel.

Where they were going, the Blade said, the Wasichu put much value on this rock and sand, and since the hunting and fishing might not be so good in this new place, they could barter what was in the basket for food and clothes—and whatever else the Wasichu possessed, I thought—his land, his home, his wife, *his soul*.

Early the dawn of the day before we left, I was hurrahed out of a dead sleep by a great pother outside. I lifted the lodge flap: in the middle of the compound a gathering crowd of squaws, braves and kids milled like spooked stock. I got dressed and joined them. Out of their center rose Manuel's totem. But where it came from no one and everyone knew (from the carving), the crowd abruptly silent, holding their breath for the holy time, the day's rebirth, the sun starting now to feel up over the mesa's eastern shore, an ocher lip of light fingering the crest of the White Cow Buffalo Woman's hair, slowly crawling down over her face as the sun rose, down over spotted eagle, down the cottonwood, the rabbit, the grizzly and buffalo. Like painting. Or, it came to me, like writing. So, suddenly, I knew: this, Manuel's message to them, his scalp lock. They stood rooted, awed. Big medicine, big. Manuel had written:

The foundation of the world is the buffalo, which must be protected by the great strength and ferocity of the grizzly, yet beware the haughtiness and arrogance that begets the sightlessness of the powerful; rather, be humble and meek and so forever wary as the rabbit and look to the gods as does the cottonwood, from whose trunk the tribe, too, must thrust out its branches to grow and multiply, covering all the land as does the sacred seer from the cottonwood's topmost branch, spotted eagle—crowning all with love, Light Hands' love, for it is the lodgepole that shelters the family and so holds up the world—even unto death.

Feeling—I don't know what—I turned away, knocking over the Blade's basket of rock and gravel, with which they were to barter for food and weapons if the hunting and fishing were poor. And what was in that basket would finish them off quicker, I knew, than all the troops Sam the President could muster, and I stooped to gather it up, above me the totem glimmering golden in the morning sun, the people saying over and over, hah wacan, hah wacan, *a holy work, a holy work,* but it was, I knew, more than that. It was Manuel's scalp lock, his legacy to them . . . for Manuel didn't expect to return.

BOOK THREE

The Stone Prairie

I I

::::::::::::::::::::::::::::::::::::::

Red Man Need Ticket

During the Moon When the Ponies Shed, that month when the mesa mats with the green of seedtime, when the air is like drinking and the sky vaults high and washed over the sun, I set out for Dodge City and Senator Mathew Devlin with three wagons of hides, two drivers, the Chosen Four and the Blade's blessing.

The McMurtys were waiting for me at the head of the draw. A week before, Tom had given me a parfleche on the inside flap of which he'd scrawled a message with charcoal saying to whoever read this that they were alive and to come and get them. He'd also given me his wife's wedding ring and his daughter's bracelet to prove what the parfleche said was true, because folk don't always believe a squawman.

"Come back," was all Tom said. Mrs. McMurty cried. The only time I was ever to see her give way. Faith kissed me, and the little boy, Jed, wanted to go along. It was the last time I was ever to see any of them.

Where we'd fought them in the gorge, I couldn't make out anyone but Pock Face, who, almost bald, hadn't been scalped, the others stripped and burnt or eaten by the wild things beyond knowing.

Behind, walking, a crowd followed us to the first rise: Gray Owl's wife and kids, Little Rabbit's sloe-eyed bride, two widows and a divorced woman Sonofabitch had been seeing to of nights and the Blade, all up close, touching and rubbing against their men's legs, behind the families, packs of kids and dogs and the curious, the Chosen Four never once looking down or back but straight on as though unaware they weren't alone, not even when they went over the rise and the crowd stopped, the women's tremolo fluttering out across the prairie—all except Little Rabbit, whose mare shied at something in the undergrowth so he had to jerk her sideways and looked down into his bride's eyes. But, of course, that had been none of his own weakness. Just the same, all that day and the next, except for the clump of the horses and the creak of the wagons, it was quiet as crying.

We followed the Big Red to Denison, where the Chosen Four broke off east, me and the others continuing north up the Washita and Canadian rivers over a tributary of the Rattlesnake.

On the other side of the Rattlesnake, we lashed the three wagons tongue and axle and I went on into Dodge alone.

The senator wasn't there. He'd lit out, the townsfolk said, with his daughter three days earlier for Hutchinson, so I sent a telegram on ahead explaining my purpose, asking the senator to wait for me in Independence, then settled down to some gentle intemperance and to wait for buyers.

There, for a couple days in Dodge, I was the big bull in the lick, everyone buying me drinks, with me telling how we'd fought them off in the gorge, how I'd come by the hides. Telling it all except about the Chosen Four. Showing around Tom's parfleche, the woman's wedding ring and the girl's bracelet. Everyone talking about going after the McMurtys, but they never would, not that they all believed me, some muttering how I'd murdered the Frenchman and skinners to keep it all for myself. Which had happened often enough before. Murdering the McMurtys to keep them quiet. Until the muttering got loud enough for me to hear, besides which it was time to pull stakes, and the next morning at the Atchison-Topeka I bought five tickets—the four extra, I said, for my wife and kids.

That afternoon I sold the hides out of a back room in Surrey's Saloon to a buyer from Cincinnati, top dollar; the wagons, the horses, the harness and fooforah to an advance agent for a big buff outfit headed south, most of the town and all the nighthawkers and light-traveling, heavy-fingered gentry in the territory, it seemed, looking on so there sure wasn't no seal on the size of my stash, and after setting up all around a half dozen times, Surrey slipped me out back through his storeroom, for which I paid the old barman with my second pair of boots, an old crescent gun and whatever else Surrey found back at my hotel, where I figured a *remuda* of night visitors was right now gathering awaiting my return—ducking down the alley, slipping across main to the depot, where I gave the stationmaster five new silver dollars to let me hole up in his office until train time, because, mister, I was now a rich man!

Fourteen hours I holed up in the stationmaster's, until just before noon of the second day, when I heard her pull in, hissing and blowing cinders and soot, the steam carving cracks in the windows. I looked out. A short hitch . . . the baggage car flush up against the tender, two passenger coaches strung out behind.

The stationmaster unbolted his office door and ushered me out on the platform like I was the new ring boss. Which, with my new pockets, I now was. I looked around. I didn't see any of *them* from Surrey's, and I handed five more silver dollars to the stationmaster, who called up, introducing me to the hogger leaning on his elbows out the engine-cab window, a round, red-eyed man who nodded down at me, his engine with its yellow spokes and blue boiler, its red stack and green tender and a bear's head, mounted, snarling, teeth glinting, up front just below the head lamp, the brass, the handrails, the ribbon leans and part of the drive shaft all polished like the fine work of God (hoggers then taking a great pride in their engines)—the outside of his engine prettier than the inside of the passenger coach, a dull, butt-brindle brown with soot-streaked plank benches and a wood stove at one end but very fancy with kerosene lamps along the walls.

A rangy lot in the passenger coach: traders, trappers, buffalo hunters, prospectors, land agents. I took a seat at the rear facing the front to see just how ambitious some of them nighthawkers might be, but I was the only one to board out of Dodge, and when that first light little tug from down underneath shuddered up through my seat from the rails, I unlocked all the way to my heels. I'd done it. I'd made her! And I lolled back stroking down inside myself . . . watching the conductor checking tickets down the aisle, a little man in a long, black funeral coat and a high, black silk hat with a CONDUCTOR sign pinned to the front, ticket stubs like colored fingers pushing out from beneath the band . . . shucking back and hugging myself. Oh, I was one fine, clever fella.

During the day, I slept, staying awake nights, when, close to thirty-six hours out, just the other side of the Arkansas River, about three in the morning, at a bend where the track worried through low hills, the wheels caught hard, steam whipping back past the windows, and we stuttered to a stop.

Everyone was asleep. Which was how I'd reckoned that, too. Outside, the hogger and fireman stood looking at a freshly severed buffalo head atop a pile of rock blocking the track.

The hogger was raving. "Go back an' wake ever'body up, help git this shit off the tracks."

"No," I said, "we can do it."

"You can, I ain't," said the hogger, when up from on either side of us they came, Manuel and Little Rabbit out of a barranca; Gray Owl and Sonofabitch from behind a stand of scrub.

"We do," Gray Owl said.

Horses and men streaked with paint, in the light from the engine they looked savage.

The hogger and fireman stood numb. The conductor whirled to run. I caught his arm, and his high, black silk hat fell off. Gray Owl dismounted to pick up the hat and hand it back to him.

"They're all right," I said. "They won't hurt nobody."

The other three dismounted to unpile the rock.

"Wh-What do they want?" said the conductor.

Gray Owl pointed to the train and brought his right hand fluttering down over his palm.

The conductor turned to me.

"They want to ride yer train," I said.

The conductor looked like a man with a mouthful of cayenne sauce. "Ride the train, for Christsake! This one?" he said looking around as if it weren't the only train in a thousand miles. "Well, they can't."

Manuel started forward.

The conductor moved closer to me, voice softening. "T-Tell 'em they can't ride the train."

I stepped away from him. "You tell 'em," I said.

Against the dark, the little conductor, enshrouded in his funeral coat and high silk hat, looked lost. He held out a white hand to me as though I should take it. "Tell them they need tickets. Tell them they—" Taking a ticket stub from his capband, the conductor turned to Gray Owl, explaining how "Red man need ticket. You go buy."

I held out to him the four tickets I'd bought back in Dodge.

He gawped at the tickets, then lifted a hand against the light from the engine to study me. "What—how? Who're you?"

"They won't hurt nobody. They just want to ride the train."

"Why?"

I handed him the tickets.

He pushed them back at me. "Mister, back in that coach, if they was to find out I let these four on—Christ!—they'd throw me under the cowcatcher."

"No one needs to know," I said. "Stick 'em in the baggage car. They're all right. They're goin' to Washington."

"What for, to scalp the President?"

"They're civilized," I said.

The conductor turned again to look at them, and I had to admit *civilized* wasn't maybe the word, the flames from the firebox etching out their savagery in gleaming garnet, paint-slashed bodies glistening, all feathers and buckskin, glinting bow tips and knife edges and Sonofabitch's wild, glittering eye. Going to Washington. The conductor was right; they looked like a war party.

The conductor turned to the hogger and fireman.

"I sure won't say nothin'," the fireman said.

"Let's go," the hogger said as though someone might change his mind.

Little Rabbit clucked into the darkness, and the boy who'd spilled water over his chin and chest that day up on the ridge came out of the barranca to gather up their ponies' reins. And for half a thousand miles they rode in the baggage car. Over a week and a half before they were discovered, when it was just like the conductor said.

::::::::::::::::::::::::::::::::::::

They—Ate—My—Babies

We caught up with Senator Mathew Devlin and his daughter just outside Osawatomie, Kansas.

In the passenger coach it looked worse than it was, loud mostly, a lot of blaspheming, some gambling and drinking, but bad enough so that when the senator and his daughter boarded and I introduced myself, the senator grasped my hand like I'd just found the deed to his jump claim, so that, later, telling him about the Blade and the Chosen Four, he was downright longing to help, saying that, come the proper time, he'd intercede for us with the President and for us not to worry.

(I hadn't, of course, mentioned the blind freight behind us in the baggage car, lest I jamboree the stock.)

I got to like the senator in the next couple days. He wasn't a mistletoe politician and he hadn't bloat in the jaw. He liked a drink and a quiet hand of stud, and he spoke his thought. He'd been down the road a piece, and you could see that, along his own trap lines, he'd done well, but he'd cut new territory now, and he wasn't sure.

An appointee of President Grant's to investigate Indian Affairs —I never could get used to calling Sam that, *President*—the senator had been herded from fort to fort, where he'd talked to none but generals, Indian agents and whatever *good* Indians the generals and agents could fetch him. So, after six months, he didn't know a lot more than his daughter, who'd come along, she said

laughing, to see her daddy took his liver pills—her name Honor—
that girl prettier than four of a kind in a pat game, so the next
morning the gambling was down to a little genteel red dog, the
white lightning under the planking, the language a marvel to the
ear, and though you just never slipped that yoke of soot seeping in
and around, under and over and through the floorboards, the over-
head and windows, there were still more sweet-smelling faces and
trimmed beards next morning than in a St. Louis sporting lodge,
but then, too, the farther east, the more civilized the folk board-
ing. Everything fine until just after we crossed the Missouri, when
this woman, frog fat and blowing, came winding down the aisle in
full croak: "Where's the conductor? Where's the conductor!" the
conductor just entering from the opposite end of the coach.

"Oh, conductor, my babies, they've been, been—" She caught
him by the sleeve of his funeral coat, pulling him after her down
the aisle toward the baggage car. "What about yer babies?" the
conductor said. I stood up. The conductor glanced at me as they
went by. I followed. So now did a lot of others. The baggage-car
door, always locked, was ajar, the conductor the only one in or
out, piling folks' luggage outside to pick up whenever anyone got
on or off, so even I hadn't been inside, knocking four times late at
night to see how they were, and they'd answer.

"The clerk," the conductor called to me back over his shoulder.

"What?" the fat lady said.

"What about yer babies?" the conductor said.

What the conductor meant was that at the last stop, instead of
throwing the mailbag up into the vestibule like the others, the
clerk had boarded, unlocked the baggage door, tossed the mailbag
inside and left leaving the door unlocked.

The fat woman pushed into the baggage car.

The Four sat huddled in a circle on the floor eating, almost
black, the soot in the baggage car worse even than in the coach.

She went up to Sonofabitch, his fierce, black eye dancing from
me to the woman to the crowd.

"There," she cried, "see, see. . . ."

Sonofabitch frowned up at the woman.

"What?" said the conductor.

"My baby's necklace," the woman said, "he's wearing it."

And Sonofabitch was, a necklace.

Lord amighty!

The conductor went white. "Yer baby?" he said.

I looked around.

The woman began to cry. "They—ate—my—babies."

Christ!

I forced myself to look down at what they were eating. You could accuse them of a lot, I knew, the Plains People, but, except for the Tonkawas, cannabalism wasn't in their draft.

"Yer—babies?" the conductor said again dumbly.

I picked up one of the bones. It didn't look human. It was too thin, too small even for a child. The meat on it too stringy. It looked—

"Pudgy's collar," the woman said.

"Whose?" said the conductor.

"Pudgy and Caroline, my dogs."

Lordy, her dogs!

Sonofabitch was wearing the dog collar all right—two dog collars.

Puzzled, confused, the Four watched the fat woman, a crowd beginning to gather behind us in the entrance, when Manuel, a half-chewed dog leg in one hand, lurched to his feet.

I moved up beside the conductor.

Gray Owl brought his right hand down, sawing across his wrist with the opposite hand, a *mistake*, and he began to try to explain:

What had happened was they hadn't brought any food, thinking that Eater of Fire, the train, would chase and kill the buffalo for them. So they'd had to eat the dogs. A delicacy to an Indian. Later I found out that back somewhere between Broken Wheel and Independence they'd eaten a whole circus—a tame wolf, a trick riding horse, a dancing bear, a porcupine and a four-foot bullsnake.

I turned to explain when the fat woman threw herself into the arms of a fat man pushing through the crowd, her husband.

"Let me tell you, sir," the fat husband said to Gray Owl, "those animals of my wife's were valuable."

And then it began, or, better, *they* began: a whiskey drummer from Boston; a big, bushy-headed gun trader I knew from selling guns to the Indians in the Bitter Roots, and a gambler in a shoestring tie.

"What the jumpin' Jesus are Indians doin' on a train anyway?" demanded the whiskey drummer.

"Lucky we still got our hair," said the gun trader.

"I'll tell you somethin' else, sir," said the fat husband, "I expect to be fully reimbursed," and he glared around.

"How'd they git on in the first place?" said the gun trader.

The conductor batted his eyes.

Everyone looked at the conductor.

"They had tickets," he said after a while and looked away from me.

"I bought 'em," I said.

"*You* hoss!" said the gun trader.

"They ain't done nothin'," I said.

"Ain't done nothin'!" half-shouted the husband.

The gambler stood over them: "Bad enough fightin' 'em out there, without livin' with 'em in here."

"Not me," said the gun trader, shaking his bushy head, "I ain't ridin', not another goddamned yard, with no Kiowa at my back," and he reached up and pulled the emergency cord, the train squealing to a stop, throwing everyone, bag and baggage, forward in a heap, everyone cussing, grabbing hats and untangling themselves, when of a sudden it got so quiet you could hear the whiskey drummer's watch ticking over his belly.

All four were standing now, Gray Owl trying to understand; Manuel's eyes cutting across to their weapons in a pile at the rear of the car; Sonofabitch's left hand stealing down along the seam of his buckskins to a fish knife on his blind side, so I knew I had to do something but didn't know what, when Little Rabbit came forward to peer into the fat woman's face. She held up her hand as though to ward him off and backed away. Little Rabbit started to follow, when the husband stepped forward between them, but it wasn't the husband so much as another face that drew the Rabbit away from the woman, the Rabbit turning now to the crowd, going from face to face, peering intently into each as though one of them might hold the answer to whatever it was he was looking for. Savages curious and open as children that way.

It threw the crowd off bead, so that whatever had been about to happen, didn't. The faces startled, staring back, waiting, when the Rabbit began to shake his head into the face of the husband and somebody snorted and somebody swore, so by the time the whiskey drummer got back to jabbing his arm at them, it was again just talk.

"Teach 'em to bother decent folk," the whiskey drummer said.

The gun trader drew himself up. "I say flog 'em an' throw 'em off."

The gambler pushed me into Little Rabbit. "All of 'em!"

From the crowd came a slosh of agreement, everything starting to build again, when, in that instant between doing and not doing, Gray Owl stepped up to the fat woman, who shrank back against her husband.

"We much, much—" Gray Owl couldn't think of the word and shoved his fingers at his mouth in the sign for *hungry*. "Sad eat dog. Here," and shyly he held out a rock to the woman.

"What's that?" said the husband.

"Christ!" said the gambler.

The gun trader spat. "A medicine rock."

Insulted, the husband pushed his wife away from the Indian. "You're right," the husband said to the whiskey drummer, "teach 'em a lesson," and for the first time the crowd commenced to burn in earnest, when someone shouted, "Hold it," and a tiny old man, gnarled as truth, pushed forward.

The crowd reined in and the tiny man reached out and took the rock from Gray Owl and, like that, it got quiet.

"What is it, Sol?" said the whiskey drummer to the tiny man.

The tiny man held the rock up to the light, licked it with his tongue, dug at it with his penknife, licked it again and squeezed a grain between his fingers.

"Where'd you git this?" the tiny man said to Gray Owl.

"From Chief," said Gray Owl. "Wakan Tanka."

The tiny man turned to me.

"The Great Spirit," I said to the tiny man.

"We no more ride eater-of-fire," Gray Owl said with great dignity, and they began to gather up their gear.

The crowd, silent, watched.

"May I see that?" It was the senator.

The tiny man handed the senator the rock, the crowd falling back, loosening now, that other feeling starting to build.

With his thumbnail the senator scratched at where the rock

had been gouged, then looked up at the tiny man, who nodded at him.

"Well?" called a voice.

The senator fetched the rock back to the tiny man.

"Yeah?" another voice called over the heads of the crowd to the senator working his way back to the entrance.

"Sol?" the whiskey drummer said to the tiny man.

"Ma'am," the tiny man said holding the rock up to the fat woman, "what he's offerin' you here, it'll buy you a half dozen of the best goddamn dogs in the country, and a buggy an' six fer each of them to ride in whilst they lick whipped cream outa silver bowls."

The husband reached out for the rock and said it: "Gold!"

The word went off like a dynamite cap.

Gray Owl drew himself up tall, tall. "We go now," Gray Owl said.

The Four started toward the entrance.

Gently the gun trader caught Gray Owl's upper arm. "Ah, Chief . . ."

Gray Owl lifted the gun trader's hand off him like it had sores, but the crowd wouldn't let them through, the Four staring at the now kindly, warm, smiling faces—the Four wondering, puzzled, confused—into the glittering eyes.

13

Hetchetu Welo

Little Rabbit was the Queen of Sheba in a cocked hat.

Wrapped head to toe in a scarlet swatch of cloth, ajangle with beads and bracelets, four and five rings to a finger, a great, spreading Japanese fan and an ostrich feather stuck in the back of his head, colored ribbons threading his hair, the Rabbit stood putting on an enormous pair of looped earrings, the gun trader grinning up at him.

On the seat between them, a carpetbag spilled out the wondrous glories of a dime-store universe; next to the carpetbag Little Rabbit's pouch of raw gold, into which the gun trader dipped each time Little Rabbit put on another geegaw. Everyone in the coach grinning, nodding, "Oh-ing" and "Ah-ing," egging the Rabbit on to greater glory. The senator's daughter, Honor, beside herself, squirming, saying over and over into a handkerchief held up to her mouth and nose against the soot, "Look, look at what he's doing, look." As though it weren't hard enough *not* to look. The senator and I into a little quiet stud with me losing steadily, an eight and nine up, a lady in the hole, the senator with a king showing and another in the kicker the way he was sandbagging me.

"Mr. Benton . . ." the girl said to me.

The senator bet low enough to suck me in, high enough to make me think he had it.

"That man's taking everything your friend's got," she said to me.

"Same as yer father's doin' to me," I said, calling the senator's bet, thinking how a man's twice stupid doing what he knows is stupid.

The girl took the handkerchief away from her mouth and stuck her face into mine. "That man's cheating him," she said.

Her breath smelled of mint.

The senator dealt me a double saw, a possible straight, and caught his third king.

"Clay," she said dropping the formality of my last name so I could feel her heating up, "he's being robbed."

Drawing to an inside straight, I thought, a greenhorn's play:

"Jack o' diamonds, jack o' diamonds
    I know you of old
You've robbed my poor pockets of
    silver and gold."

She laid her hand over my cards. "Clay!"

I glanced at the senator to get her off me.

"King's bet," the senator said, again laying out enough to hurt but not drive me off.

I had to face her. "What's goin' on there between them, Miss Honor, it's not how it looks."

"What," she said, "the stealing?"

"Not necessarily."

She flushed. "Oh, what would *you* call it?"

"To Little Rabbit it's just dirt he's givin' away, worthless. . . ."

"But we know better."

"The beads are real."

"The beads are glass."

"It don't matter to him, ma'am, what they are."

"Of course it does."

"To the trader, the beads are worthless, the gold's real."

"Stop hedging, Clay."

"They're stealin' from each other."

"Oh, stop it. Now, will you please stop him!"

Again I glanced over at the senator to call her off.

He smiled. "At home, Clay, she's got a cross-eyed saddle pony and a one-legged canary."

She took her hand off my cards and the senator flipped me the knave. An inside straight!

Off his three kings the senator raised, I raised back, he raised and I raised. I had him.

"Clay!"

The senator looked at his daughter, sighed and threw down his cards. I waited. Without turning over his cards or letting me turn over mine—so sure he'd won—the senator was quitting the game.

I sat a moment looking at the straight, my first real hand, then at the girl watching me, and past her to the gun trader.

From all the gun trader still had in his carpetbag, I opined he'd had a bad season. This more likely than not the gun trader's stake.

"What they're doin' there, miss, that's serious business."

"It's theft."

"Could be Little Rabbit'll be more agin' stoppin' it than the trader."

"If you won't, I—"

"Miss, I seen hair lost fer less."

She started to get up.

I caught her arm.

"Aren't you supposed to be looking after them?" she said.

I let go of her arm. In the last eight hours—ever since the fat woman and the baggage car—I'd thought a lot about that. But what exactly was I supposed to be looking after?—because an Indian's the most hard-set, willful independent on God's green crust. No one, leastwise a Wasichu, tells a brave anything. Only, this was one spread, I thought, God hadn't a whole lot to do with. Even the Blade, however dimly, had foreseen something of that. 'Ceptin', just how far down that pipe did he expect me to draw?

The senator thought it was over and begin to shuffle the cards.

"Well?" the girl said.

Stampeded, I stood up.

The senator smiled at me. "I never win either, Clay." He still thought it was funny.

I didn't want it. I didn't like it, nosing another man's hunt. Neither would Little Rabbit. Neither did the gun trader, eying me all the way down the aisle.

"He's mine, hoss," the gun trader said.

"Sure, Lew," I said, "but don'tcha think you got enough there now?"

The trader laughed. "There's a long line ahead of you, hoss."

"Hell, Lew. . . ."

"After me—you!"

"He's gonna need some of that when he gits to town."

"So am I."

The whole coach laughed.

Little Rabbit turned to look at the laughers, starting again to go from face to face, peering. Only, this time it was all joshing and trading him rings and stickpins and whatever else they had for his dirt, the gun trader fuming enough to work a bellows.

I followed after, telling Little Rabbit in sign and Arapaho how he was wasting his medicine. I reminded him it wasn't his to give away like this. He was violating his pledge. He was not only betraying the trust of the four tribes but also that of Wakan Tanka.

The gun trader jerked me around. "That's enough, hoss."

Little Rabbit took a ring off of each finger and dropped it back in the carpetbag.

"Hetchetu welo," I said, *that is good.*

"I tol' you to leave him be," the gun trader said.

"Hell, Lew, you got enough there to retire."

The gun trader moved into me wagon wide and wormy. Back in the baggage car, he hadn't just been going on about throwing us off. He was mean and he was randy and he had me by a good fifteen year. He cocked his head at me. "What's eatin' you, hoss, got a twist in yer bit?"

"You got yer share."

"You mean leave some fer you."

"I mean you don't have to clean him out."

"Oh, you turnin' missioner, hoss? In the mountains you never traded 'em fooforah fer pelt?"

I felt suddenly like I'd been caught up short on a snubbing post: I *had* and I *did* and I *would.* Same as him. Only, up there at rendezvous the play went both ways, and I glanced back at Honor and the senator, when from the back of the coach came a WHOOP that lifted the hair on the nape of every neck in the car.

The gun trader pointed. "There's another one fer you to see to, missioner."

Again the car laughed. I headed back toward the rear of the coach. My out. Though I wasn't fooling anybody.

He stood vomiting drunkenly off the rear observation platform, Sonofabitch, the bullsnake thong down around his chin so you could see into the empty socket of his eye.

I pulled the patch up over the hole, caught him under the arm and swung him back toward the door into the whiskey drummer stuffing a satchel with Sonofabitch's gold.

The drummer held out a jug. "Here, this is his, bought an' paid, an' when he finishes that, you tell him there's plenty more in the well."

Letting Sonofabitch go, I made a grab for the satchel, Sonofabitch starting to topple off the back end of the train so I had to catch him with both hands, the drummer swearing, scuttling back into the coach, the satchel clutched to his chest, "Here, now, you just be careful . . ." and the drummer grinned, "or you'll lose yer boy altogether."

In the baggage car Gray Owl helped me with Sonofabitch.

From the rear of the car came the sounds of a crap game. "Git it down. Come on, before she cools." It was the gambler's voice. "Chief?"

I looked across at Gray Owl wiping Sonofabitch's face.

Gray Owl shook one hand against his ear as though throwing dice. "Manuel want play," Gray Owl said.

"Gimme another drink," a second voice said. "How 'bout you, Chief, more panther piss?"

"Roll 'em."

The dice scratched across the floor.

"Gawd-damn!"

"Too bad, Chief."

"How long, sweet Jesus."

"All in a day's work, gentlemen," came the gambler's voice.

We bedded Sonofabitch down behind some packing crates, and I went out to look at the game.

Above them hung an Evans lamp, the gambler smiling, holding the dice, in front of him one of the whiskey drummer's samples, a watch, some rings and Indian jewelry, a pair of boots with socks stuffed in the tops, a handgun and most of Manuel's raw gold. The three others looked like trappers, one with but one ear, hair growing partly over the hole so it looked like he was wearing an ear muff, claw scars all the way to the nose as if a beast, a bear, had ripped it away.

One of the trappers, the one who belonged to the boots and socks, the barefoot one, drank from a jug, then held it out to the one next to him, a man with a thick gun-barrel beard. The bearded man took a long pull at the jug and handed it to one-ear, who handed it to Manuel, who took a short suck at it.

The gambler squinted up against the light at me. "Git wet, mister?"

I shook my head, no.

"The pistol's hot, boys," the gambler said. "Tell you what, Chief—how much you got there?" He fingered through what was left of Manuel's gold. "I'll cover yer whole pile with this," and he shoved out all his winnings. "Whatta you say?"

"No," I said.

Manuel nodded, yes.

"Git her down, boys," the gambler said, "we're goin' fer a ride."

I stuck my boot on top of Manuel's pile so he couldn't bet.

The gambler looked up.

"You can keep what you already won," I said to the gambler, "but not all *that*."

"I can do *what!*" the gambler flared.

"Not all of it," I said.

The gambler nodded at my boot on Manuel's pile: "You wanta lose yer foot, mister?"

"All I'm askin' is—"

"You ain't *askin'* or *tellin'!—nothin'!*" the bearded trapper said dropping his hand inside his coat, but that wasn't what decided me. It was Manuel's eyes glistening up at me. I'd plain out insulted him, and in about one second I'd lose not only my foot but my whole leg, and I lifted my boot off his pile.

"Awright," the gambler said, "here we go . . . fer all the hides," and he went through a long, drawn-out rite of blowing on the dice, rattling them, cupping them in front of his mouth, whispering to them, and then he started to throw. Manuel caught his wrist.

The gambler looked as though someone had just pulled his plug. "Huh?"

"You no throw," Manuel said.

The gambler tried to jerk his wrist away. "What's the matter with you?" The gambler turned to me. "What's eatin' him?"

"You change dancing dots."

"What?" Again the gambler swung around at me.

"He says you switched dice on him," I said.

The baggage car went still as stealing.

The gambler jerked his arm free. "Now, what would a bush buck like him know about somethin' like that?"

Manuel knew, all right. From some of the best teachers in the world. The mountain men.

The trappers sat tick-tight, waiting, undecided.

The gambler tried to shuck it off. "We'll just pertend you ain't said nothin', Chief—this time!"

The barefoot trapper laughed too loudly. "Ah, come on, Chief. . . ." Barefoot held out the jug to Manuel, who made the short, hard *no* sign.

Again the gambler started to throw, and again Manuel blocked the throw.

The gambler's eyes crinkled at the corners, sweeping the circle. "Yer forcin' my hand, boy," and the gambler, insulted, made as though he were quitting the game, starting to get up, when he snatched at the handgun in the center of the pot. Manuel started across at him too late.

"Manners, Chief," the gambler said holding the handgun on Manuel, "manners. I'm just gonna have to teach you some manners," and the gambler slid back to give himself room. "Huh, boys?" The trappers bristled like cats.

I moved to the side. This was one woodpile cut to size. And a lot less trouble. Invading, drunken, lying Indians—they'd loot, kill and brush them off the train like flies.

Against my thigh the tiny palm gun in my right pocket burnt heavy as a hot ingot. I let my hand fall over it.

Lordy, I thought, it was going to be a mess.

"You," the gambler waved the handgun at me, "under the light." He pulled back the hammer.

"The boy's right," cut in a voice from directly behind the gambler, who started to swing around.

"No!" the voice rang like a mule skinner's. The gambler caught himself. "Just as you are, that's fine."

I leaned back squinting into the dark, but against the brightness
of the Evans lamp, I couldn't make out a thing.

"You'll never git off the train," said the gambler over his shoulder, so I thought how if, like the gambler believed, it was a
holdup, it was like trying to steal poison from a copperhead, and
again the gambler started to swing around and again the voice
rang.

The gambler froze. We all froze.

"The gun," the voice said, "drop the hammer and lay it down."

"You ever been keelhauled over railroad ties?" the gambler
threatened.

"Behind you," the voice said, cold. "Easy."

Unmoving, the gambler stared down at the pot, then, to see
what he should do, up at the trappers, searching back over the
gambler's head into the darkness for the voice, and, not liking either what he saw or the odds, the gambler eased the hammer forward and lay down the handgun.

"Now," the voice said, "slide it across the floor to the wall."

Head straight on, the gambler thrust at the gun with the side of
his hand, the gun clicking where it hit against the wall. Then,
very slowly, the gambler swiveled around.

Like the head of an animal, cautious, wary, peering up out of its
hole, came the single eye of the handgun.

The gambler's handgun!

Whoever it was, he'd just bluffed the gambler out of his handgun. The gambler swore.

"Twice you switched dice on the boy . . ." the voice behind the
handgun said.

The voice was followed by a hand.

"So clumsily, I might add," said the voice behind the hand,
"that it would lead me to believe *all* you gentlemen were a party
to this."

And from behind the hand, an arm:

"So if you'll all unbuckle your gunbelts . . ."

And following the arm—the senator:

"If you please."

Some cardplayer!

The trappers, like the gambler, didn't want to give up the pot,
hanging back, so you could see what was going on in their heads

when the handgun went off slamming the barefoot one, scratching at his shoulder, back up against the wall, the hands of the other two shooting up into the air.

The senator stepped up under the light.

"The door, Clay," he said.

The gambler gave a start, looking from me to the senator, and came to his feet.

I wasn't sure I'd heard.

"Now, hold on, Senator . . ." the gambler glanced over at the sliding baggage door along one wall. "You know how fast this train's goin'! If you think yer gunna—" He looked around at the others. "Well, you ain't!"

"Clay . . ." the senator said.

The gambler dropped back between me and the door, crouching, hands out in front like he'd fight.

The senator drew himself up. "The way I see it, sir . . ." the senator began and took a little half step to the right and drilled a hole not a finger's width above the bearded trapper's head, the bearded trapper's hands leaping up into the air from whatever they'd been doing at his waistband.

It frightened the gambler. It frightened all of us. The gambler shrank back against the wall. The senator motioned the trappers to their feet.

"You've got two alternatives," the senator continued, "out there, or I turn you over to them in here," and the senator nodded back at the passenger coach.

The ridge line along the gambler's jaw went slack. The gambler had been winning, taking from them at cards and dice all the way out from Olathe, Kansas. I shoved the sliding baggage door open. The black outside hissed past beneath a piebald sky, the wind pulling at our knees. Tiny clouds scudded across an appaloosa moon, the prairie cream flecked to the timberline, when of a sudden there was a roaring and I jumped back. A jagged stream of silver flashed in at us. Suddenly it was as though we were running rapids. In that half moment I swear I smelled spray. I looked back out. We'd stampeded a herd of buffalo, that appaloosa moon frosting over their humps till it looked like white water a mile down the track.

Along with what the senator said, or maybe he figured to do it now, while it was all clear, the barefoot one, the one with the senator's slug in him, took a little hop and step and, hand still to his shoulder, went out the sliding door.

The bearded trapper lurched to the opening to look after him. (What he'd been fumbling at in his waistband when the senator caught him was one of those tiny, single-shot derringers. I could just make out the handle in his belt with the letter *D* on the butt.)

"It's all sand and rock out there," the bearded trapper said. "Desert."

"The Kaskaskia River's not more than a forty-mile walk."

"If you don't break yer back landin'." The bearded trapper peered down into the darkness, head switching sideways with watching the sage whirl past, then he braced himself against the door, mouth working. Just before he jumped, he looked back. "Fuck you, Senator," and, pulling at the door edge, catapulted himself out of the car.

Far off to the west, the silver humps continued to flash and flow.

The last of the three, the wildest-looking of the three, the one you'd never thought it of, the one-eared one, like a man next in line at the paymasters, quietly, carefully sat down in the doorway, feet dangling outside like a kid on a fencerail, head cocked as though listening with his one good ear for where to jump, then cautiously, very gently, he pushed himself feet first out of the car. "A gentleman," the senator said and turned to the gambler, who ran back to the rear, Gray Owl and I following, wrestling him to the floor, where we tied his ankles, carrying him—the Owl at his shoulders, me at his feet—back to the opening, where he began to scream and where, swinging him in a short arc, counting . . . one, two, three, we threw him, arms flailing, out the door.

"With feet tied, dancing-dot man make big jump," Gray Owl said.

I think Gray Owl meant *bounce*, and in the sudden quiet we stood listening, but, of course, we didn't hear him bounce or anything, the only sound the slapping of the moths up against the Evans lamp. I leaned out and looked back. I couldn't see anything.

"Close the door," the senator said and went over to Manuel, who, through it all, hadn't moved.

"The pot, boy, is yours," the senator said. "By default." And Manuel commenced to gather it in, when, just as I shoved the sliding door closed, the door at the end of the coach opened and the senator's daughter, Honor, walked in under the Evans lamp, Manuel down over his knees looking up, so we all saw her happen to him.

14

::

Sell Me Your Daughter

Orange rags of burning gas from the kerosene lamps along the walls ballooned up or dimmed or spurted obliquely outward at every sharp curve, at every hump or chasm, at any abrupt change, the jagged shards of light flapping in tatters across panels and faces or deflecting off window glass so that in the car's semi-darkness you started up now and again at what appeared to be the coach catching fire.

Late at night and cold, we sat at the far end next to a stove stuffed with buffalo chips, Manuel and I across from the senator and his daughter, the senator and I next to the windows, all around us the snuffling and shifting of sleeping.

I held out the screw-top shot cup, the senator pouring brandy from a flask.

"Manuel?" the senator said, holding out the flask.

Knowing Sonofabitch was passed out in the baggage car, I still looked around for him. Sonofabitch could smell it.

Staring at the girl, Manuel, I don't think, saw, much less heard the senator's offer.

"Manuel," Honor said half joking, "Man-u-el . . . what kind of a name is that for an Indian? I mean it's not like Little Rabbit or Gray Owl. It's Spanish, isn't it?"

Manuel went on staring at her in that open Indian way so she must have known, because she wasn't uncomfortable or embarrassed.

"How'd you get a Spanish name like Manuel?"

Manuel didn't understand, and I tried to explain how an Indian might have no name or one or two or three or four or even five names: first, the name given him by his mother or father or relatives or friends in childhood; then the name he got during his hanblechia, *vision quest*, his initiation into manhood, the most important event of a young man's life, during the four to seven days of which, without food or water, naked atop a mountain to be nearer Grandfather Sky, he seeks his vision, which, when it comes, *if* it comes, gives him his adult name. So if, like Gray Owl, he dreams of an owl, *owl* becomes a part of his name: "Owl Man" or "Owl That Walks" or in Gray Owl's case, he dreamed of a gray owl leading a herd of antelope, his full name "Gray Owl Antelope Leader," a very religious name (which was part of why he became something of a medicine man), a young man sometimes given a third or fourth name, very secret, never spoken aloud. This his good-luck, long-life name, usually given him by a *winkte* (men who dress, look and act like women either out of their own choice or in obedience to a dream, *winktes* with the gift of prophecy.) A *winkte* name most powerful of all. Or sometimes he's named by the whites—and I thought of Tom McMurty's thirteen-year-old daughter Faith naming Sonofabitch—but mostly it's because the whites can't pronounce the Indian name. Or maybe it comes from something that happened on a hunt or in battle or in camp.With Manuel it came while the men were away on a hunt, when a renegade Mexican, Manuel de Alba, tried to rape Light Hands, Manuel's mother; Manuel, nine maybe ten then, snaking up from behind the Mexican to slam the rowels of one of the Mex's spurs into his throat, strangling him, so thereafter the tribe called him "Manuel Choke Breath," a name of much honor, and Manuel kept it.

The girl was staring at Manuel. "Man-u-el . . ." she again slowly sounded out his name, smiled and pointed proudly, "Man-u-el."

"To your health, sir," said the senator and we drank.

Manuel pointed back at her. "You—you much—you—" His hands fumbled, clutching at his knees to find the words. "I like—give—to—give—" Turning to me, he burst into Kiowan and sign, then abruptly he laid the pouch of gold in the senator's lap.

"Wh-What—?" the senator began.

"He wants to buy yer daughter," I said.

Course the senator didn't understand. He darted a look first at Manuel, then at his daughter, at me, down at the pouch and back at Manuel as though he weren't sure he wasn't the jestingstock of some high-wrought horseplay, the edge of a smile on Honor's face as though she weren't any more sure than her daddy.

Then, after a while, the senator said without smiling:

"Tell him that's more than I have ever been offered for her."

Manuel went on talking at me and the girl in sign and Kiowan.

"He says," I said to the girl, "you are made of twilight . . . your hair like the fingers of the moon on cornsilk . . . your eyes full as dawn."

The senator hefted the pouch. "Tell him I'm flattered that he'd want such a homely, spindly woman," said the senator and handed the pouch to Manuel, who shoved it back at him.

"He says he knows the yellow dirt is not worthy of such a woman, but that he also has many fine horses, many guns, many furs and blankets to trade."

Honor took Manuel's hand. "Oh, Manuel, I am *so* flattered. I am, but—"

"He says he will git more horses, more blankets. His tipi is large and snug," and softly Manuel commenced to sing her his love song:

> "My sweetheart, we surely could
> have gone home,
> but you were afraid,
> When it was night, we surely
> could have gone,
> but you were afraid."

. . . singing so low and soft it was hard to pretend you weren't straining to hear. The senator, caught up in the cleft of his embarrassment, had two quick drinks and stared at his knees. I leaned back watching them through my reflection in the window, as much off bead as the senator—savages, for one thing, shyer, more henhearted than the girls at flashing their tail feathers.

Twice Manuel sang his song to her. It didn't make a lot of sense to me, but, then, most of their poems and chants don't.

Manuel, the second time, reaching across to take her by the elbows, holding them tight to her sides so she couldn't turn away, his eyes smudged in the lamp glow, ember hot on her, drawing her face, so in that moment something dropped from her—like my stepping out on that hook of the Republican, seeing Fleet Fawn the first time—so in the same way now the girl wasn't funning or fussing or the great lady, her lips moist where, when he'd grasped her elbows, she'd bitten down, parted as if she might cry out. But it wasn't that. You could see that. He wasn't hurting her. She didn't try to pull away. A tiny crease furrowing up the cloister between her eyes so, for the first time, I thought, she was looking, *really looking* at him, so I, too, turned to look . . . Manuel with the high cheekbones but without the slit Indian eye, round like his mother's, the nose straight too, like the mother's, the chin and jaw square and chopped off like the Blade's. Smiling now at how she studied him, his teeth even and white, the eye molars sharp, strong from tearing at sides of buff . . . the way some of the old ones died without a single tooth missing. And I saw—by way of her—the way men don't see other men—that Manuel was handsome.

They sat like that for maybe ten seconds, his want of her so upsurging and singing I wondered it didn't wake the coach. Then she dropped her eyes, her head falling forward toward his chest, in that moment the whole of her yearning forward into the circle of his arms, Manuel letting go of her elbows to reach out for her, when she jerked back. It startled me. It startled the senator. He yanked back up in his seat. "What do you think of that?" she said to her father, who didn't know any more than I *what to think of that*, and I turned to the window, shamed at spying on their moment, Manuel's arms still outstretched for her. He looked like he'd been slapped. But— I shook myself and glanced up and around . . . at the lamps along the walls, at the yellow glimmering of the coals in the cracks around the stove door, at the sleepers mumbling and dream twitching, at the senator, at Manuel. And I sat up. I was awake. Then at the girl. The senator's daughter! . . . with bloodlines back to before the revolutionary war . . . elegant, refined, softly smiling and asking again of her father, or was it me, or just anyone who cared, "What do you think of that?" so I thought how I'd fancied it, *them*, the whole of it dissolving like the whiteness of what was left of the pieces of my face in the glass behind the dying lamps, Honor's voice echoing, reaching out from some place I had to look for, repeating to Manuel how honored she was but she couldn't marry him, and she tried to explain, but you could tell from Manuel's face how hopeless it was, the senator finally pulling her against his shoulder, where, tired, she mumbled some more about being honored and sorry and closed her eyes, Manuel sitting straight up over her, watching, as though keeping guard.

The senator and I had another drink. Outside, the night rushed by black and silent. We smoked.

"He's not going to change anything, you know," the senator said after a while.

"Who?"

"The President."

"A coon don't diddle snakes," I said.

"For what?" The senator, face whiskey red, pointed the bottle at me. "Money? They don't know what to do with it. Land? They won't work it. School? They won't go. Protection? From what? Grant's own constituency? Ha! So tell me, what can the President do?"

"I'm not the President."

"And if you were?"

"Neither are you." I sipped my drink.

"Clay, do you know how many of these Indian delegations Grant's seen?"

I didn't want to talk about it.

"You know *why* he sees them, Clay? To impress on them the Great White Father's strength, that's all. You know what'll happen? He'll have them taken out to the navy yard to see some ships, then over to the barracks to see our cannons and soldiers, and after that maybe a trip to New York to show them how many of us there are. And you know something, my friend, it works. After that, *they know!* We have too much, and we're too many.

"Clay, they've already lost. Just now to men like you, the buffalo hunters and trappers, and tomorrow to the others, the cattlemen and sodbusters. 'Manifest Destiny' the President calls it. And he's right. That dice game in the baggage car; could you blame them? If not them, somebody else. The same for the others, the gun trader and the whiskey drummer."

"You welshin', Senator?" I said smiling to take the edge off.

"How's that?" The senator sat up in his seat, tall with injured dignity, half waking his daughter.

"You sayin', sir, you won't help us?"

"I am saying, sir—" the senator was beginning to sound like a senator—"are you aware of the President's problems. They are manifold."

I was aware, all right. The papers had been full of it. . . . Sam had got himself tied in with some banking discrepancies along the eastern seaboard. But I didn't believe it. I was beginning not to believe the senator. It wasn't that a-tall. He was hedging.

"Just don't expect me, sir," the senator said, "to cast out devils."

I wasn't sure I wanted to drink with the senator any more. I stared at myself in the window, behind my reflection trees and mountains ghosting by so the pieces of my face, my nose, one eye and my forehead, looked like they were flying.

For a long time after, it was quiet, quiet, then the senator said, "The beaver an' buffalo, Clay, they're going fast. A year, two more at the most. . . ."

I couldn't reckon his drift.

"You're too old to be standing in water all day up to your balls or scraping buffalo hides. . . ."

The clickety-clack of the wheels over the rails was lulling me.

"What I'm saying," the senator said, "is they depend on you. But you, *you* should oughta also be able to depend on them."

How, I sure couldn't imagine. I wasn't even sure of what he was talking about any more. I stared out the window.

The senator laid the pouch back over the knee of Manuel, who, unmindful of everything around him, went on sitting guard over the sleeping Honor.

In the window the reflection of Sonofabitch lurched by. In a seat across the aisle, Little Rabbit sprawled asleep in all his beaded, beribboned, ostrich-fanned splendor. The pouch of gold fell off Manuel's knee onto the floor and lay there . . . after all we'd been through for it, I thought . . . a near carnage, Gray Owl, I found out later, behind one of the packing crates with

Manuel's rifle. Bodies all over the baggage car if the gambler or one of the trappers had gone for it. I picked up the pouch and laid it on the seat next to Manuel.

(I didn't like it a-tall, not a-tall, that feeling of being bound to them.)

I hunkered down in the seat behind the fading lamp glow. The senator was wrong. It wasn't the buffalo hunters or sodbusters but here on the train—it had all been right here—in this coach!—the whiskey, the dice and fooforah, the lying to them, cheating them, stealing from them, the corruption and drunkenness, that's what would finish them, not men, but *man*.

A week later we pulled into a big brownstone station off New Jersey Avenue and C Street. Off to the left you could see it, the Capitol—Sam Grant's new home town: District of Columbia, Washington.

15

Cat Run

I tried to hurry them along, a crowd gathering in front of us on the platform, gawping up at Gray Owl, first off the train, lordly, around his neck his medicine bag, over one shoulder his bow and arrows, under his arm a gunnysack of corn, the crowd sniggering at Little Rabbit following in all his beribboned ostrich-fanned finery, carrying a goose, stopping on the landing to gawp back down at them, so I pushed him on ahead before he got to staring, Manuel glaring, his rifle, bow and arrows in one hand, in the other a crate of clucking chickens. Last off, Sonofabitch, a pig in the curl of his arm, over his head and shoulders his bow and arrows plus all of Little Rabbit's arrows and bow—so as not to ruffle Little Rabbit's attire—Sonofabitch carrying all their spears, looking wild and monstrous, his fierce eye impaling everyone in his path.

(The corn and animals—a cow, even, in the baggage car—had all been bought from a farmer outside Wheeling. That farmer, if he knew it, with enough gold he'd never have to look up a mule's hump again.)

The crowd was commencing to push in around us now, next to me this small, middle-aged woman staring open-mouthed up at Sonofabitch, who walked up to her, opened wide his fierce eye and whooped, frightening her, so she whooped back, frightening him.

I looked around for the senator and his daughter. We'd lost

them back somewhere between the coach and the platform and I ran back—our only entry, Lordy, to the President—but I dared not leave the Four alone out there too long either. A pyrite pity. The Four, this one time good as gold, bunched together out in front of the station, church still and staring, when it dawned on me: This was their first time butt up against the city.

The first half of the trek they'd been in the baggage car, the second half looking out windows, seeing little, the railroads skirting the towns days, passing through the big cities nights—so where were the great herds of Wasichus they'd heard about? Manuel and Sonofabitch boasting at the beginning of how easy it would be to take and hold this empty land. Gray Owl and Little Rabbit not so sure. Neither were Manuel and Sonofabitch the farther east we got, finally not talking about it at all any more. But here, now, corralled on all sides by Wasichus, by horses and buggies and buildings blocking out the sky and even the sun, they knew. It depressed and frightened them.

The first thing, I decided, so we could move about without looking like a walking sideshow, was to get them clothes. Only, once they'd gotten over their fright and wonder, they were off—except for Gray Owl, anchored to the cow—like cats in a covey of quail.

"Ah-ma-na bah hah," Gray Owl said, looking up and down the street—the *stone prairie*, Gray Owl called the city.

The first one to disappear was Little Rabbit. Manuel pointed across the street to a saloon.

The saloonkeeper stood white-faced behind the bar, so I thought how Little Rabbit had probably pushed, peering into his face, the barkeep nodding toward the rear. Outside the men's room I heard the goose hissing.

Inside, Little Rabbit sat on a box washing his feet in a toilet bowl, the goose paddling around in the toilet bowl next to him.

"What in the Lord's name . . ."

"Pull vine," said Little Rabbit, "wash face, hands, feet in bubbling well. You want drink?"

Outside, the cow was halfway down the block, in the middle of the street, alone, wandering, on its back their weapons, the gunnysack of corn and all their gold, Gray Owl down on his hands and knees examining the metal car tracks when, clanging and banging, it came.

"Gray Owl!"

The horse-drawn streetcar almost on top of him, the driver, laughing, whipped the horse at Gray Owl. I yelled. Gray Owl rolled to one side, the streetcar's metal undercarriage catching the front of his buckskins, pinning and dragging him down the street. I gasped. Those wheels could chop him up into leavings, and I took off yelling, when abruptly the car stopped.

Manuel had caught the horse. He stood holding it by the bit, Gray Owl bleeding from a gash on the chin, the knees tore out of his leggings.

It took the driver a while to stop laughing before he looked down into the flat eyes of Manuel.

"Hey, whatta ya think yer doin'?" the driver yelled. "Leggo there."

Softly Manuel blew in the horse's nose to gentle him.

"Turn loose," the driver yelled. "Leggo my horse."

Manuel's marble eyes never left the driver's face.

"You gonna turn loose, or do I git down from here!"

That driver, I thought, was about two breaths away from being disemboweled, and I started forward.

"Awright!" the driver yelled and lashed down with his whip. Manuel took the leather across his shoulders, at the same time seizing and yanking the whip out of the driver's hand, Manuel halfway up the side of the streetcar when I caught him from behind.

"No, Man, no." I held his knife hand. I yanked him down. "You make big trouble, big. You ruin all, all."

He jerked back from me, agate eyes pulling at the driver, in whom some primordial instinct had surfaced, warning him that here was a man who wanted to *kill* him. Now! That was how it once had been, how it still was out there, and it frightened him.

He stepped back down off the driver's platform into the car, casting about at the passengers for help, when Manuel brought the whip down across the horse's rump, the beast lunging into the traces, plunging wildly down the street, the passengers inside yelling with terror.

I glanced up and down the street. We'd taught them clothes and counting and all, except police.

"Let's git outa here."

Still holding Manuel, who was helping Gray Owl, I started after the cow, when I missed Sonofabitch.

"With Pawnee," said Little Rabbit pointing.

Sonofabitch stood in front of a drugstore Indian, the pig tied to its wooden ankle. Twice I yelled at him.

I sent Little Rabbit with Manuel and Gray Owl down the street after the cow with orders to wait at the corner.

At the wooden Indian's feet lay a leather loincloth Sonofabitch had cut away—the sculptor a stickler for realism—Sonofabitch hacking away at its oaken genitals.

"What in the Lord's name . . ."

I knocked his hand away.

"Pawnee," Sonofabitch said.

"I thought I tol' you to stick with us."

"Pawnee steal many ponies, take squaw, very snaky."

"Sneaky."

"Traitor, scout for white balls."

"It's only wood. Come on."

"Pawnee steal sister's son."

I pulled at the big Comanche's arm.

"Pawnee put out eye."

"What in Christ's name!" the voice said, same as me. He stood in the doorway in a white apron, the druggist, a round man with wattles. The druggist pointed behind the wooden Indian. "Look. Look!"

I looked.

Sonofabitch had shoved his skinning knife up the Pawnee's wooden behind.

Lordy!

With only the knife handle sticking out.

I looked up and down the street, thinking again how we should have taught them police. "Come on," I said.

The druggist began to shake his wattles and shout.

I yanked Sonofabitch, grinning broadly, down the street toward the others, waiting at the corner.

"Hey, you. You! Come back here. Whatta you think yer doin'?" Wattles started to yell for the police.

We were halfway to the corner when Sonofabitch stopped. "Sow," he said.

"Let the pig go."

He ran back.

I started after him.

The druggist had two helpers with him now, the three starting for Sonofabitch, who, forgetting the pig was tied to the wooden Indian's ankle, snatched it up, yanking, pulling at where it was tied, the wooden Indian starting to topple, so the druggist and his two helpers had to scramble to catch it and Sonofabitch broke free. The five of us running around the corner: Sonofabitch with the grunting pig; Manuel with the crate of clucking chickens; Gray Owl pulling the bawling cow; me yanking at Little Rabbit, who, with the hissing goose, wanted to stop and look into all the passing faces. And Lord, Lordy, that's how we made our getaway.

When the clerk in the department store turned around and saw us bearing down on him—I kept forgetting how they looked to others—like a war party, the way the clerk blanched and ducked behind the counter; I went on up to him alone. "Some work clothes," I said, and tailed after the clerk to a bin, where he fumbled at some shirts.

"I think these are what you—"

I followed the clerk's look over my shoulder.

They were gone.

Only, this time it took two hours, two store officials and two hundred dollars to round them up.

Little Rabbit I found in HOUSEHOLD gawking at himself in a mirror long as a spring pond. But it wasn't Little Rabbit who fretted me. The Rabbit, I knew, would go back to where the store had set up this sort of base for us—once they'd appraised our gold—and where we'd tethered our animals.

The scream led me to Sonofabitch in WOMEN'S WEAR, a feather boa about his neck, in a lady's hat, a great floppy fruit-covered thing with a black lace veil falling down over his face, grinning down at the poor woman, who, trying on hats, had looked up into the mirror to see this great, one-eyed mountain looming down over her.

Sonofabitch led me to Manuel in the GUN DEPARTMENT, on the counter in front of him an arsenal over which Manuel insisted Sonofabitch help him stand guard until I got the others to come help him tote it off.

It was one of the store officials who took me to Gray Owl, wrapped in a beautiful patchwork blanket, turning to the pretty sale girl, not for help in buying, but admiration. And he got it.

"Yes, yes," the girl said, one of the few in this land, as long as we were there, to recognize in this tall, stately man, savage or no, what truly he was—what they all were, but especially Gray Owl— a prince of his people.

When I backtracked for help, I found the other prince, Little Rabbit, still making faces at himself in the mirror, a crowd forming behind him, chuckling, so I thought how, for a fact, they were funny: the Rabbit there with his faces; Manuel with his arsenal; Gray Owl in his bedspread; Sonofabitch gone when we returned to the GUN DEPARTMENT, striding somewhere through the store in that great, floppy, fruit-covered hat, the black lace veil down over the bullsnake eye thong, in a woman's dress he'd picked up along the way, a huge fur coat over it, about his neck the feathered boa, to which he'd added a half dozen scarves, three store officials jabbering after him to pay for all he'd taken, when he stumbled into the LIQUOR DEPARTMENT.

I mean, walking into that department store, they saw everything they'd ever dreamed, plus giving them some dreams they'd never had.

"I take," said Manuel to the clerk looking numbly on. In front of Manuel on the counter, pistols, rifles, shotguns, scatterguns, boxes and boxes of ammunition and knives—long knives, pocket knives, bowie knives, skinning knives, axes, harness, saddles. The department store like a visit to the spirit land. Like the Good Lord setting us up in one of those many mansions he's preparing for us, and we loaded up, later waiting in HOUSEHOLD for Little Rabbit, still in front of the mirror, peeking now and again around the corner of the glass at himself, then jumping back as if he would surprise his reflection, when, like a man with a nail in his boot, the Rabbit stopped to listen to the laughter behind him, and, like in the train coach, turned to the crowd.

For a full five seconds the Rabbit studied the laughing faces, then turned again to himself in the mirror, the laughter growing, and in that instant Little Rabbit saw—I don't know what—himself or them or something, and he reached up and pulled off first one earring, then the other, then the beads, the laughter now a howl, then the ostrich feather, the fan, the ribbons and rings and scarlet robe.

He was undressing and I started forward to stop him, when I felt Gray Owl's hand on my arm.

When Little Rabbit finished, he stood before them in a breechclout and leggings, all his grandeur on the floor around him, and then, very deliberate, kindly, he went up to them to look close into their faces.

Again they howled, but they weren't sure any more, their laughter cracking, then breaking to a titter and silence.

I had to get them settled down somewhere.

And quick.

Besides which—what the senator had hinted at back on the train, those banking discrepancies—well, the senator was right: Sam had gotten himself in real trouble there and was laying in for a tour of the country to explain himself to the people.

16

....

Learners of Police

To help us cart off everything we'd bought, the department store
sold us a wagon and horse, a mule-hipped old shadbelly with a
white eye. The wagon equally falling apart, pyramided to a peak
on top of which teetered the crate of chickens, the pig and goose,
the cow hitched to the tailgate, Gray Owl handing up more pack-
ages from the pile on the sidewalk to Little Rabbit and Manuel,
when out of the department store lurched Sonofabitch in the
woman's dress and fur coat, the black lace veil gathered in a ball
down over his good eye so he couldn't see where he was going,
chanting, weaving drunkenly to some silent ceremonial drum, tot-
ing a case of white lightning between two policemen.

The policemen fetched Sonofabitch up to Manuel and the Rabbit, who gently propped him up, still holding tight to the case of
white lightning, in a corner of the driver's seat, when from up the
block came the god-awfulest ruction: the wild clanging of a bell,
shouts, the thudding and stampeding of horses.

Like no rig I'd ever seen! Though I'd heard of it from a mountain man in Shawnee. Nor was I sure I'd believed him, because I
didn't see how it could work. But there she was: shiny and drawn
by three horses abreast. In its center a boiler or firebox or something with black smoke pouring from the stack, steam from the
back. Men with big hats hanging from the side of her. Everybody
tearing to get out of its way. The whole of her hell roaring down
on us.

The Rabbit leaped from the wagon. Gray Owl stood in stark, gaping shock. And Manuel snatched up his carbine and took dead-on aim at the driver.

I started around the wagon for him. I still wasn't sure what it was or why. But I *did* know what Manuel was about was worse. I was halfway over the front wheel when Sonofabitch awoke with a yell, hurtling himself from the driver's seat into the middle of that poor old shadbelly, all but collapsing the poor beast, whooping war cries, beating at it with his feathered boa. The old scrag pitching into the traces, throwing the pig, squealing, from the top of the wagon, bouncing the crate off onto the pavement, where, breaking open, chickens ran squawking three hundred degrees to the pole, the cow bawling, Manuel, jerked sideways, firing, missing the driver, hitting the smokestack or whatever it was.

Geysers of steam and water gushed out front and back, the men in the big hats bumping into themselves and each other in their panic to get out of the way of bullets, boiling water and spouting steam, and if that wasn't enough, the goose, hissing and flapping, had somehow gotten itself entangled with them.

It was a drabble-tailed melee of men, horses, chickens, pig, cow, goose, bells, yelling, squealing, blaspheming, blatting, baying—and they learned police.

Two nights, a day and a half, we spent in what the inmates called Heartbreak Hotel, the kaska, *drunk tank*. Sonofabitch being drunk, the police reckoned, I guess, 'specially after what had happened, that we were all drunk.

The old District Jail it was called, eleven of us in a windowless cell 8 × 10 without water closets and one tub of water for an entire corridor of prisoners to wash in.

Right off I thought of the senator, but, Lordy, it sure wouldn't help our cause none either with the senator or Sam or anybody else if it got around, and I decided to keep shut and bear up.

The Four were like caged birds, flitting and darting, touching the bars, climbing them to see was there a way over the top and what was the ceiling made of. Sniffing at the corners for a way out. Frightened now. Sitting in a circle to chant and pray, all that night and the next day, over Gray Owl's medicine bag, till the rest

of the prisoners couldn't take it no more—could you fault them?—
and they began to bang on their toilet buckets for the guards.

The big hog in the stoop was a giant of a man who kicked Gray
Owl's medicine bag, sacred to a savage, across the cell, yelling at
them to shut up so they could sleep. Sonofabitch, in a rage, picking up the giant like the gunnysack of corn, "No, Sonofabitch,"
throwing him up against the cell bars, where the man's head
cracked like a melon, and they went on chanting.

I rushed over to the man, unconscious, his head at an angle,
blood seeping out both ears, so suddenly what we'd been charged
with—drunk and disorderly, malicious mischief, discharging fire-
arms in the city, resisting arrest (mounted on the old shadbelly,
Sonofabitch had charged one of the policemen), and attempted
homicide—all that seemed pretty tame next to manslaughter.

I bandaged the man with one of Sonofabitch's scarves.

Then the guards came, but they thought the man, still unconscious, was drunk, since most in the tank were, many of them also
with bandages (a lot of them, I'd noticed, with hands and feet
missing or on crutches, probably, I thought, from being run over
by streetcars or that hell-howler we'd barely escaped and all else
you found out there in their roadways), besides which the guards
hadn't come because of the banging on the toilet buckets but to
take us to court.

The judge, a frosty old buck with a full beard, allowed as how,
since we were ignorant folk unused to civilized ways, he'd only
fine us for the boiler Manuel had ventilated and the outhouse the
fire engine hadn't put out—which was what that hell-howler was,
a *fire engine*—but not the next time . . . and the judge brought
down his maul on his high-topped desk and we were free.

I was still wondering how the man Sonofabitch had thrown up
against the cell bars was when Little Rabbit started to climb the
high-topped desk to peer into the judge's face. I yanked him down
and got them out quick.

Back out on the streets, I now knew the most important thing
was to find them a place to live.

The City Park, by their lights, was pluperfect. In the Wasichu heartland, it was out in the open with plenty of shelter, trees and brush, but, best of all, running water.

We might even have made the night there if someone hadn't reported three men taking a bath in the fountain, one of them naked, which was Sonofabitch, the Rabbit and I holding him under the water to sober him up.

The zoo was even better. Everything, the park had—and game too. But, of course, just as impossible. But how they loved it!

(Ever after, whenever we went on an outing, they started at the zoo, and always with the elephant. The rhinoceros and hippopotamus, the baboons and camel, the giraffe and painted ponies (zebras), they'd stand bobble-eyed in front of for hours, but the elephant—'specially at first, when they weren't sure he wasn't feeding himself at the wrong end—I don't think they ever believed.)

After the zoo came another park—Washington's filled with parks—then a woman's garden and an old man's pea patch, the police on us all the way, so it would seem like I wasn't doing too good a job fending for them, but what you got to understand is— like with Little Rabbit in front of that department-store mirror— you can't tell an Indian anything. Not because he's stubborn or bullheaded or not sabe enough to understand what you're saying, it's just how he's been fetched along. You see a squaw with a child over a fire, you don't hear her telling it do this or that to be careful of the flames. When that kid burns himself, he knows. The things you sometimes see they let their kids do would turn your hair. And anything else, *telling*, is bad form. (Which is why, when Honor asked me shouldn't I be looking out for them, I couldn't answer how you look out for someone won't be looked out for.) But, finally, after the old man's pea patch, they turned to me—the first time—and I found them a campsite along the banks of a marsh southwest of town, and from then on things between us commenced to change.

They didn't treat me no different, no better. It was just that now they'd decided somehow I was a necessity, and I began to itch the way it is in the mountains when the birds go still and you know something's in there—which is what they were doing with me, someone's eyes always on me, someone always with me, even to the slit trench we'd dug out back.

It's an oiliness I can't abide. It's why first I'd taken to the mountains, and one night I cut stake.

Gray Owl caught me just outside camp. He brought his right hand up and away, *why?*

To seek a place for us, I said. (Which it wasn't exactly at all and Gray Owl knew it wasn't exactly.) We go together, Gray Owl said. We are too many together, I said. So many frighten the Wasichus.

Gray Owl looked around, then, hands in front of him, palms down, he pushed out and away, bringing his right hand up to his left breast in the casting-away motion—*this place is bad for us.*

"That is why I go," I said.

"Here we cannot hunt, we cannot find berries or roots. The land is scarred. Life is dead to life."

I tried to step around him. He caught my arm.

"The Wasichu medicine is not to be found in this place, Face on Water."

I pulled away. "Have I not told you this," I said.

He held out both hands to me, palms up, bringing them from me to himself, slowly closing the fingers.

But twice before had I seen that sign. And never to a Wasichu! To have made it at all had taken the whole of his pride—*we need you.*

I turned to go.

Again the sign.

He was all but begging.

"Please, Gray Owl," I said, ashamed for both of us. "I will be gone only a short time, quick, short."

Then he held his right arm out full length, and, bending his elbow, brought the fist back to his shoulder so the big muscle in his upper arm bulged strong. "Hetcheto aloh," he said, *it is so indeed,* and he motioned me back to camp.

He was right: I wasn't strong enough to fight nor fast enough to run. "We must have the senator subchief," I said, "to lead us to the Great White Grant Father."

"Is that why, like the spotted coyote, you steal away?"

"You do not trust me. You do not listen. You would watch me like the black hawk. You dishonor me."

Carefully, very deliberately, with both hands, he made the pushing, pulling sign with the fingers out: *That you have already done to yourself, Face on Water.*

17

Wasichu Is She

They came in an elegant, shiny-black, fringe-topped carriage drawn by matched blacks and driven by a colored coachman: the senator; his daughter, Honor; and a young man, tall and well dressed, who jumped out to open the door for them.

"Senator, Miss Honor . . ." I said.

"Where you been?" the senator said.

"Well, now, Senator, that'll take some tellin'."

The senator looked around. "What're you doing way out here?"

I told how we hadn't been able to find anything in town, and this was close to the river, where the fishing was good. Which was why, the senator said, he and his daughter had come: to offer us a place to stay until we found something, because didn't we know these marshes off the Potomac were malarial, every President and his family from James Madison on with a touch of either dengue fever or yellow jack? Only, it was beneath Manuel's dignity to live in a squaw's tipi, Manuel never taking his eyes off Honor, balking at shaking her hand or even greeting her. Which never stopped her passing out food and tobacco, laughing and joking with them, saying how happy she was to see Sonofabitch walking the straight red road and Little Rabbit without earrings, and would they all come to her wickiup for a big feast? They would be she-saw-ka, *honored*, Gray Owl said very formal, too quickly, and they all made the finger crooking below their mouths in the *yes* sign, nodding and grinning, all but Manuel, who walked away to look at the matched blacks.

The senator asked how things were progressing, and I made the wavery, *so-so* sign.

An insult, Manuel's walking away like that, the others silent now, embarrassed.

The senator chuckled. "I can imagine," he said.

But he couldn't.

Honor followed Manuel over to the horses.

"Stick with 'em, boy," the senator said and slapped me on the back as if we, him and me, had this pact.

"At this point, sir," I said, "I ain't got a lotta reach around here."

Out of the side of my eye, I saw Manuel make the *no* sign and shake his head.

The senator studied me a moment, face to one side against the sun, then he took out a cigar, sniffed it, held it up to his ear, rolled it between his thumb and forefinger and nodded at the crinkling as though it had said something with which he agreed, and handed it to me.

"You talked to Sam—the President—yet?" I said.

We had to be patient, the senator said shaking his head, because we hadn't been invited to Washington like all the others and this created problems, which, he said, I couldn't imagine.

Nothing like the problems, I said, I could imagine if the Blade got shuck of waiting and did what he said he'd do.

Which was exactly *why* we had to be patient, the senator said, because it was so important, because him and me had all this responsibility—to the Plains People, to the settlers, to the Chosen Four, to our country, to each other, to ourselves and Lord knows who all, and again he held out the cigar to me.

He'd also been able, the senator said, to get a message through to Tom McMurty's brother in Ohio.

Lordy!

The McMurtys!

He never missed a card, the senator didn't, and I guess I turned away, because I felt his hand on my upper arm.

"Anything you need, Clay, money, advice, any trouble, anything—you come to me, hear?"

He stuffed the cigar in my vest pocket.

"Daddy."

Honor and the young man were waiting for him in the carriage. The senator handed me a card. "You can get me here, Clay."

"Senator—"

But he was gone.

The colored coachman layed the lines lightly over the shoulders of the blacks and they leaned into the traces.

"Manuel?" Honor called from the back of the carriage.

But Man didn't answer. He stood quiet, black eyes pulling after her.

"Please, Manuel?" she called again.

Very still and Indian, Manuel watched them go.

I had the feeling that, like on the train, we'd been talking about different things, the senator and I.

I took out the cigar. I wondered why I hadn't been able to take it from him earlier. But what the hell! I licked the end. After those cheroots from the forts, you forgot. An honest-to-Jesus Molina.

Unmoving, Manuel continued to look after the girl.

I wrapped the cigar in clean newspaper and put it back in my vest pocket for later.

The next two weeks on the outskirts of the city were a renewal of the spirit decreed by Gray Owl, who said we'd become "pollute" and must reaffirm our vows.

We built a sweat lodge to purify ourselves and gathered sage for grace.

Mornings we prayed to Grandfather Sky for humility and wisdom; afternoons we danced for perseverance and insight, and nights, contemplated for greatness and truth, the whole last week fasting for submission and tranquillity (so I damn near starved) all in silence, which, if you can keep from talking to yourself (which I done plenty of in the mountains), I never minded, for, unlike us, the American Indian has never claimed the power of speech, though an awesome gift, as proof over the dumb creation.

"And what," you ask, "is silence?"

"His voice," they answer, "the great mystery."

"And the fruits of silence?"

*"Courage, endurance, self-control, patience, dignity—the cor-
nerstone of character.*

*"In the hush of man, the perfect equilibrium, the absolute
poise, the true balance of mind and body and spirit by which man
maintains his selfhood. Neither a twig to be shaken by the vagrant
breeze nor a ripple to be purled across the surface of serenity. Silence."*

And silent we sat that night across from one another over the
fire, Manuel and I—their camp within my ten-foot square, I
thought, so I could help with the chores—the others asleep, Little
Rabbit coughing his light, dry, hacking cough (a condition he'd
had since catching cold trying to sober Sonofabitch up under the
fountain), Manuel far from Gray Owl's inner tranquillity, brooding into the flames. Over the girl, I knew. Like that since the
train. His hands working over his knees in a kind of smothered
sign, so after a while I said, "She is much wincincala, much,"
pretty girl.

Palm down, he pushed up and away from his left breast for *her
heart is good,* which could also mean wincincala, *she is most
pretty.*

We sat for another long time; then, looking into the fire, I said
—because I couldn't say it flat out to him, because he had to
know I said, "She will not come, Man—to your blanket."

He stiffened. "Am I not the son of a chief?" he said softly.

I nodded.

"Am I not a brave warrior?"

"You are."

"And a fine hunter?"

"Yes."

"Is not my lodge full and warm?"

"All that . . ."

"Then—" He made the wide circle, *why?*

"Because all of those things—" I wasn't sure why—"don't
matter."

His head came up at me, stunned. "Are not a man's mother
and father of importance . . . ?"

"Yes."

"—to have beautiful children?"

"That is so. . . ."

"Is this not also important to the Wasichu?"

"It is."

"Is it not important to be courageous?"

"To many, yes."

"Must a man not provide for his own?"

I nodded.

"The lodge, must it not have food and all things for warm living?"

Caught up in his reckoning, I could only nod and wonder.

"So—" Again he made the large *why* sign.

"I cannot tell why except that . . . it is different. She is different."

"She is a woman."

"She is a Wasichu. She is—" I decided I'd been too long in the mountains. It had all gone by me. I'd begun to mold . . . out there now streetcars and fire engines, trains with kerosene lamps along the walls, and people—the senator and her, the conductor, the judge and jailers and people I wasn't even sure of any more. Hell, caught between here and there, I wasn't even sure of me any more. "I cannot tell the why of such things, Manuel, I don't know," and I looked away from his hands, still suspended in the *why*, a sign that, the longer we stayed in this land, the more I saw of until, like now, looking at Manuel, it was enough to make you weep.

Along the horizon the night shone mossy and secret, diluted by the city, its forged glow veiling the stars, the Capitol dome off to the east alight like a second moon, so suddenly I wondered how the senator had known where to find us.

After a while I said, "Why will you not go to the lodge for the feasting, Manuel?" The fire was green and it began to crackle and spit. "The others will not go without you," I said. "You slight us all, Manuel." Manuel made spitting sounds back at the fire, the flames churning like little lightnings in his eyes. He wasn't going to the feasting, you could see.

Gray Owl woke and squinted into the fire. He'd had a dream of a bear beaten off by a porcupine, and he announced that the praying and dancing and fasting were now at an end, because, like the porcupine, we were now sufficiently armed.

I took out the senator's cigar and cut it in two. One half now, the other maybe over a drink tomorrow with Sam in the city if— But then, looking around at them, remembering the senator's words, I knew we were a long way from Sam's palace.

18

The House and the Wickiup

I found them a place, a sliver of splintered clapboard caught between the cliffs of a dye factory and a woolen mill, a tired spine of tenements pushing in from behind, the whole clotted as cold clabber.

A picket fence, toothless, surrounded a tiny front yard of dirt. The gate, without hinges, balanced against what remained of the frame as a sort of silent tablet to privacy so, when you entered, if you didn't step over the fence, you set the gate aside or walked through or over it. The landlord, a breed, was part Cherokee, part white and all thief who, knowing the trouble we were having, asked three times what the place was worth.

Little Rabbit wouldn't go inside.

After the first dozen peeling rooms smelling of urine and dirty socks, he'd refused: the tipi more better, more clean, warm in winter, cool in summer, the Wasichus' house like a big cage, the Rabbit said, that shut out the sun and the wind and the air, which was why the Wasichu was always sick when even the animals knew better, and Little Rabbit hacked his light, dry cough and stayed outside. Brooding, Manuel refused even to accompany us.

Of all the places we'd seen, this was the worst. A basement, it was dank, without windows except for a grate at street level, the smells from the dye factory and woolen mill suffocating; in the corners the scuffling of rats; roaches long as your finger crawling the baseboards. But they liked it. It had a dirt floor for the chickens and pig to root around in, and a place out back for the cow and horse.

Still, the Rabbit wouldn't go inside.

"To be like Wasichu," I said, "we live like Wasichu."

"To kill snake, you live *not* like snake—like chaparral cock."

"Prairie long way off, Little Rabbit."

He shook his head. "Brave, squaw, Wasichu, all same two-legged."

I was through arguing. Here was a place would take us even *after* seeing us. "Now, here," I said, "in this place shall we live! So come."

Instead he sat down in the dirt of the front yard, the others filing out of the basement to sit down around him, so I knew it was a Mexican standoff; the moment I sat, the Rabbit stood, starting to gesture.

It's what most irritates the Indian about the white man, *his bad manners*, the white man's forever wanting to get directly to the point, the Indian believing that if a man has something to say, of however little worth, he should be listened to, his words, face, gestures, even his pauses studied, the time and place savored, the talker doing the listener the honor of thinking the listener worthy of his words, the talker to the listener thinker, doer, teacher. Which was all the Rabbit had really wanted—to make a speech.

Little Rabbit jutted a finger at the house. The Wasichu lodge could not move: "If the Great Spirit would have man be still, would he not have made the world so? But always he makes the world change so birds and animals can move, have green grass, ripe berries, sunlight to work, dark to rest, summer for flowers to bloom; winter to sleep; everything changing; everything moving for good." He glanced sideways at the house. "Nothing for nothing. The Wasichu does not obey the Great Spirit. That is why we cannot agree."

The house and the wickiup—it was as good a rendering of their troubles as any.

When we got back to camp, Manuel was gone.

Manuel's bow and arrows, his spear, hunting knife and muzzle-loader, the eating bowl he'd bought, his flint and fire rock, everything was gone.

Sonofabitch swept his arm west, peaking his fingers in front of his chest. "Manuel go home," he said.

Gray Owl sank to his knees, praying and lamenting . . . their medicine irrevocably stained, the mission betrayed, perhaps destroyed.

Little Rabbit began to circle the camp, tracking.

I sat down behind the lodge. I didn't know what I felt or even what I should feel. Relieved, maybe, Manuel as much a vexation as Sonofabitch, yes, but where the big Comanche was curious and into things, a child, Manuel galled.

Sonofabitch grinned. "Manuel have long walk," he said, "long, long."

"No," said Little Rabbit. He pointed at the ground. We followed him to the campfire. It had been doused with coffee grounds. "See, see." Little Rabbit pointed. "Big, little."

What the Rabbit meant was there were two sets of tracks: the big ones, Manuel's; the small ones, a woman's. In high-heeled riding boots, the way the ground dug down. Little Rabbit trailed back to the edge of camp. The woman had tethered a horse to a scagbush, then had coffee with Manuel, who'd gathered up his necessaries, mounted, and, Indian fashion, pulled the woman up behind him—you could see by the deeper hoofprints—after which they'd ridden off together.

Little Rabbit made a full, sweeping motion: they'd made a wide circle away from town, not west, south, down toward the channel.

Little Rabbit looked at me. I held out my hands and shook my head. I didn't know, either. Sonofabitch chuckled and made the bad man-woman sign. Gray Owl frowned and went into the lodge. Gray Owl knew. We all knew. I wondered if the senator did. But why? Where? What had she come back for? To see if Manuel wouldn't change his mind and come to her feast? And after that, what? What in the Good Lord's name had he said to her? What did she think she was doing? With a savage! Jesus! And I remembered that night on the train, out of Osawatomie, when Manuel had sung her his love song . . . the way she'd been drawn, how, singing, he'd held her elbows close, her head dropping toward his chest and her reaching into the circle of his arms before jerking back so I'd thought how I'd only fancied it.

The marsh grass was beginning to spike up into the setting sun, and I put on my coat. She hadn't been the first, no . . . even to marry and have families and live good lives. But most of those white women were prairie women, not that far theirselves from the land and the wilderness. And then there were the others, like the Girdon girls, Swedish girls, twins, Mini and Maud, from up around the headwaters of the Purgatory, they'd run off with some Cheyenne. I'd seen them a couple summers during rendezvous in the Tetons. Take up with anything as long as it was red and wild enough. Little better than sporting women. All day and night carrying on in their lodge. It's how they got a handful of young braves around them, killing and looting all through the Dakotas until a band of farmers trapped and wiped them out in the Coahuila Gorge, all but Maud, who turned around and married one of the farmers. Shameful! Only, Senator Mathew Devlin's daughter was a core from a different root. I went back over the ground. Man hadn't forced her. You could see where she'd waited at the fire for him while he'd gotten his necessaries together, then while he'd mounted. Besides which, that wasn't the Kiowa way. Then I remembered how they'd murdered Manuel's brother Black Horse, saying how Black Horse had violated the fur trader's wife, the tribe saying behind their hands how it was in the blood, Man's mother, Light Hands, being so fair.

South along the skyline the mare's-tail was building to thunderheads. I walked out in the marsh grass, the earth spongy under my feet, the mosquitoes rising. The air smelled of salt and dried fish and the tobacco growing across the river. Whatever was to be done, it had to be *now*. But what? It wasn't one of those things you inquired around about. You sure couldn't go to the senator. Because if it ever got out . . . who'd believe it? The same as happened to Black Horse, to Manuel. But maybe it wasn't Honor. Maybe it was somebody else. Maybe— But who else? I went in to talk to Gray Owl. He made the thumb-and-finger circle, tapping around it with the opposite hand—*we wait and watch*. Only, Lordy, the longer we waited, the worse, and I decided to go after them, laying out for the morning's first light (it being too dark now to track), but sometime around the middle of the second watch the thunderheads burst, the rain washing out sign two inches down, so there was nothing now but *to watch and wait*.

Six days we took turns sleeping at the old campsite so if Man returned, somebody'd be there to tell him about the new place, all the time thinking about what if something happened to them? to her! a senator's daughter as well known and liked as she! With the Apaches and a band of Pawnees burning up the Southwest, we'd have about as much chance as an icicle in hell and twice the heat, so the next day, the seventh day, I decided that for him and her and all of us I'd go see the senator, when Manuel came slogging up out of the marsh grass. They'd been out there together, Lord God, almost a week.

19

Without Pride of Ancestry or Hope of Posterity

"The city of Washington," Colvin McCullough said looking at me over the tops of his cards, "is like a mule—without pride of ancestry or hope of posterity."

"Go home," he kept repeating at me and raised, and Lord knows I wanted to go and called, laying down three ladies. He had bullets over. "Ain' nothin' heah," he said watching me rake in the pot, "ceptin' tedium, typhus an' treachery. This heah's the genitalia of our generation, the pudendum of our principality, a vulva of vipers. You come here to violate or be violated." He waved a hand. "Nothin'."

Tall, with white side whiskers and wearing a wide-brimmed white plantation hat, Colvin McCullough was a representative in the House who'd been sent "tuh this heah fevah hole by the perceptive voters of Jaw-jah," him and me bucking heads all one afternoon in a gambling drop off Constitution Avenue.

I hadn't understood all Colvin had said, but he was right about one thing, *nothin' heah*, no hunting, no trapping, no industry, just politics; Washington, like Pap said, little more than one of those sleepy little southern towns with some horse racing Saturdays along E Street or across the river next to the Government Hospital for the Insane, which, Colvin said, should be under the Capitol dome, that and some opera, which, of course, I never consid-

ered, though I did take the Four to see *Pocahontas* at Grover's
Theatre, which they didn't understand but argued all night over
her dress and which nation she belonged to; I also took them to
dinner one night at Willard's Hotel, where, except for Little Rabbit's drinking all the water out of the finger bowls, the McMurtys
would have been downright proud of their behavior—being always
more than careful to keep them as far away as possible from
"Hooker's Division"—the whorehouses down in the triangle next
to the Treasury Department—the Four liking the town even less
than me.

The Moon When the Cherries Turn Black, it was hot and
muggy, the streets along New Jersey, Independence and Maryland
so wheelrutted, the carriages were all but scraping their axles, so
dusty that, when you weren't coughing or blowing your nose, you
were slapping at yourself to get off the grime, so I thought how,
when the rains came, the town must stop, mired to the hubs, a
full-grown bull supposed to have disappeared the winter before in
a sinkhole off Constitution Avenue. Cattle, goats and pigs wandering everywhere, fouling the streets and sidewalks, eating all the
grass and shrubbery, tearing up all those elm trees Tom Jefferson
had planted along Pennsylvania Avenue, a herd of white-face cattle grazing on the monument grounds.

So, whenever I could, I got them out of town, which wasn't
hard to do. An hour's walk south of the Capitol grounds and you
were in some of the prettiest country you ever saw: thick, green
forests with game—deer, bear, wild turkey, pheasant, partridge.
We'd stay out sometimes a couple weeks. And once we trekked
over to the Chesapeake, the lower half of the bay crawling with
shallow-bottomed tongers and the tall-masted skipjacks and bug-
eyes crisscrossing from shore to shore for oysters. The fishing like
no place I ever saw—terrapin, strawback, hardmouth, spotted
belly, grayfin—over a hundred and eighty different kind of fish in
the Chesapeake, an old jacker told me. Reach down and scrape up
oysters by the handful. Crab twice the size of your head and tasty
as butter . . . so we were more often out of town than not.
Prowling all that summer and into the fall, hamhocking up and
back and around, driving stakes wherever the game ran hot and
the water fresh, one of those little drop stops our first real clue to
her and Manuel . . . because Manuel sure hadn't, *wouldn't* tell

me nothing—which way they'd gone or where, how long they'd been out together or even that they'd been together. And, Lord knows, I'd tried, worming and worming at him. But unless you been ear up against a stick wall, you don't know how stiff-balled a savage can be, mule mute and harder to move than beaned bowels . . . because I sure enough wanted to be prepared with something for when the senator came looking for us with a troop of regulars. But the senator never came. Until, after a while, because the whole thing seemed too hard to credit anyways, I began to doubt it had ever happened. I mean, tracks as easy to misread as anything else—until that hot, still afternoon in the glade:

Manuel had been walking point, pushing hard all day, so, a good part of it, we'd had to dog-jog to keep up—though I never thought nothing of it then; they all had their ways: Gray Owl, working point, relished clocking off the miles, so with him you moved; Little Rabbit liked to poke and pry; Sonofabitch a dawdler, though, one morning, Sonofabitch lit out on a dead run, going like that until noon just to see which of us went to the wall first, which, of course, was me, or they'd zigzag or take a cliff route when they could just as easy gone around. But, mostly, an Indian on trek, unless it's a war party or a hunt, likes to enjoy soaking up and putting down, savoring.

So I never thought nothing of Manuel's pushing until we hauled into that little closed space—he had a way, Manuel did, of finding them, like that little cranny under the chokeberries where he'd carved the totem—Manuel reaching up and pulling down and away at a tall cranefern and, like opening a door, we stepped into this tiny glade, where, tired as we were, we just stopped and stood and looked, because there's places, no matter how many hundreds of sites you camped, you'll never forget. There's one I remember on the Apashapa River, another on the Stillwater, and, of course, that little nook under the hook of the Republican where Fleet Fawn, my wife, and I first met. And this place we were standing in now, *this* was one of them . . . sunk down in a sort of coomb, the trees arching over so the sun yellowed in off the leaves like warm molasses, a tiny waterfall warbling in behind, a stream curling down and around like an embrace, moss, moist dry and carpet thick, eeling up over your moccasins, the whole hushed as chapel. Manuel pointed off left to a tiny fire site, then to the right, where pine needles overlay the moss for a bed no feather down ever matched. Beautiful!

Four days we holed up. The fish running up the bank into your pan, deer nuzzling you awake mornings, berries, figs, and sweet apples for the reaching, laying around all day, eating and gambling, sometimes in the midday heat soaking in a little pool Manuel had found downstream, at nights telling fortunes or acting out hunting stories and battles and other lies. All but Manuel, up and out mornings before anyone was awake, or standing on the bank gazing out over the little stream or peering up through the trees; once letting the water from the tiny waterfall run over his arms; nights staring, humming into the fire, so I began to have an idea. Then, the dawn of the second morning, Little Rabbit woke me, four fingers up to his mouth, pointing down the bank, and I followed, squatting next to him in the reeds. He sat a moment, arms straight out over his knees, then he reached inside his leathers, holding out—it looked like a *spur*? . . . not a Chihuahua, nor Texas star, nor OK nor Army nor Spanish nor like any spur I'd ever saw, gut hooks all compared to this, fine-lined as an ink drawing, the holders and shaft goosenecked of solid silver, the rowels tiny and sharp and delicate as squirrels' teeth.

Little Rabbit held it up before my eyes and spun the rowels in opposite directions so, when you looked close, it spelled out the letters H D.

He'd found it, *felt* it, Little Rabbit said, under his back when he'd lain down . . . hooked into the moss beneath the pine needles. I spun the rowels, Honor Devlin, *H D*.

As I'd opined earlier, Manuel was in full moon: He'd brought her here the same as, straightaway, pushing and beelining, he'd brought us, the same as, without looking, he'd pointed out the fire site and the pine pallet . . . trying to get it all back, to relive it, so for the first time I began to think how it had been with them . . . awakening mornings, her breath kneading with his, licking the dew from her eyelids, chasing one another through the high grass to keep warm or holding to one another until the sun had tongued the wet from the leaves, eating from each other's mouths the plump, round cheekberries that, when you bit into, exploded down your throat like wine; breakfasts catching the delicious little rainfish upstream in rock traps (I'd seen two above the falls), the crisp, speckled outsides oozing down the spit, melting over their teeth like honey; forenoons contending with the squirrels for the tiny, tasty limenuts, hoarding them up for later, or hunting, spearing the wild turkeys gossiping stupidly in a line along the branches, flushing the partridges, wing-shooting as they upwhirred (you could see their remains in the fork of a young oak, where the ants had finished them); in the long, lush afternoons lazing along the banks, lipping the spot grass off one another's bodies, listening to the broken buzz of the water flies; in the heavy heat playing in the waterfall or swimming in the pool downstream until, tired, drowsed by the fume of the bellflowers and long purples, they'd turned to one another, intertwining beneath the laceleaves; and later, in the mauve dusk, baking the small, hard ears of wild corn and the tiny potatoes that burst in the burning coals like white flowers, the juice from the partridges running down into their cottony centers, stuffing themselves on the rich, brown meat to stretch out long yet strangely light on the moss, drifting thigh on thigh up and up through fern and leaf skinned over by a milk-soot of sky and stars. Or had she refused all that, seeing only the gutted game and the dirt rimming the hand, smelling the wildness and feeling only the cold and hardness? And the talk. . . . Had they talked? Oh, the long nights of talk, trekking along the ledge of sleep, the soul upwelling from the dark heart and upwelling until the great crab had crawled down the surf of the night to the first white waters of dawn. But, about what? What had they said? Or was it, all of this, my own reliving? What could they have said to one another? "*My* daddy's a United States senator?" "*My* daddy's a half-naked chief with a palsied gun hand and hanging breasts; my mother died of the plague and my two brothers were murdered . . . ?" and before he'd asked her to his blanket, had he done the pointing *in truth* next to his mouth and told her—what? —of winters hunkered down under the drifts for warmth and summers that seared the milk of the eye, of droughts when the young died and of horses floundering in floods that flashed down the arroyos like cataracts? Of sandstorms shredding the flesh and blizzards that cracked lodgepoles while people disappeared in the deadly dance of the winding wind? The wild land—of deserts and forests and gorges and canyons and ranges and the devil's own grid, of peaks so high the breath froze in pants, and valleys where the sun never shone? Of mesas to forever and prairies past the horizon? Or had he, *not-telling*, lied, speaking only of the high days of the tall cream skies and the burnished meal bending and rising like waves on a sunlit sea? And the early springs—the Moons of the Blue Buds Appearing—When the Ponies Shed, the grass higher than a man's head, the snuff of flowers like drinking to make you drunk and the moonlit nights when, bewitched, the tribe went reeling off into the noonday dark chasing after peacocks screaming in the trees? And always the great herds and the long hunts, had he told her of them? With the kids squalling and the old women making water on their hands for luck? Of fleas and flies and maggots in the pemmican? And the smells!—of horse, of wet hides and dry dung, of fresh blood and stale bodies and dragging the sick on travoises, leaving the old behind, nights licking the blood from sticky wrists, holding the lodge flaps close to keep from blowing away? And always how quick death came? Had he told her all that? Singing his love songs at dusk. And the nights, the nights.

Around midwatch of the night before we left, I fronted Manuel.

He sat cross-legged at the fire, carving something on metal.

"Manuel . . ." I said and lay the spur on the ground between us.

He glanced at it but never picked it up. He never stopped carving.

I picked it up and spun the rowels.

"It's hers," I said. He dug at the metal. "Isn't it?" The knife slipped and he grunted. "You were here before with her, weren't you, you and her?"

Still he went on carving and I told him how dangerous it was and what would happen to her and worse, to him, but even worse to the *find-out* itself if they were ever discovered, and they must never do it again, and carefully I lay the spur at his feet and left.

For a long time after, I lay and doubted and wondered and worried up at the Milky Way draped over the shoulders of the night like a lamb's-wool shawl. But, the next morning, the spur was right where I'd left it.

If we hadn't trekked too far out, we'd bring back whatever game we could before it spoiled, but mostly we'd nigger-fish off the Potomac or sometimes in the Tidal Basin, the best fishing down where the Channel and Anacostia met, Little Rabbit boiling up some mighty tasty concoctions nights—Little Rabbit, once he'd had his say, the most amenable of the lot, doing most of the housework (mainly cleaning up after the animals), most of the milking and all the cooking (squaw's work and a real mortification to a brave; I think it had something to do with the Rabbit's manhood vision and debasing himself), a lot of the animals in the neighborhood, cats and goats and such disappearing, along with the rats in the corners—the Rabbit had a way of trapping them with a drop loop, some of those stews he compounded pretty pungent until Honor and the tall young fella from that day in the carriage started bringing stuff over—Elbert Davis the young fella's name, a nice young fella—the young fella—I think, her way of telling Manuel how things stood between him and her. The closest to any mention of her and Manuel when once, in passing, I'd said, half joshing, what a fine trek down to the Anacostia she'd missed and named that week the two of them had been gone. Yes, she'd smiled back, half joshing too, but that particular week she'd been visiting her cousin in Baltimore, but maybe we could make it another time, and she'd glanced at me so I still wasn't sure but felt a whole bellyful better knowing how she'd handled it with her daddy and whoever else might have gotten curious—all of us, she said, expected come Saturday at her lodge for the big feast, which, if I'd known *how* big and what they intended, I'd never have let them gone to . . . and no mention from Manuel of *not* going.

The day of the eating, I went on ahead to scout the time and terrain, and let me tell you, it sure wasn't what I'd fancied, the senator's lodge with more rooms than the Princess Hotel, servants passing in and around with drinks and little trays of food you could eat a dozen of at a bite, an orchestra in one corner of the room, the women in evening gowns, the men, all, except for me and this jack-a-dandy with the senator, in tails. I looked again. *Him!*—I'd never met him, I'd never seen him, but I knew *him*. Rory-cum-tory in full glory. A cavalry officer, you'd've said from the cut of him, but like no cavalry officer nobody'd ever saw: a tasseled sword clanking off one hip, a ruddle-handled .45 swung off the other, down the seams of his trousers a broad pair of stripes, orange and blue, his shirt a flare-collared sailor's blouse, a red silk cravat flaming out from under his chin, with more interlacing loops of gold cable down his sleeves than a braid of snakes in a birthing blind, raked over his forehead a great wide-brimmed hat (which he hadn't yet made no move to re-move) and from under which a fall of yellow hair cascaded down his neck to lay along his shoulders in a nest of golden ringlets. I mean he was a Mandan medicine man in a mud mask—standing, grinning down on the senator, everyone, especially the women starting to gather around him, when the senator raised both arms to announce, "Ladies and gentlemen, General George Custer," and the general flourished off the great, wide-brimmed hat and smiled around to a sprinkling of applause, saying in a high voice how honored he was though for what exactly I didn't know, it being my notion that all this was for the Four and the general sure wouldn't have come for that, the fact being that General Custer wasn't now no general, nor rightly no nothing at present, Custer having just been court-martialed at Fort Leavenworth for abandoning his command, for ordering the shooting of twelve deserting men who from all I'd heard had every right to desert, for appropriating government property for personal use, for failing to pursue attacking Indians and leaving the dead bodies of his men on the prairie to rot. For all of which General Custer had been court-martialed and put down for one year, which, come to think on it, was probably why the general was here tonight—to get the senator or whoever to get that court martial rescinded. Except, looking at him there, you'd've swore he'd just won the war—a-lone, with a loose spoke—the three of us, the senator, the young fella Elbert Davis and me, watching Custer charm the room while we waited on the Four, when down this high winding staircase came Honor in a green gown, little pearls all over her, in her dress, in her hair, around her neck, the young fella's eyes glowing. Oh, she was a beauty for a fact and spitting mad.

"Papa! All these people. I told you it was to be something small. Why?"

"Because, daughter, *all these people* can do for your Indians what you can't. Colvin McCullough, there, knows everyone worth knowing. . . ." (You could hear Colvin all over the room competing with Custer, going on about a "vulva of vipers," and for the girl's sake I hoped that Colvin was better at politicking than cards.) The senator pointed. "Stacy Kingle's on the Indian Commission, Tom Evanston's in the President's Cabinet . . ." which, I thought, was why Custer was here all right, "an' Bill Fineman over there's—"

"Why not go right to the President?" I cut in.

"Yes, why not," a heavy voice said, "go right to the President!"

"Governor . . ." the senator said, the two men smiling first at one another then at me, so I was beginning to see how simple it all wasn't.

The governor was red-faced and windy, with a large, bosomy woman on his arm. "My missus here wants to know where's your aborigines, Ed?" the governor said to the senator, who at that moment was gesturing across the room over our heads at her . . . in a red gown with sparkles down the front, cut low, low, so many of the men, Custer among them, were watching her (one of the things that later used to bull me wild) . . . only a little older than Honor and almost as pretty, with candy-gray eyes and soft as sinning. Her name was—I came to call her "Buff," a birthmark the shape of a buffalo climbing her right hip, so I thought of her— Lord help me—as good medicine, her eyes well black and moist on me, taking my arm like we'd known one another from before the flood, telling how she'd heard so much from the senator about me, and she had—about the fight in the gorge, about the hides and the Four and the train . . . only, the way she retold it to the governor and his missus I was some high-flying fandangle for a fact, until of a sudden there was only her voice, so, self-conscious, she stopped . . . a gasp, some giggles and then a stillness—even from Colvin and Custer—so we all turned.

They stood in an uneasy knot on the foyer landing: Little Rabbit in work shirt and pants; Gray Owl, tall and dignified, in his patchwork blanket; Manuel in leggings, shirt and browband; Sonofabitch in a frock coat, fur around the collar, his eyepatch also of fur to match his fur collar, in knickers, the feathered boa about his neck, on his head a derby, eagle feathers punched through the crown.

The senator gestured. "Our guests."

....

20

Of Yourselves Fools

Followed by Honor and the young fella, the senator crossed to greet them, clasping both hands over his chest in the sign for *peace*, placing his middle finger at his mouth then one finger up for *brother*, sweeping his right hand around the room for *welcome*.

They answered in sign, and palm down he brought his right hand up in an arc from his chest for *good*, the senator troweling it on a little thick, I thought, even for the crowd.

The senator stepped up on the foyer landing with them. "Ladies and gentlemen, my friends: on my right, Gray Owl; next to him, Little Rabbit. This young man is Manuel. And to my left is—is—ah . . ."

The big Comanche lifted his head defiantly. "I are who, a big, red-eyed sonofabitch."

In the next half second you could've caught enough flies for a frog ranch.

"That's all right, boy," Colvin McCullough called, "you ain't the only one here tonight," and everyone laughed.

"Our honored guests," the senator said; "come and greet them."

The music started and the evening gowns and white ties—all except Custer—commenced to move in among them, Buff still hanging on my arm.

Honor took Manuel's hand.

"You're mine, Man," Honor said and started through a small

side door, the young fella Elbert Davis following when Manuel jerked away to stand glaring at the young fella.

"Him?" Manuel said.

"Of course, *him*," said Honor. "Man, this is my young man. You know that."

But Manuel didn't know.

The young man's lips stretched into a nervous smile.

"Man, this is my number-one brave."

That Manuel understood. He looked from Honor to the young fella and back and stalked away.

"Man," Honor called after him, "Man," and she started to follow, then let him go.

It had all happened so quickly, I doubt anyone but Buff and I had seen or heard.

If nothing else, I thought, it was the one thing Honor had learned from her and Man's week together in the glade—how impossible it was.

Buff pulled me over to where a waiter was serving drinks, Sonofabitch and the governor's wife just behind us.

"Mister Sonofa—" the governor's wife began, feeling for the ending, handing Sonofabitch a glass of champagne.

"Bitch," he finished it for her.

"I beg your pardon!"

Buff laughed.

Sonofabitch slugged down the champagne.

The governor's wife smiled, pleased with herself. "You ever tasted anything like that before?"

"No," Sonofabitch said and took the other drink out of her startled hand and slugged that down, when a second servant passed with a tray of drinks, Sonofabitch turning his back on the governor's wife to follow the drinks, me to follow Sonofabitch, dragging Buff after, when we turned into the general.

I can't say, from all I'd heard, I was in any particular push to meet Mr. Custer, nor, from his look, him, me—Buff maybe but not me.

He had chill blue eyes with slate centers, and in a glance he'd took my measure rim to root. For a full five seconds we stood before one another.

I nodded, smiling at the ruddle-handled handgun on his hip. "'Spectin' trouble tonight, General?"

He didn't smile back. He looked over me at Buff, then around the room. "Well, now," he said eyes cutting away from Sonofabitch reaching around from behind the drink waiter for another drink, "I wouldn't be a mite sur-prised, sir," and he pushed by me to Buff, bowing, asking her if she'd honor him with the next dance.

My first, last and only converse with General George Armstrong Custer.

Buff simpered and curtsied and made a little face at me, so I thought how the way I felt must show, and they went off toward the music.

The only one of the Four nobody seemed to take to was Little Rabbit. It was, of course, the Rabbit's way of staring into faces.

I started over to get him when Little Rabbit found himself staring into a face that stared back, the two nose to nostril like a pair of fighting cocks, the staring man with a head of silver-white hair, very distinguished.

"May I ask," said the silver-haired man staring back at the Rabbit, "why do you stare at people?"

Without taking his eyes from the man's face, the Rabbit made the sign for *find-out*.

The man frowned.

"Find," the Rabbit said.

"What—do you find?"

"Heart. See . . ."

"Heart?"

"With cante ista."

The man shook his head, "See?"

The Rabbit pointed to his chest.

"Can— is—" the man tried to say the word.

"See, not with eye in head," the Rabbit said, "see with cante ista, *eye of heart*—into heart."

The silver-haired man smiled kindly. "Do you really think that's wise," he said and began to maneuver the Rabbit across the room.

I looked around: Manuel had stalked out into the garden; Sonofabitch, surrounded by women, was behaving, and Gray Owl—I gawped, then followed them, the senator, the governor, Colvin McCullough and the man from the President's Cabinet, Custer lagging after—Buff wasn't anywhere around—into the library with Gray Owl.

It was the damnedest thing. Not only was Gray Owl enjoying them, but *they* were enjoying him, laughing, bantering with him, asking him why he wore feathers in his hair, Gray Owl countering with why did they strangle themselves with that string around their necks. Making him comfortable in a large leather chair, sitting around him over cigars and cherry wine. Marveling . . . till it occurred to me how it must almost have been instinctive their being drawn to one another, recognizing in Gray Owl one who, among his own kind, was one of them. Colvin McCullough, joshing, wanted to know what Gray Owl was doing in this citadel of the enemy?

"Change," Gray Owl said serious and thought a while, sucking on his cigar. "Much change. Buffalo soon gone. Wasichu all places with spotted buffalo [cattle]. Wasichu house near waterhole. Wasichu village on river. How we live?"

"Like we do," the governor said.

"No. You have no law."

The governor didn't so much answer as bluster, like some big bird, I thought, puffing out its feathers.

"You say law for all man . . ."

"That's right," said the governor.

"You tell us not drink whiskey." Gray Owl lifted his glass. "All same you drink whiskey; trade same for fur, for robe. You say not have gun. You have gun. You say sign treaty, say land ours then take back. No law."

"Those are bad men," the man from the President's Cabinet said.

"Yes," said Gray Owl, "good, bad Wasichu. But bad most strong."

"Why do you say that?"

"Bad men rule."

"Are we bad?" asked the President's man.

Gray Owl pointed to himself, then, with his right hand over his left breast, made the casting, downward motion.

The President's man turned to me.

"He asks," I said, "do you know if *he's* bad?"

The President's man glanced sideways at the others, who pretended not to have noticed.

"What is bad?" asked the governor.

"Bad do as wish all time. Make slave if not agree, same color, same Wakan Tanka. Not trust words. Indian, enemy in war, friend in peace. Wasichu say, 'My friend, my brother,' then—" He thrust his right hand forward and downward to the left, opening and closing his fingers in the sign for *kill*.

Oddly, without asking, all seemed to understand the sign.

"Hold on, boy," Custer burst out—from the moment of the Four's entrance on the foyer landing, you could see Custer hadn't liked any of it, either what he was seeing or hearing, the senator stiffening at Custer's tone, and the general dropped his voice. "I've a mind to say that door swings both ways, boy."

"History, Gray Owl, history," the senator said smiling, smoothing it over, "she's our teacher. The red man must stand aside for progress or be overwhelmed. That has been—*is* our destiny . . . manifest in both our houses. The white man was made stronger by Providence, and so he's accountable for that strength to the red man. We want to help."

Gray Owl made the *no* sign.

"Not for red man. For red man land, for red man forest, red man metal in ground!" and he turned and stared at Custer, who, sipping cherry wine, acted as though he hadn't heard.

The good feeling was gone now; then the senator said, "Gray Owl, you oughta be in Congress . . ."

"Wouldn't last," said Colvin McCullough, "he's too honest," and everyone except Custer chuckled and it was all right again.

I went out to see about Sonofabitch—and Buff—passing Little Rabbit and the silver-haired man in a roomful of paintings, the two standing before a painting of a knight on horseback.

"Picture no good," the Rabbit was saying, hacking his light, dry cough around his words, "can no touch pony, no feel, smell, talk to, ride."

"How long have you had that cough?" the silver-haired man asked.

"Horse too much heavy, buffalo run off."

Through the window I saw Manuel headed for the stables.

I found him in the half-light in the stalls stroking the muzzle of a beautiful sorrel—Honor's cross-eyed pony, I wondered?—when there was a tinkling laugh, and I followed Manuel to the stable door.

Out in the garden at the edge of a clearing where the moonlight splattered down through the trees, the young fella and Honor stood talking, then the young fella put his arms around her and they kissed. Manuel started for them. "No, Man. . . ." I moved into the entrance. He tried to shove past me. I caught and held to either side of the opening. "Man, no!" Twice he pushed hard at my chest, then raised his arm to hit me. I dropped my head, waiting, but held on. If he got by me— A boy against one of the most vicious manslayers on the plains. Then I saw his moccasins step back and raised my head. Manuel looked like a man cut in half: the bottom of him braced, legs spread to fight; the top of him falling away, elbows loose down his sides, staring over me at them. Then, once again, her tinkling laugh and the young fella's deeper laugh and the awful look in Manuel's eyes, and I got a more solid grip on either side of the door, but it wasn't as I thought, because Manuel only stood. A long time watching. Then his hands came up in the ancient sign with all the old *why* arguments. "She chooses him," I said. But I don't think he heard me, his eyes suddenly glittering, reaching out for her, so I dug in for his charge, but the glitter, too, died and there was only the deep Indian melancholy, and he reached behind him and I began to sweat . . . he was reaching for the sheath strapped under his shirt to his tailbone. All this while, he'd been holding a skinning knife.

I stayed in the doorway until he turned back into the stable, until Honor and the young fella had gone. Except for the horses shifting in the stalls, it was still, the moon whitewashing the harness along the walls. Then I heard Manuel in the rear of the stable and started to feel my way back when I heard them—drums. From the house. Lordy! I called softly into the darkness, "Man, Man . . ." but I knew: by now he was back somewhere in that Indian place yonder words, yonder thought, yonder which only the birds and dumb things went. Even as I found him, he'd have been lost to me, and I swung back toward the house.

As I entered, they were just coming out of the library, Custer

and the others—I looked for Buff—the President's man telling a
story to Gray Owl. The drums seemed to be coming from—

"Clay. . . ."

It was the senator, with the silver-haired man.

"Clay, this is Dr. Domars."

The silver-haired man's hand was soft, like a woman's.

"I wish you wouldn't, Doc," said the senator, "not yet." The
silver-haired man ignored the senator. "Not till you're sure."

The silver-haired man took my elbow and steered me into a
corner. "I'm afraid, sir, I've some bad—"

I looked around for Sonofabitch.

"Your Indian's got consumption, sir."

"Sonofabitch?"

"I just examined him, Mr. Rabbit."

"Little Rabbit?"

"I'm afraid so."

"Con—sump—"

"Tuberculosis."

"You're not sure of that, Doc," said the senator.

"But—when?" I said.

"Just now," the doctor said.

"No, I mean we've only been in town a little over—"

"Doesn't matter," the doctor said, "they've no resistance. Runs
through them like the plague. It *is* the plague to them. They
bring in some tribe to sign a treaty . . . in three months half the
tribe's got it; in six, the other half's got it; in a year three quarters
of them are dead. So if you want to keep the rest of them alive, sir
—*except* for Mr. Rabbit—I'd send them all home."

"Now, wait a minute, Doc," began the senator.

"Now," the doctor said. "Tomorrow."

It was coming too fast for me. The senator kept looking away
from me, then back. The doctor still had my elbow, squeezing it.

"Nothin' I c'n do," I said.

"They'll die," the doctor said.

"Doc—" the senator cut in.

"They *must* leave."

"They won't," I said, "not till they git what they come for."
And it hit me: "What did you mean, Doctor—*except* Little
Rabbit?"

"I mean, he can't go back. Ever. He'd infect the entire tribe."
We thought of it the same time:
"Little Rabbit's just been married, hasn't he?" the senator said.
I nodded. "Then, he'll never agree to—"
I tried not to think on what I'd have to say to Little Rabbit, or to Little Rabbit's sloe-eyed bride, the doctor's words like a mist, dim and fading out at the ends, so I thought how doctors had to cover themselves like executioners.
"A fine man, Mr. Rabbit," the doctor said.
The senator started to pour me a glass of cherry wine, when over the drumming came Gray Owl's voice, chanting, and I headed for the sound.

In the ballroom the guests had formed a great circle along the walls, clapping. In the center Little Rabbit, coughing, sat cross-legged on the floor, drumming on the back of a bull fiddle; Gray Owl stood over him chanting; Sonofabitch in nothing but a breechclout, his clothes all over the room, the eyepatch down over his nose, whooped, body glistening with sweat, dancing drunkenly.
It was one of the few times I ever truly thought Indian, hating, wanting to rub away the gray grinning along the walls, when Manuel, also probably brought by the drums, stepped out on the floor, the cheers and clapping louder, pushing him also to dance.
Manuel stood like a dark slash out of the night, till first Gray Owl's chanting, then the drumming and clapping and finally Sonofabitch's jiggling stopped.
"What do you?" Manuel demanded of them in sign.
Gray Owl spiraled his right index finger upward from his forehead in the sign for *medicine*.
"No," Manuel said, "you do not make medicine, you make of yourselves, for them, fools!"
It was a serious charge.
"Look around," Manuel said.
Tittering, the crowd was calling out for more dancing and singing, calling for Manuel not to be a spoilsport and join in, and, seeing that there was some sort of argument, calling to be let in on it, half hoping, I thought, to see someone scalped.
The three looked around, saw what Manuel said was true. They

were being ridiculed. Manuel arrogant, tall, staring the crowd down, a fighting brave just out of the bush. Then, very deliberately, Manuel lifted first one bare foot then the other, the bare sole sss-padding along the floor.

Four times to the four powers he made the sss-padding, bowing to Grandmother Earth, tilting his head back to Grandfather Sky, now motionless, then again sss-padding but faster, Little Rabbit sliding in behind, palms feathering over the back of the bull fiddle, Gray Owl's voice insinuating, soft as rain, caressing the beat—like I'd never heard them before—and Manuel, arching his back, commenced to dance—that, too, like no dancing I'd ever seen. I could read it, but not understand it: Manuel's feet now fragile as leaves over the wooden surface, a whisper, the beginning, a day made of dawn, when abruptly he stiffened, body rigid as dying, arms starting to reach up and up, widening, circling with the sun—Giver of Time, Grower of Life, Withdrawer of Night, Flame of the Universe, the SUN, the DAY, the LIGHT! and, risen, Manuel danced the sun people awake: the child leaping and flashing, the young girl mincing and making pool eyes, the mother scolding and summoning the old man, withered and trembling, to the fire, and then the warrior: Manuel's feet starting to stomp, thudding and pounding—like the buffalo before the horsebacks, the heart cracking at the chase, the lungs bursting in flight, the awful thrashing of battle, and then the sudden silence in the aftertime, the long still with the great breath, and now the return, the heroes, faces blackened in victory, strutting, the wounded holding wounds and grieving, the women of the lost throwing dirt and dung over themselves, Manuel despairing, bent low, almost to the floor, body undulating, head, belly, back, arms snaking, sinuous as the crawling things, suddenly unfolding, upswirling like grama grass before the wind and tall and tall, arms out, wheeling and swooping with the wingeds, he flew at the figures along the walls, then, up-reaching, up-stretching, up-thrusting up and up with the growing things, glorious, fingers fluttering in the way of the leaf children, he up-rose tall and tall, only to freeze with the moon in the dark time that is always with us, that is always near us, the time of forever.

It was dancing such as they'd never seen—as I'd never seen—and knew we'd probably never see again, spring soft and winter wild, tender and harsh, savage with dignity and achingly graceful, and they never once clapped, the women's eyes shining, the men uneasy. That's when I saw her, Honor, along the wall, starting gently to sway with him. Behind her the young fella, puzzled. And suddenly I knew what I hadn't understood before—though in all this time he hadn't gone near nor even glanced at her, though, Little Rabbit and Gray Owl, they'd known: *Manuel was dancing his world for her, inviting her*. This, his love dance, his offertory— his people, the hunt, the land, his manhood and gods. Dancing until, when he'd melded them to him skin and soul, he chopped it off, Little Rabbit following Manuel's lead, hands caught in mid-air; Gray Owl, taken up in his song, withering in the midst of a phrase.

And, tall, gleaming with perspiration, chest rising and falling, Manuel turned to them. "Ga-ha dang!" he hissed, and the three filed from the room after him.

"Clay . . ." the senator nudged me after them.

After what we'd just seen, the senator's want of grace galled and I flared. "I can't hold 'em forever, senator."

The senator shook his head.

"The President," I said, "git us in to see Sam," I said and saw Buff working her way along the wall toward me, and I started toward her.

The senator stepped between us, nodding me after Manuel and the others, and I went—whether because he'd told me to or just wanting to be quit of them all I'm not now sure.

At the door I looked back once more for Buff and saw Custer swagger out from the crowd along the wall into the center of the dancing place—the Great Protector—as though he'd driven us out.

::

21

The Long Find-out

In the weeks following, they seemed to settle in. Each in his own way during the day, while, at night, seated around a small fire in the dirt floor, they swayed to some unsung rhythm, Gray Owl, a gourd rattle in either hand, solemnly circling them, making medicine to the snake god and the gods of the antelope and buffalo and rain and sky. Giving thanks for the benefactions of today, asking for the humility to accept tomorrow. Praying like his fathers for the chase, for strength and endurance, honesty and goodness and all the things they wouldn't need in this new land. The four of them on a hunt few whites and no savage had ever been on before, this the greatest of *find-outs*—the search for civilized man!

But as the weeks went by, the Four began to unhinge, then to fall away and break up: since the train, Sonofabitch hadn't been twenty-four hours off the laughing milk; Little Rabbit's cough, like the doctor said, worsening, terrible now to listen to; Manuel lying about all day every day on the potato sacks, brooding up at the ceiling; while Gray Owl—I hadn't seen Gray Owl in weeks. Already we were into the Moon of Popping Branches, the trees bare, snow on the ground, their gold almost gone, and still nothing done. The senator forever "working on" getting us in to see Sam—the President—while we waited and waited and waited, until, one day, a crawful, I decided to go out there and see Sam myself at the Palace (which was how it was called before they splashed whitewash all over the new one in '17 and called her the

"White House"; the "Palace" all I ever knew or heard it called by Pap, who was through D.C. in '14 after jumping a British merchantman he'd been impressed aboard during the War of 1812, trekking up the south bank of the Rappahannock from Norfolk and crossing over from Fredericksburg, Jimmy Madison President then, "a withered little Apple-John" Pap called him, his wife, Dolley, one of the sauciest mares Pap said he'd ever laid eyes on, with pretty blond curls and cream-white arms and shoulders and a sparkly way to set a man dreaming nights . . . in her carriage when Pap saw her, riding from Lafayette Square to the Presidential Palace—just one week to the day, Pap said, afore that limey barnburner, Admiral George Cockburn, put the torch to it. . . . "August 24, 1814, a day long to live in infamy," Pap recites with all the flourish of a Fourth of July highbinder . . . ol' Georgie Cockburn reared back in Dolley's favorite chair giving orders to "burn down the Palace," which folk don't much like to hear it called no more because it sounds too much like royalty).

Anyway, all fused and fired up, I lit out down Pennsylvania Avenue, only the further I rode past the saloons and whorehouses, past the dry-goods stores, the barber shops and gambling drops, the closer the Palace, the farther off Sam and the Columbia. There'd been so much in between: Shiloh and Vicksburg, Chickamauga and Spotsylvania, Kenesaw Mountain and Yellow Tavern, Cedar Creek and the battle in the wilderness, and Lee and Appomattox and ol' Abe and of a sudden I was looking straight up into the palace portico, and I reined about and rode back to the senator's.

"We're goin' home," I told the senator.

Too bad, said the senator lighting a cigar, because, he said, our meeting with the President had been all but arranged.

"How long?" I said.

The President wanted to see us, the senator said, had been looking forward to seeing me—us, but—

"How long!"

"A matter of days now," the senator said.

I reminded the senator of what would happen to the Central Plains if the Four—Three—went home, and indirectly whose fault it would be.

"Perhaps hours," the senator said. A shame, didn't I think, to throw it all away when it was right in our hands?

I was beginning not to believe the senator. I was beginning not to believe the President wanted to see us. I was beginning not to believe the senator had the *come-on* with the President he said he had. I was beginning to believe the senator was bluffing. But why? To keep from having to prove he wasn't as all-fired important as he said he was? But he *was* important. He was a senator. But, then, so was I bluffing—whatever control I'd had over the Four going fast.

"A shame," I agreed and moved downtown into the Princess Hotel, which the senator didn't like a-tall. He said I was deserting them. Though *how* I couldn't reckon. I mean, I couldn't ken how sleeping nights curled up to a pig or waking mornings chickens walking across your face was one of the necessaries of this lashup. And then there was Buff. I'd found her again through the senator. Fact is, he'd arranged a little dinner party for us. But how could I take her down in that basement! Besides which, I could never get the chicken-cow-pig smell off me. Besides which, by my lights, I'd lived up to my end full dog. What'd he expect? Which was something else I never figured out until that thing in the alley with Sonofabitch.

For Sonofabitch it was all in the *water-that-burns*, ol' busthead when he could get it, ninety proof, some of that solution so powerful you wondered how they kept it corked, but then, with his gold gone, Sonofabitch had to go to the grape, mostly skulky red, Muscatel mustn't tell, the red water *mini-sha*. And yet mni-waken, *holy water*, that's what the Indian first called liquor because, like with the peyote eaters, it created visions, sacred to a savage. So in the beginning it was a religious experience, though how much real alcohol they got from those old French traders is pretty much a question, the stuff being mostly Missouri water laced with rattle-snake heads, frogs, flies, vinegar, lots of cayenne pepper, gunpowder for a kick, with just enough whiskey to color it. All the same I seen many a blunt-eyed old pishko, *wino*, spill a last drop on the ground for the spirits of the departed, saying, "Here, old friend who's gone, here's something for you," or "Here, my old love, share this last drink with me." And maybe in the beginning it had been that way with Sonofabitch too.

For five days now Sonofabitch hadn't been home. I tailed him down through all his old haunts, the railroad yards, the packing sheds and nickel flops where the grape went for two pennies a bottle and found him in an alley sitting on a garbage can sucking at the neck of a jug, drunk enough to have to open his collar to pee, his eyepatch gone, the empty socket clotted, a white paste frozen down one corner from his eye to his cheek.

It was dark in the alley, so I didn't see them at first, four of them, dirty as lying, shivering in the snow, filtering in around Sonofabitch. I kept to the shadows.

"How's it goin', Chief?" said the closest to him, teeth chattering, a thin man with a head like an ax.

Sonofabitch knew exactly what they wanted and held the jug closer to him.

"Oh, come on, old boy, we're all old friends down here," said another, an Englishman from his accent, a rag knotted under his chin.

"Share an' share alike down here, Chief," said the third, wine cherries bulging out his face like walnut warts.

"Yep, we're all the same tribe," said the fourth, a great, shambling man. He reached for the jug.

Sonofabitch pulled it away.

"Don't be that way, old man," said the Englishman.

"No," Sonofabitch said.

The four began to fan out around him. The one with the wine warts blocked off the alley. The other three, angling for position, started to move in.

Sonofabitch backed through a clutch of garbage cans up against the brick wall.

"One way or another, Chief," said the big, shambling one.

To free both hands, Sonofabitch set the jug up on a window ledge behind him.

"This way, old man," said the Englishman, "you get nothing."

I'd picked up an angle iron at the entrance to the alley. Down here, my boots alone could keep them on the hard for a week, in juice for a month. I lay back against the wall but inching forward, when, upon some signal I hadn't seen or heard, they erupted, axhead squirting in from the right at him, the Englishman from the left, the big, shambling one straight on, and then there was a

whoop and I took off at wine warts, the nearest to me, with the
angle iron, Sonofabitch, too, whooping, so I thought how the first
whoop must have been my own, thinking also how buttwitted I
was, when something—a club or fist or something—took me dead
center under the ribs to stretch me flat out, my head in a pile of
garbage, my feet in a snowbank.

Cold conscious, I could hear, talk, see everything that was going
on, do everything but move, my legs dead as candle ends. I hol-
lared at Sonofabitch to watch out for the wart coming up on his
blind side and sat up and threw the angle iron at warts and hit
Sonofabitch just over his good eye, so it could've been over right
there.

"The Battle of the Jug," I always think of it as, a vicious, gouging, crotch-kicking yahoo: the five of them rolling in the snow
among the garbage cans and garbage, clubbing, clawing, using
anything they could lay their hands to. The fight as funny as it
was savage, hands forever clutching at the jug. Sonofabitch slapping, dragging, knocking them away. You could see why he'd been
made one of the Chosen Four. Drunk or sober, Sonofabitch was
one fighting sonofabitch.

Axhead charged head down, Sonofabitch picking up an empty
garbage can, holding it so axhead ran right up into it, lifting the
can, axhead inside, bodily up over his head, throwing it, hitting
the big, shambling one in the chest. The Englishman came at him
from the opposite side, the wrong side, the side with the eye,
Sonofabitch whirling, smashing him in the face with a handful of
slush and old bacon rinds, punching him into insensibility as he
tried to wipe it out of his eyes. The wart took a running kick at
him. Sonofabitch sidestepped and the wart landed astraddle an
iron railing taking all the balls out of his fight. The big, shambling
one, recovered now, lumbered at him like a runaway coal wagon,
Sonofabitch waiting till the last minute, then bringing together a
pair of garbage can lids like cymbals on either side of his skull,
and the fight was over.

Swaying, Sonofabitch stood a moment, the single, fierce eye
rubbering around for more but closing fast from where I'd hit him
with the angle iron. Twice I called to him but he didn't hear me.
He was bleeding from a claw mark down one cheek. Then he stag-

gered back up against the wall for support, gave a single victory whoop, vomited, and passed out under the jug.

The feeling was coming back in my legs now—I could move my toes and bend my knees a little—and I tried to get up, when there he was, like a ferret, out of the shadows, a fifth, a small man who'd simply waited, and now picked his way through the garbage and bodies toward the jug. I lay stone still. Finding me like this, he'd peel me like a pear. So small, he had to step up on Sonofa-bitch's chest to reach the jug, and then he ran off down the alley. I sat up. Somehow, though I couldn't tell why, it was fit it should end thisaway.

For Little Rabbit the *find-out* was in the streets. Always in faces. But, of course, Little Rabbit didn't know about such faces. Day after day in the cold he roved, peering into startled eyes, coughing into frightened faces, coughing continuously now.

Twice the police picked him up, but no one would press charges. First they called it vagrancy, then malicious mischief, and settled on disturbing the peace and put Little Rabbit away for a day. But they could see it wouldn't do no good, and afterward looked the other way.

I'd see him on Pennsylvania Avenue or off on one of those side streets. The last time on Seventh Street with Manuel, who stood shivering before a store window studying a tuxedo on a store dummy, which, when you looked close at it, resembled Honor's young man, so I hung around in case Manuel decided it was an evil totem and started to take it apart, when Little Rabbit burst into spasms of coughing that sent him reeling down the street, doubled over, trembling, Manuel hooking a supporting arm under his shoulders, the two staggering along through the slush next to the buildings—to be protected on that side against ambush—looking as out of place in this new world as a ruby in a goat's ear, exiting around the corner like a vaudeville team.

Gray Owl I heard before I saw, a bull grunt, then pah-ha hay-say, *let me enter*, and through the glass doors leading into the lobby, I caught a flash of the blue and green and red of the patch-work blanket.

Buff held me back. "You promised, Clay."

I'd promised to buy her a new fur coat.

The doorman held the door shut so Gray Owl couldn't enter. Buff tugged at my arm. Gray Owl could see me now and, face pressed against the glass, he made the short, urgent arm thrust, *I must see you*, then the gentle forefinger sign, palm out, *please*—it can also mean *pity me*. Buff pulled at my arm.

The doorman yelled through the glass that he was going to call the police.

"Come on. Come on!" Buff said. *She*, I knew, the reason why—after weeks since any mention of that meet with the President "only hours away"—I'd stopped pushing the senator. I liked it too much this way. With her. I didn't want to go back. Chance leaving her, losing her. Lordy! I was twice her age. I spent too much on her. And I was so taken with calico fever for her that, right now, had you given me a choice between her and Fleet Fawn—everything Buff wasn't—Lord help me, I'd have taken the Wasichu!

"Later, Buff," I said.

"Now," she pouted, "you know you promised."

I shook her hand off my arm.

The doorman held the doors shut. "No," the doorman said to Gray Owl, "you can't come in here. No! Now beat it. Before I call the police. . . ."

I handed the doorman a bill, and Gray Owl, white with the cold, shouldered into the lobby. Everybody was staring.

"You come, Face on Water. Now. You come!" He pulled at my sleeve.

Buff was embarrassed.

"Many boxes, Face on Water. You come!"

There was an urgency in him I'd never seen.

I called to Buff to go on without me and pick out her coat. She made a face and flounced off, so I knew that coat would cost plenty.

Like a man branded, Gray Owl hauled me out of the hotel, dragged me across town to the LIBRARY OF CONGRESS it said out-side. Inside, books, everywhere you looked, books: floor to ceiling along the walls; around the windows and doors; special racks in the center of the room. Hundreds and thousands of books. I'd never seen such a place. The Wasichu power. *His mark.* The Wasichu medicine. "Re-dah-nah so"; Gray Owl gestured around the room. He wanted me to learn him what then I couldn't even do for myself—*read.*

22

Yuwipi
(the little lights from nowhere)

In the basement a darkness, a raven's wing of blackness, lowering, palpable, flowing in and around and through, a river of ink, intense as the grave, suffocating, driving deep within, the inbeing isolate, damning all to see with cante ista, *eye of the heart*. This the ceremony of the *yuwipi*. For Little Rabbit, who'd decided to die.

And so we sat in the swart still. Waiting. Praying. Silent. Desperate, desperate. Praying. When out of the unholy hush the dark footfall of drums, the faint wash of chant and song, of the women's high tremolo and voices, tiny voices, spirit voices whispering from clabrous throats through spectral lips. And then the lights, tiny dots, fireflies flitting, bright, then bursting, little flashes of lightning going off before the eyes and in ears. The drum roar gathering, throbbing, filling the awful darkness, driving out the body clutter and mind chatter, purging for the Great One. Underneath all, the rattles, *the yuwipi*. Praying, desperate, desperate praying. To the ghost voices. Murmuring. Like bees threshing. And swishing through the air. I ducked at the whish of flying-by things. A rattle knocked against my right temple and chest. I held my hands up against the whirr of wings and the brushings along the skin—of cobwebs and willowtips and childfingers until, spooked, I started to my feet, and in that quartered instant of fear and rising smelled him—the dust and dung and sour sage—and the middle of me exploded in reds and scarlets, the huge head slamming through me, caroming off my shoulder blades, the great horn grazing my ear, the muzzle, hot and moist and slobbering, snuffling across my cheek, the hump and flowing shag of mane, of caked earth and bark, blanketing one whole side of me, slamming me backward across the hole Little Rabbit had dug . . . a hole so large there'd been space for hardly anyone else in the room. Little Rabbit coughing, digging the hole in the basement floor.

"What the hell, Little Rabbit," I'd said, watching him dig the hole, scolding.

From the tip of his nose hung a plop of sweat that all his coughing and exerting couldn't seem to shake loose.

"What're you doin'?" I'd said.

Unseeing, unhearing, the Rabbit had dug.

"What's the hole for?" I'd said, unable to accept it. "What're you diggin'?" I took his arm. "Little Rabbit?"

The plop of sweat dropped into the hole.

I went over to Manuel, lying on his back on the potato sacks, arms crossed behind his head. For days now, or anyways since the senator's, he'd been like this, the pig and chickens scuffling around him in the dirt.

"What's Little Rabbit doin'?" I'd said, still not able to stop the pretense. "Man?"

Manuel grunted at the funk in me and rolled over toward the wall. I turned to Sonofabitch, who walked away.

"For Lordsake!"

But that's how they did it. One day they decided, and the next they went off alone up into the hills and lay down behind a rock and did it.

Only, mostly it happened with the old, the very old, and rarely even with them—and never the young.

Then, in the dimness, I saw the tiny stones with which the Rabbit had outlined himself in the dirt.

He didn't look well, no, what with the coughing and shoveling, but he didn't look like that, either. Digging his own grave! I didn't know what to say or how to stop him.

Carefully he laid the shovel, an old buck-blade he'd scrounged

someplace, along the lip of tiny stones, pushing gently into the
earth, humming softly to himself. His death song.

I brought my fingertips together in *apology* for speaking to him
as I had.

The thing, though, was that Arapahos don't bury their dead but
elevate them on scaffolds, where they are closer to the Great
Spirit, where the sun and wind, the rain and snow can honor
them.

Little Rabbit was afraid, Manuel said, that here on the stone
prairie the Wasichus would desecrate his spirit, and so he'd chosen to take his chances in the bosom of Grandmother Earth.

I closed my right hand over my heart and brought my left
across my eyes and shook my head to let him know I *hadn't
known,* and sat down to keep him company in his time.

Like an old dog I'd had, Daniel, I thought, watching him.
We'd grown up together, Daniel and I, so by the time I was seven
and old enough for the fields, Daniel was ninety, white-muzzled
and arthritic and almost blind. Pap and everybody said he should
be put away. He was starting to smell and he couldn't eat. But he
was mine, and I said no, always keeping one eye on Pap, the other
on the dog, until that spring when I saw him limping out into the
meadow. I followed and called, forgetting he was also deaf as a
turnip. When I got to him, he was walking in a circle, trampling
down the spring grass, then he rolled over it, making it smooth,
and lay down, and I knew. Nice and easy, in his own day and
hour. So I learned early how dying was only another living.

Gray Owl had taken one look at the hole Little Rabbit was digging and declared a *yuwipi* (the little lights from nowhere) to find
out what was taking place, Gray Owl now across from us in the
darkness face down before the altar, fingers laced with rawhide,
body ceremented in a buffalo hide—Gray Owl, through whom the
spirits would talk. Then abruptly the lights, the wingings and
drums all ceased, out of the silence a voice, high and wailing:
"My grandchild, you shall pick of the sacred fruit," then more of
Gray Owl's prayers, and suddenly Gray Owl called, "Hasten to
make light. Make light!" and the dry grass was lit.

I looked around. At first in the dimness all I could make out
was the altar, a mound of powdered earth, on either side the
wagmuha, the holy rattles, inside which were the yuwipi stones

(the stone, without beginning or end and lasting forever, sacred to a savage, the sound of the rattle neither music nor rattlesnake but the spirits talking, 405 of these little stones gathered from the anthills); in front of the altar the holy rectangle, at the four corners, bags of deerhide filled with kinnikinnick, *tobacco*, next to the four bags the four colored flags—black, red, yellow and white for the four races of man, for the four great powers of place; but between the west and north staff, a fifth staff, the top half red for day, the bottom black for night, at the top an eagle feather for wisdom.

As more dry grass was lit and the fire blazed, I made out Gray Owl standing in the center of the room, at his feet, in a pile, the buffalo robe. How he'd gotten out of it, no one could tell. I'd seen Manuel and Sonofabitch bind Gray Owl, arms behind his back, each finger tied to the other with rawhide. The separate finger-tying wakinyan, *the thunderbirds*, the lightning. Gray Owl was then wrapped up like a mummy in the buffalo hide and tied with the long thong in the seven sacred knots.

(The tying, the tobacco and thongs ending the isolation between one human being and another, creating a line from man to the Great Spirit. The man is tied so the Great Spirit can use him. But it is most perilous. Tied, Gray Owl was now as one dead, his spirit perhaps hundreds of miles away, talking with the ancient ones—which is why everything must be done exactly, for if it is not done exactly, he may never find his way back and so die—the ancient ones telling the yuwipi many, many things. The yuwipi, through the ancient ones, able to see into the unknown past and sometimes the future. So he might find a missing brave who has been killed by a wild beast or an enemy and so bring great grief to a family. Or find a stolen robe and so humiliate the thief and his people. Or see a man kill another man. Or foretell the death of a relative or friend and so himself endure great sorrow. It is why so few choose to be yuwipis. The yuwipi brought back only through wace iciciya, *prayer within*, the reason for the desperate, desperate praying.)

Now, alive and returned, Gray Owl stood before us looking about. The rest of us sat back against the basement walls—Sonofabitch west for the black power, Manuel north for the red power, me east for the yellow power and Little Rabbit south in the place of dying, because the soul travels from north to south along the Milky Way to the Spirit Land.

And now came the time of talk and the asking:

"I heard many drums," said Sonofabitch, "yet we have but one drum. How is this?"

"It was the huge heart of the Great One beating," said Gray Owl. "It was He in the blood of your ears."

Manuel got to his feet. His face was white. He stood unspeaking, frightened, I thought, looking past Gray Owl.

"My friend?" said Gray Owl.

Manuel went on looking past—*through* Gray Owl.

"Yes?" said Gray Owl. "Speak."

Manuel's eyes were red as though burnt by the sun. "I—saw—my—father," said Manuel.

Gray Owl did not reply and Manuel sank back down in the dirt, covering his head with his blanket, his body shaking, making crying sounds.

I did not speak until the crying noises stopped. "I was hit by the rattles," I said to Gray Owl. "I felt things on my face. I was struck from behind by—" I couldn't say it because there wasn't a buff within a thousand miles, and even if there had been—I made the sign. "His horn grazed my ear. I was knocked down."

A corner of Gray Owl's mouth lifted. "That is because you are an unbeliever. You doubt the *yuwipi*. And so you were chastised. Be thankful. You could have been trampled to death. It has happened before."

(For a month after, I couldn't raise my arms where my back hurt.)

And now all, even Manuel, turned south to the dying place of Little Rabbit. You could see Little Rabbit was afraid to ask. Little Rabbit said: "What does it mean, Gray Owl, I shall eat of the sacred fruit?"

Gray Owl frowned. "I do not know," said Gray Owl.

"It is what you said," said Little Rabbit.

"I said nothing. I am but *their* voice."

"What, then, Gray Owl, do you think it means?"

"I cannot say," said Gray Owl, "only that the sacred fruit is to be found only in the great green hunting lands above."

Which meant, we all knew, Little Rabbit was to die.

Little Rabbit thought long and long before he said, "Then was I right to return to Grandmother," and he pointed at the hole he'd dug.

After a while, when there were no more questions, each of us said in his turn "mitakne oyasin"—*all my relatives*, which means each and every one of us, and we all stood, and, though later that night we would eat of the dog with the holy red spot, the *yuwipi* was over.

Just before dawn I heard Gray Owl in the rear of the basement making medicine to the books I'd been unable to read (but, then, Pap couldn't read neither, and Ma, except for those parts of the Bible she'd memorized, wasn't much better. Pap said it didn't matter, it was all in the ciphering anyway. Still, it's always been a fret to me, not reading, a dentist from Boston once starting to learn me when a yellowstone Sioux lifted his hair, and, once, in the Bitter Root Mountains we buried a fella, all his possibles wrapped in newspapers in one of which was read me of this fella in Philadelphia teaches lettering to folk never had the advantages of scholarly pursuits but who I never got to know till later), so the best I'd been able to do then for the Owl was negotiate a lien allowing him to take home enough boxes (books) to make medicine —Manuel also banging around in the back, getting dressed, from the sound of him, so I guessed Gray Owl had told Manuel how we were going to the senator's.

Honor answered the door in riding clothes . . . a black bowler and the tight English trotter coat and flared breeches, very trim, only something was wrong, something—

"Clay, Gray Owl . . ." She could tell straight off from our faces. "What is it?" she said.

I told her about Gray Owl and the reading.

"Of course," she said. "Come in out of the cold," she said, but you could see she could see that wasn't all.

I moved back for Gray Owl to enter the same time he moved back for me, so we stood looking at one another, waiting, then Honor moved back from the door, all three of us waiting.

"There's one more," I said, and Manuel stepped out from the side into the doorway.

"How—dew—yew—dew . . ." Manuel said in near perfect English and held out a silver bracelet to her.

Honor could only stare: Manuel was wearing the tuxedo I'd seen him looking at in the store window, the pants too long, the coat too short and narrow in the shoulders, no collar, the tie a gnarl, the shirt half open down the front, where he'd been too proud to let me help him with the studs, feet bare, wearing leggings.

Gently Manuel took Honor's hand and slipped the bracelet over her wrist.

Honor, trying not to stare, began to stammer: "Oh, Manuel, you—" She held the bracelet up for us to see. "It's beautiful."

So Manuel hadn't just been lying on the potato sacks, after all. He'd bought himself a tuxedo; he'd learned himself some English and carved Honor a bracelet.

Manuel was as pleasured with himself as a kid in hip boots, strutting a little, turning this way and that, smiling a lot, holding up her wrist with the bracelet so we could all see.

Honor's face looked as if it were coming apart across the nose, the top half working in disbelief, the bottom half with pity and remorse and sorrow and what all I couldn't say, the whole bending into a smile that said, "Come in, Man . . ." and, still holding her wrist, Man started through the door, then stepped back. He stood studying her.

"Man?" she said.

He went on looking at her.

"What's the matter?" she said.

Lightly he shook her wrist with the bracelet. "Yew dew not like?" he said with the perfect English words.

"The bracelet!" she said, "why it's beautiful, beautiful, it's one of the most beautiful gifts I've ever—" and with her opposite hand she started to reach up to touch the bracelet where he held her wrist, when he let her arm drop, and in that moment she realized, along with the rest of us, that all this while she hadn't been looking at the bracelet a-tall, but at him, at his mad getup, and she said softly, "I'm sorry," and hugged the bracelet to her breast turning it around and around on her wrist, the tears sliding out the corners of her eyes down the bowler chinstrap so it glistened black on either side of her face.

For a long moment Manuel studied all that was going on in her. The way, I think, he read it, the bracelet and the near-perfect English hadn't meant anything to her (savages as thin-skinned and crackly as dry onion that way), and the clothes—he looked down at himself—the same, I thought, as that day with Little Rabbit before the department-store mirror—at the too-long pants and short sleeves, the open shirt and bare feet, then he jerked off the tie and ran down the drive, but not really ran so much as loped, as though he knew he had a long way to go and shouldn't waste himself.

Honor didn't call or try to stop him. It wouldn't have done any good, she could see. (Nothing any more after that did any good with Manuel.) And I touched Gray Owl's arm to go when a voice, hearty and full of itself, called from behind Honor in the hallway, "Well, now, well, well . . ."

It was the senator.

"Come in outa the cold," the senator called, and Honor closed the door after us.

The senator was sipping at a hot, steaming cup of brandy. "Just in time," the senator said, so I thought, "not by half," and the senator smiled broadly. "Tomorrow," the senator said, "tomorrow, the President'll see you all tomorrow," and sipped at his brandy, as pleased with himself, I thought, as Manuel earlier; then he pointed with the cup of brandy, "What's that?" and Honor held out Manuel's bracelet to me to give to the senator and it was, for a fact, beautiful. Like the totem. In the center a turquoise big as a blood plum, carving the length and width and circle of it: an eagle, a tree, a buffalo head, clouds, all overlaid on signs of the Thunder People . . . the same as Manuel had been carving that night in the glade when I'd fronted him with the spur. The spur! I looked down. That's what had been wrong with her, I thought, when she'd opened the door. It made her look lopsided: On the heel of her right boot a Chihuahua, a great Mexican gut-gouger with sunset rowels; on the left . . . tiny, fine as a web, the rowels set in goosenecked silver shaft and holders, the same as Little Rabbit had found hooked in the moss under his back in the glade.

I handed the bracelet to the senator.

23

....

Sam the President

Dressed in white doeskin for peace and purity and carrying gifts for the Great White Grant Father, they stared up at the Capitol dome but refused to believe the Wasichus had built it—the Wasichus must have found it already made. So, since it wasn't possible for human hands to have made such a lodge, it could only have been the work of the Great Spirit, they said.

Expressionless, the commissioner of Indian Affairs glanced at me but said nothing. Probably, I thought, because the commissioner was himself an Indian, a Seneca, Donehogawa his tribal name. Not one of Sam's more welcome appointments. Every time there was a massacre—which was every time the Wasichus lost a battle—the papers were full of the Indian commissioner, whose fault you would have thought it had been.

A tall, nice-looking, well-dressed man but with the black Indian eye, the commissioner was once as wild a young buck as any, they said, which made it all the harder to believe that sometime, somewhere out there in the bush he'd been washed in the blood of the Lamb—he'd got both civilization and an education, becoming a lawyer, who they wouldn't let practice because he was an Indian. So he'd become a civil engineer. That's when he'd hooked up with Sam. In Galena, Illinois. He'd been with Sam at Fort Donelson, at Vicksburg and the battle of the wilderness; he'd been with Sam at Appomattox, had campaigned for Sam for President, and Sam had taken the Seneca—Samuel Ely Parker—with him to the Palace. Who a better commissioner of Indian Affairs, said Sam, than an Indian! Just as now, watching them, crook-necked before the Capitol dome, the commissioner had known why they couldn't accept the white man as creator of this marvel: The Wasichu could not, *must not* be that mighty.

The commissioner had picked us up earlier at the home of the senator, who couldn't go with us because, the senator said, he had business with a Cabinet member on the floor of the House.

Little Rabbit pushed into the commissioner's face, peering—the Rabbit sweating, pale as a winter moon, yet insisting on looking into the face of the Great White Grant Father and his subchiefs, all of whom I'd offered to bring to the Rabbit's lodge, a visit of great honor, great (which, of course, I couldn't do, but anything to put him off until he got better, because suddenly that little Arapaho, with his crazy staring into hearts and seeking after lost truths and forgotten virtues, meant more to me than I knew how to say). And I said, "You are much ill, Little Rabbit, much, much." And he'd said, "Thus, Face on Water, would you have the Wasichu see me!" And I'd said, "But thus are sometimes all men," and argued how one must first serve oneself to better serve Wakan Tanka. Which was exactly why he must go, said the Rabbit, shriveled, hacking now constantly into an old torn strip of potato sacking, tottering, so weak Gray Owl and I had to all but carry him, the others never taking their eyes off him, the Rabbit's medicine powerful, powerful to them now that he was dying, the commissioner, unflinching, staring back into the Rabbit's coughing face, the Rabbit finally nodding his approval, and they all piled into the commissioner's buggy, the commissioner driving them over to the Indian Bureau to show them portraits and pictures of some of the other delegations to Washington. A mistake. Sonofabitch spotted an old enemy, a renegade Cheyenne, Cut Hand, and while no one was paying him any mind, Sonofabitch peed on Cut Hand's photograph.

From the Indian Bureau the commissioner took us to the CORCORCAN MUSEUM OF ART, which bored them, then to the Palace.

At the Palace they kept us waiting downstairs in what the commissioner called the Grand Saloon—long enough for Gray Owl to admire the President's lodge and proclaim it to be well furnished with "everything good and pretty and strongly built." Then a man came in and whispered to the commissioner, Manuel right off suspecting an ambush despite the commissioner's protests that the man had merely whispered to him that the President would see us now. So we all, including the President, had to wait while Manuel went outside to scout around for an ambush.

He stood behind a great oaken desk, Sam, smoking a cheroot, talking to a man he later introduced as the Secretary of the Interior.

Sam looked more stooped, his beard without the red lights in it, blacker now and thicker, speckled with gray, the eyes bluer but with more flint in them than I remembered.

When he saw us, he came out from behind the desk, holding out his hand: "Clay."

"Hello, Sam—Mr. President," I said; Sam, unchanged, as easy as an old shoe, asking about Pap, about my brothers and sisters and old friends, telling the Secretary of the Interior about the old days on the Columbia, about how our potato crop had been washed away and the chickens all dying en route to San Francisco. Snakebit Sam. And we all laughed, Sam apologizing to Gray Owl and the rest for going on like this, but I was an old brother he hadn't seen in many moons and it so gladdened his heart to see me—the way Sam handled them, you could see he'd had practice —which little speech hereinafter made me a sachem of much power *if all went well*, Sam asking how long we'd been in Washington, so I wondered who the senator had been talking to all that time he'd been *working at* getting us in to see the President, and if this was why the senator had suddenly had business on the floor of the House.

When I introduced the Four, Little Rabbit, the same as with the commissioner, raked Sam's face like an eight-disc harrow, Sam trying hard not to blow cheroot smoke over the Rabbit or be coughed on, Little Rabbit finally placing his right hand palm down across his left breast, pushing upward and away for *his heart is good*. Then, very formal, Sam sat down behind his desk and with great solemnity began to speak:

Sam said that the Chosen Four's journey had been a long one, that he knew they had undertaken it as proof of their friendship and to be at peace, and he thanked the Great Spirit and welcomed them, after which we all sat waiting.

—and waiting and waiting for Gray Owl. A gesture of much respect, for though each was top cock in his own coop, each now, for the first time, was affirming Gray Owl as their headman, their spokesman, because, though there is no pecking order in Tribal Council—whoever wishes can at any time have his say—the privilege of speaking first is usually reserved for the chief.

It rawed me because Gray Owl knew well enough what could happen if Manuel or Sonofabitch spoke first: our meet with Sam over before we'd opened the gate. Then Little Rabbit stepped forward, tall and straight, the tottering gone, eyes narrowed. Something was galling him.

He stood uncertainly before Sam's desk, looked around at the others, then moved to one side so Sam had to swivel about to face him.

"I come from where the sun sets," said Little Rabbit. "You were raised on chairs. I want to sit as I sit where the sun sets," and walking to a far corner of the room, he sat down on the floor Indian fashion. "This is the way He raised me. He raised me naked," and the others followed, sitting, forming a half circle facing the President.

I couldn't reckon it. It wasn't like Little Rabbit to be rude. Sam now had to come out from behind his desk, the rest of us following. The commissioner and I sat on the floor with them, Sam and the Secretary of the Interior on chairs, when, suddenly, seeing Sam flopped back in the chair like that, I knew: standing before the President's desk, Little Rabbit had felt as he had back in court before the judge, a criminal before the bar. It was how, the Rabbit knew, the others would feel too, and to cancel it out, he'd smoked the President out from behind his desk.

Wily little rabbit.

From his medicine bag Little Rabbit took out the Pipe of Tranquillity.

Holding up the pipe, Little Rabbit told how with this sacred pipe man walks the earth; for the earth is Grandmother and Mother, and she is holy. Every step taken upon her is a prayer. The bowl of the pipe is redstone, the earth; carved in the stone and facing the center is the buffalo calf, who represents all the

four-leggeds; the stem, of wood, is everything that grows upon
Mother Earth; the feathers hanging from the stem are from
Wambi Galesha, *spotted eagle* and all the wingeds of the air:
"All the things of the universe are joined when we smoke—all
send their voices to Wakan Tanka, the Great Spirit."

Little Rabbit was impressing on all the seriousness of what was
about to take place. It was a pledge of the heart to justice and
truth. Little Rabbit lit the pipe and passed it around.

The smoking took a long while, each blowing smoke to the four
directions, up to Grandfather Sky, down to Mother Earth and
Wakan Tanka, Sam and the Secretary going along with the full
ritual so I thought how Sam was snubbing in his lines. This could
just be the most powerful, the most important delegation ever to
have come in. Here was the Blade's only son, each of these men a
representative of a great nation. Handled wrongly, as Andy Jack-
son had done, they could cost the country millions, set the plains
back a hundred years, belay progress there for another hundred.

And when the smoking was done?

I looked at Gray Owl. As yet, nothing. Nothing had been done.
Nothing had been said. What was holding him? Already Manuel
was casting about with that same look as when he'd challenged
his daddy. He could blow us out of the barn before we'd closed
the door. Gray Owl knew that! But, Lordy, you can't rush a savage. And there was Sonofabitch feeling his eyepatch to see was it
in place, which meant he, too, was preparing to get up and ruffle
his feathers.

I'd almost rather Manuel than Sonofabitch, I thought, when
Sonofabitch was on his feet. "Brothers," Sonofabitch began, "I
would tell you a story told me by my great-grandfather in the long
way past."

I could only hope Sonofabitch took after his grandmother.

Sonofabitch threw out his chest like a great chief. "When the
Wasichu first came over the waters, wide, wide, he was but a little
man . . . very little. His legs were cramped from much sitting in
his big boat from over the long, long water. He begged for a little
land to light his fire on. But when the white man had warmed
himself before the Indian's fire and filled himself with their hom-
iny, the white man became very large.

"With a step the white man crossed over mountains. His feet

covered the plains and the valleys. His hand grasped the eastern and western sea. His head rested on the moon. Then he became Great Father. He loved his children, and he said, 'Get a little farther off lest I tread on thee. . . .

" 'Brothers,' said my great-grandfather, 'I have listened to many talks from many Great Fathers. But they always end thus: Get a little farther off; you are too near me.' "

A good speech. I let the air out. When Sonofabitch sat down, all grunted their approval except Manuel, stung, I thought, because Little Rabbit and Sonofabitch had gone before him. Gray Owl, motionless, silent, when Manuel leaned forward to get to his feet, and Gray Owl rose.

Gray Owl stood as still as stalking, looking full into Sam's eyes. "Father, the Great Spirit made us all. He made my skin red and yours white. He placed us both on Mother Earth. *But* he meant we live different ways:

"You work the earth and feed on spotted buffalo; we rove the woods and plains and feed on wild animals and dress in their skins.

"You love your land; you love your people; you love the way you live; you think your people brave. The same do we think ours. So let us enjoy Mother Earth together differently.

"We will trade skins with your people. We have plenty of buffalo, beaver, deer and wild animals; we have plenty of land if your people will stay away. But you send the steel snake among us. This we do not like. It drives away the great herds, frightens the antelope and deer, brings more Wasichus into our midst. Now also do you build forts. If you want peace, why do you build forts? If you want our friendship hand, why do you steal our homes?"

Sam never flicked an eye.

"There was a time, my Father, when we did not know the whites—our wants then were few. We had seen nothing we could not have. Before the Wasichu, we could lie down to sleep and, when we woke, we would find the buffalo feeding around our camp—it was all we wished—but now hunters kill all for their hides, and wolves feed on their flesh while our people cry over the bones."

Too full to go on, Gray Owl stopped. Sonofabitch grunted and the Rabbit lifted the pipe up toward Tunkashila, *Grandfather*

Sky, when out of the silence like a malediction, foul, profaning, damning, drawn out and rasping, the single word: "Wah-si-chu!" *fat takers.*

Sam's expression never changed.

Gray Owl went on. "Stop the hunters, my Father, stop the forts, stop the steel snake. Leave us our land. We are happy. We can no longer remain so if you permit the intrusions." Gray Owl looked from Sam to Sonofabitch and back. "We can no longer get farther off."

A humble speech but with much grace . . . direct, cautious, wise. It left much to think on, and for a while all was quiet. Then Manuel stood and it was right. Little Rabbit had staked the fire site; Sonofabitch had dug the pit; Gray Owl had fueled it, and now Manuel would ignite it.

Manuel stood, not as tall as Sonofabitch, but high, high. Solemn. Like the Blade. His voice low and respectful. "We do not beg," said Manuel. "We do not cry." He lay the flat of his hand against his chest. "We are men! We keep what we have. If you pull from us what is ours, shall we not pull back?" His eyes were in Sam like skewers. "And maybe we shall pull away what also is yours." His voice softened. "We would to you what you would to us. Is not that the way of men?

"We would be friends, but as you would not be friends—" he took a step toward Sam—"so would we be what *you* make us," said Manuel flat out, his eyes glinting black, and he turned and went back to the others, very Indian.

But Sam was the President, the Great White Father, the giver and taker and holder of souls, and he rose solid as a man in church, the flint turned frosty in his blue eyes. And whether he was aware of what Little Rabbit had done to him or not, Sam went back around behind his desk so the room, with us at one end and him at the other, broke in half.

Sam stood behind his desk, regal, kingly, the President Chief: "My friends and children, I welcome your words as now I hope you will receive mine. I wish us to be brothers of the same family to live in peace. How much better it is for neighbors to help than to hurt one another! If you will live in friendship, you can employ all your time in providing food and clothing for yourselves and your families. Your men will not be destroyed and your women and children will lie down to sleep in their lodges without fear of being surprised by enemies and killed and carried away. Your numbers will increase instead of diminishing and you will live in plenty and quiet.

"Your lands are good. Upon these you may raise horses and large flocks of cattle by which you may procure the conveniences and necessaries of life in great abundance, and with less trouble than you have at present. You may, by a little more industry, raise more corn and other grain, as much for your families as for the support of your stock in winter.

"My children, all who have followed this advice are increasing in numbers, are learning to clothe and provide for their families as we do."

Sam paused, looked closely at each in turn:

"You have seen that all men here receive you as brothers. I wish you, my children, to see all you can and to tell your people all you see, because I am sure the more you know us, the more you will be our hearty friends."

I remembered what the senator had said about frightening them.

"I have now opened my heart to you. Let my words sink into your heart and never be forgotten. If ever lying people or bad spirits should raise a cloud between us, call to mind what I have said and what you have seen, and the clouds will fly away like the morning fog, and the sun of friendship appear and shine forever bright and clear between us."

A good speech, good. Had style. Sam had given it many times before, you could tell. *Except* that it was as though Sam hadn't heard anything Gray Owl or the others had said. It made sense, yes, Sam's sense, logical, reasonable. Included much of what plagued them, sound, sound advice—*if* you lived in a house with tables and chairs, cooked at a stove and drew water from a cistern, with a barn with chickens and pigs and an ox and a plow to work the land. But what of a nomad who'd never sat on a chair at a table?

The Four sat unmoving, thinking, I thought, what I thought— *and what of the buffalo hunters, what of the forts and the steel snake and the sodbusters?*

Then Sam came out from behind his desk carrying what at first looked like bandoliers of ammunition. The Four came to their feet. Sam was carrying medals, each about the size and shape as the back of your hand.

Solemnly Sam explained the medals: on the front was a likeness of Sam and an Indian facing one another, above them the legend IN GOD WE TRUST and, below, WAKAN TANKA LOVES ALL; on the back an engraving of a buffalo.

With great seriousness Sam hung the medals about each neck and shook each hand. And the medals made everything right. All except Manuel commenced to smile and chatter.

To them, the medals with God and Wakan Tanka were, I think, a sort of pledge of trust and good faith telling them all they'd asked for would be granted, and immediately they came forward with their own gifts, stacking them in a heap on Sam's desk, Manuel hanging back so it embarrassed them, Gray Owl finally piling Manuel's gifts with the others, the Rabbit last with the pipe:

"Here, my Father, is our sacred pipe filled with such tobacco as once we smoked before we knew the white people. It is the wild growth of the farthest parts of our land. It is not as pleasant a tobacco as yours, but it is ours, it is us.

"We know also that the robes and the leggings, the moccasins and bear claws, the peltries and rattlesnake skins are of little value to you, and so we wish you to place them in some prominent corner of your lodge so that when we are gone and the sod turned over our bones, if our children should come to this place, as now we do, they will see and know the things of their fathers and think on times past."

I looked at the commissioner, who looked out the window. It was the Moon of the Red Grass Appearing. Already the hills were starting to green, the cherries to turn scarlet.

The Secretary of the Interior walked them to the door. They'd met Sam the President. It was over.

Outside, in the hall, I heard a clink, turned and looked back, then down at the big, brass-bellied spittoon into which, just before you entered, you were supposed to deposit your chewing tobacco or betel juice or whatever it was they were afraid you'd spray on the President, then back up at them: The only one of the Four without his medal was Manuel.

BOOK FOUR

Manuel Choke Breath

24

Bathed in the Blood
of the Lamb

Of the Four, only Sonofabitch got bathed in the blood of the Lamb.
It began with the eye.
Then the girl.
And finally the witnessing for the Great White One.

After seeing the President, it had started out pretty much as the senator had said it would back on the train out of Osawatomie. First the commissioner took us out to the navy yard, then to the army base (which Manuel didn't want to leave), then to Congress and from there to a hospital, where, as they told it later, a woman in a stiff white dress put chilly water on their arms, after which a man in a white coat scratched the chilling place with a porcupine quill that made their arms red and festery so, the next day, they had to wear a little package over the hurting spot. But it would keep away the pox, from which the white man and all men died, the doctor shaking his head at Little Rabbit's coughing, giving the Rabbit something which, the doctor said, would relieve for a time the awful hacking. And two days later the commissioner put us on a train for Philadelphia and New York.
In Philadelphia the commissioner took us to the Moyamensing

Penitentiary to see how people were treated who broke the law. A lot different than the drunk tank. Gray Owl so upset he pushed his head against the bars, peering, like the Rabbit, at the bearded men within.

"What is the matter, Gray Owl?" said the commissioner.

"Is there one man here without spots?" said Gray Owl.

The commissioner turned to me.

"He means innocent," I said.

"Why, Gray Owl?" said the commissioner.

"I was a prisoner," said Gray Owl, "and kept a whole year once in a place like this in Santa Fe. I was without spots. I was lonely and sad, and I would not have another so unhappy. Let me speak to him."

From Philadelphia we went to New York, a sight indeed, but it wasn't the fine hotels nor the food nor the great crowds nor even greater buildings that impressed them as much as Mr. Barnum's AMERICAN MUSEUM, to which they went every day to stand mumble-tongued before the educated dogs, the trained fleas, jugglers, ventriloquist, the living statuary, tableaux, gypsies, albinos, fat women, giants, dwarfs, freaks, ropedancers, dioramas, panoramas, models of Niagara, mechanical figures, fancy glass blowing, knitting machines—like nothing I'd ever seen—two thousand and one oddments for a quarter.

But the best time they had was in the DEAF-MUTES ASYLUM, where in no time they'd worked up a sign language with the inmates that had them winging away at one another like a flock of happy jays, making signs of the cat, the dog, the horse, the bear and every animal, wild or tame, you could name. Again and again after, they spoke of the deaf-mutes as "boys who talked with their arms."

But it all paled before a glass case in a room in a large New York building, where we saw the marble things. I couldn't make them out. The commissioner told Sonofabitch to look closer. And then I saw—marvel of marvels!—they were eyes—blue eyes, brown eyes, gray eyes, cat eyes.

The commissioner asked Sonofabitch to see if he could find one to match his own good black eye. But there were no black eyes, and a man came and looked at Sonofabitch's eye and said he could make one just like it, but Sonofabitch said, no, he didn't want the black Indian eye, and he pointed, he wanted the blue eye, the commissioner hauling off to look at Sonofabitch as if Sonofabitch were a half-head or one of the poor *no-thoughts*. The room stopped.

"The blue?" repeated the man, dumbly, who made the eyes.

"The Wasichu!" Manuel was aghast.

"No, Sonofabitch," said the commissioner, "you do not know what you do."

Little Rabbit started to laugh but caught the rudeness in his throat.

"For what reason?" said Gray Owl.

"You will look strange," said the commissioner. "At least take the brown. It is closer in color. I have seen the off-color eyes. I saw a dead Cheyenne once with off-color eyes. They are not so bad. But not like you wish."

Again Sonofabitch pointed. "I wish the full-blooded blue."

The commissioner swore. "With a black eye on one side of your head and a blue on the other side of your head, people will laugh."

Little Rabbit could hold back no longer, the rudeness starting to bubble through his teeth. "Sonofabitch will be two people," Little Rabbit said and stopped, not because, like before, of the rudeness, but because in that moment Little Rabbit saw the thought and gave it to us, and we all turned to Sonofabitch, whose single black Indian eye glinted with the knowing, his mouth upcurving with the secret.

Sonofabitch pointed at the eye man's blue eyes. "To see from the eye of the enemy," Sonofabitch said, "is that not a great thing!"

There was the cut moment of wonder, then the catch of recognition and, from deep within their chests, like falling leaves, came the soft "Aaah" of understanding and all, except the commissioner, began to smile at Sonofabitch.

"No," said the commissioner, "you cannot do this. The eye is glass. It is without sight. Without power. Without medicine. You cannot make of yourself a fool. You cannot—"

Sonofabitch bristled and came up tall over the commissioner, tall and tall, looking down.

The commissioner had made a mistake, all right; you don't call a savage a "fool" or tell him "you cannot!" and the commissioner knew it, his voice softening, "Listen to me, Sonofabitch, listen. I say all for you. If you do this thing, you can never return to your people, you can never—"

Sonofabitch slapped the front of his own mouth with all five fingers in the sign for *enough*, for *silence!* But the commissioner wouldn't have it, opening his mouth again, his mouth freezing open, so you could see his lower teeth and the wrinkled underside of his pink tongue curving up to the roof making the word, his eyes darting from one to the other of them in a tight half circle about him, threatening, and sadly, wearily, the commissioner shook his head and was still.

Later, the commissioner and I went with Sonofabitch into a little room where the eye man fitted the new blue eye in beneath Sonofabitch's drooping lid.

A marvel!

When the man held up a mirror for Sonofabitch to see himself, Sonofabitch looked and looked and grinned and grinned and said he couldn't believe his eyes.

The different-colored eyes split Sonofabitch's face in two so, like the Rabbit said, whichever side was turned to you, the black or the blue, Sonofabitch was another person.

"Take it out now and then," the doctor said, "and wash it."

"No, no," said Sonofabitch. "Whoever heard of a man taking out his eye!"

When Sonofabitch walked out of that small room, he looked with two eyes at the Rabbit and at Manuel and Gray Owl, who said with disbelief, "Sonofabitch is again a boy," and they stared and stared. It was the greatest wonder they were ever to know in the white man's land. And the more they wondered, the more it frightened them, the finer Sonofabitch felt with his new blue eye in his old brown head.

If only, Sonofabitch said, he could go back now and grasp the Great White Grant Father's hand and look with his two good eyes into the President's two eyes. None of them ever to really get over it. The white man's medicine surely beyond knowing (the high-water mark of the trip), returning to the Capitol only when the Rabbit's cough began to worsen (if possible), Sonofabitch never thereafter able to walk by a window without studying his reflection in the glass. Sonofabitch, with his new eye, a full foot taller. Not that Sonofabitch had changed. Back in the Capitol he went right on drinking, but now when he got up in the mornings, hung over, the black eye would be half-closed, bloodshot, the blue looking straight on, clear and fresh as a dewdrop. Then, at nights, they'd see Sonofabitch asleep—his new eye awake, wide, wide awake and staring all night as though the Wasichu part of Sonofabitch never slept, was forever spying on them . . . the beginning of their distrust. Great, great medicine. And because the eye always felt the same in his head, it never suggested itself to Sonofabitch that it might need straightening. So one day he'd be walleyed as a bull toad; the next, both eyes looking at one another, Lord, like strangers, crossed, Lordy, as barrel staves; the next, gazing all day up at the sky, that eye swiveling in Sonofabitch's head like a loose ball bearing so, one morning, he awoke with his eye all the way around backwards in his head so they all said Sonofabitch was now able to "see inside himself," so instead of their learning the Wasichu secrets, they said, the Wasichu was now looking into theirs, all now beginning to fathom the commissioner's contrariety. For if the eye could see up, it could see down; if to the west, to the east; if the good, also the evil, so now Sonofabitch frightened them. "Ice Eye," they said of him when he was away, and "Half Face," and they could never trust him again. Not that they cut him off from them—Sonofabitch frightened them too much for that—nor was he treated any different; rather, they withdrew . . . deep into that murky Indian place to which admittance comes only with acceptance, with brotherhood and the blood and the power. They shut out Sonofabitch's soul.

Sonofabitch couldn't *not* feel it. Though he wouldn't admit it. He fought it, denied it, refused it, saying the eye was beyond them. All the same, an outsider, he became testy, drank more and, alone, took up with the girl.

How she happened was one night a month after they'd returned, the two got drunk, Sonofabitch and Manuel—after the President, after Honor and the tuxedo, Manuel had gone a little loco, taking up with Sonofabitch to become almost as much of a swill-belly, fighting and carousing and staying out days at a time (until it seemed there for a time that all I was good for was following them around, bailing them out of whatever they'd got into), until this night ride on the old broken-back we'd bought from the department store. . . .

Drunk, mounted double on her, they'd come tearing down the center of the street, whooping and hollering, Sonofabitch waving a whiskey bottle behind Manuel, shooting out street lamps with his bow and arrow. Cutting into a park, where the old mare slipped on a cobblestone walk, pitching them both up against a tree, where, if they hadn't been soaked as toads, the fall would have killed them.

They woke up next morning under a Salvation Army band marching over the top of them, Sonofabitch on his back looking up into the face of a Nigra, young, in her mid-twenties, in a Salvation Army bonnet, asking if he was hurt. The first Nigra Sonofabitch had ever seen and the prettiest he was likely to see, the new blue eye giving him confidence with her, besides which he thought she was a Cheyenne and got hisself converted, you might say, on the spot, and the Army was stuck with them, Sonofabitch around all the time courting his Cheyenne; Manuel, thinking they were a real army, snooping for guns and ammo—in the beginning more like pets than people until the Army began to use them more or less as swampers, lifting and hauling, and finally as showpieces.

They loved the Salvation Army. Every night a feast (with all that free food), drumming and singing, the red-jackets, as Manuel called them, letting them march out in front of the band with tambourines, the idea being to draw a crowd. Which they did. The two of them more often than not drunk, yipping and screeching and dancing, Sonofabitch especially. I heard him once two blocks away:

"All bad Wasichu, come." (Which in Sonofabitch's scheme meant everybody.) "Hear happy tongue, all sinner, all bastard, all no-good, come. Great Spirit save soul. All prick, all Wasichu mother licker, sister screwer, come. God want all sinner, all dirty horse fucker."

If Sonofabitch hadn't the words, he'd sure got the flavor—his first and last gathering sermon—so by the time I got there, the crowd was blocking traffic all the way up and down Constitution Avenue.

In actual fact, the red-jackets probably saved them, saved Manuel anyway, because Sonofabitch now had his Cheyenne. They still drank and fought and raised hell, but nothing like before. Then Sonofabitch's infection became serious, carrying over from his girl to her religion. (It was, Gray Owl and the others said, the Wasichu in Sonofabitch—the new, blue eye.) But if Sonofabitch was susceptible, not so Manuel, who trusted neither Sonofabitch's Nigra-Cheyenne nor her God: first, because they called themselves Army, which Manuel knew all about from the plains wars; and second, the red-jackets were all the same, Manuel said, as the black-coats (missionaries).

The highlight of Sonofabitch's conversion—they called him Steve now—was when Sonofabitch witnessed for Christ, getting up in the pulpit, his Nigra-Cheyenne holding his hand, Sonofabitch looking proudly out at the congregation with his two good eyes, face halved down the middle like a torn photograph—his Cheyenne kept the new blue straight now in his head—Sonofabitch pounding on the podium, howling and crying like he'd seen the others do, pouring out his sins: drinking and blaspheming, lying and stealing, cheating and adultery (which he'd heard the others confess but which I'm sure he hadn't any idea of the meaning of). And not a word about the dozen or more (not counting Indians) he'd murdered, scalped and more often than not first tortured. But, of course, those weren't sins.

A real whangdoodle, Sonofabitch's salvation. They'd got him up in feathers and skins, and standing up there in the pulpit, he looked savage and terrible, the saving of Steve's soul such a triumph they went after Manuel's.

But if Sonofabitch's salvation was a ringtailed roarer, Manuel's was a carnival, the church gorged to the lintels, reporters from all the papers, the choir and band hammering away at heaven, Sonofabitch in all his feathers and skins introducing his brother, Manuel Choke Breath, dressed simply in browband and shirt. Still, if they hadn't got Manuel up like Sonofabitch, they'd made the most of it, decorating the altar with chicken feathers and cowhide, beating solemnly on a drum as he came down the aisle. Everyone standing to see him, hallelujahing and amening and blessing Manuel all over the hall. Then they sang "Onward Christian Soldiers" and Manuel stepped up into the pulpit, everybody steeling themselves for Sonofabitch's hell and howling, but that wasn't the way it was in Tribal Council, Man's voice soft and respectful, now and again breaking into Kiowa:

Manuel said the red-jackets and black-coats knew the Indian couldn't read their holy box (Bible). "They tell us different tales about what is in the box," he said, "but we believe they make the box talk to suit themselves," and Manuel forked his fingers across his tongue and said that if the red man had no forests, no rivers, no land, the Wasichus would not trouble themselves about the red man's good, that the red-jackets and black-coats asked the Great Spirit for the light that the red man might see when they themselves were blind and unsure of the light.

"They want our country," Manuel said, "and in return teach us to quarrel about their religion. The Great Spirit will not punish us for what we do not know."

He then told how the black-coats ordered them to raise corn, yet did nothing themselves and would have starved if the red man had not fed them: "All they do is pray to the Great Spirit, but that will not make corn and potatoes grow. In our land they beg from us."

Manuel shook his head and made the sign for *wonder* and *not understand*.

"If your God is true, why are you false? If your God is kind, why are you cruel? If your God is honest, why do you steal? If your God is good, why are you—" he brought his right fist away from his chest twice, fingers flying open in the casting away sign for *evil, evil*.

Manuel was a great disappointment.

After the Army, Manuel spent his days in the library with Gray Owl. Which isn't to say that Manuel, being now with Gray Owl, had reformed, the Owl almost as much of a highbinder in his way —drinking, blaspheming, visiting the ladies down in "Hooker's Division"—as any, a conduct that confuses whites mistaking medicine men for priests. (But how else understand man, says the medicine man, except to experience man, to sink as low as the crawling things or soar as high as mahpiya, *the clouds?* For a wicasa wacan, *holy man*, believes medicine is sinning and sickness and despair and drunkenness and poverty and jails and joy and the magic and more kinds of love than you can shake a stick at. The spirit good and bad, and man learns from both. A Wasichu priest, to an Indian, a chi-pa-sa, a soul who, like a man in a well, sees but one way when everybody knows nature is many things, even the fool.)

Even after the half dozen tutors rounded up by Honor and the senator, Gray Owl still couldn't read a lick.

The knot in the tether was that, to Gray Owl, reading was the same as counting coup on an enemy. After you touched him, you took on all his strength and knowledge. Gray Owl each day taking great piles of books out of the stacks over to his library table, not to read, but turning the pages, running his fingers down over the print, all the while keeping himself pure for the God of the Writing to come out and enter him, when he'd know all. But, of course, Manuel hadn't the sticking for that.

From Sonofabitch and Gray Owl, Manuel went to Little Rabbit, who, as they'd known even before our visit with Sam, was dying, the trip doing for Little Rabbit for sure—but who could have stopped him!—the red roses of death flaming in Little Rabbit's cheeks, straw thin and wasted, coughing up blood and chunks of his lungs, laying all day every day in his grave, Gray Owl shaking rattles over him or all day out gathering herbs—partridgeberry and smooth sumac for his cough, jimson weed for poultices for his congestion, sometimes archangel root (better for pleurisy) when he couldn't get anything else, red cedar truly the best for bad lungs. But none of it did no good. Not that it don't work. Nothing better in the world than cranesbill for dysentery or fishweed for worms, and once, in the Bottoms, down with stomach cramps, I was certain of seeing my maker till a young squaw fed me the scrapings from some jack-in-the-pulpit, so by dawn she and I were doing our own making. Some of those old pejuta wicasas, *herbalists*, able to cure just about anything the human form can think up to plague it. (Army doctors, after a battle along the Big Red, still shaking their heads over how tribal shamans had kept alive and even cured the wounded.) But, right now, nothing was helping the Rabbit, and one day while Gray Owl was out gathering herbs, I brought in a white doctor, who said the Rabbit should have been dead months ago and whose help the Rabbit refused as a betrayal of Gray Owl. He'd also tasted, the Rabbit said, evil spirits in the medicine I bought him, spitting it out, only allowing me to line his grave, always damp, with fresh straw daily, the basement itself gone to hell in a basket without the Rabbit to keep it up, roaches and lice into everything, the pig and chickens and now a goat fouling everything else so the smell—Lordy!—rats, without the Rabbit after them, sitting in the corners like pet cats, some grown near as large as beaver, making runs at the chickens and goat, one night going for the cow, bites all over her legs and underbelly the next morning—the pig they seemed afraid of—eyes glittering in the dark as though now it was their turn, so somebody always had to be with the Rabbit, out of his head a lot now, making speeches, praying and talking to his mama and daddy, but mostly to his bride, Sweet Sage, Manuel sitting up continuously over him now on a deathwatch.

For a whole week Manuel sat up without food or sleep, rocking and nodding and falling over, until I began to think if the Rabbit didn't go soon, Manuel would, the rats, like the black mounds outside the barricade, in closer and closer each night, until one day I slaughtered a sheep, laced it with strychnine and threw it down an old coal shaft out back, so for two days and nights all you heard was them down there at the carcass. The sound like walking on gravel. Which cleared them out for a time, the only trouble now being that a lot of them had crawled back in between the walls to die, the stench for a couple weeks thick as cooking.

Then Little Rabbit had a vision. Not a dream. A vision! Gospel to a savage:

A great red eagle—red as the sun, Little Rabbit whispered, eyes closed, claws to clutch up mountains—like a thunderbolt the eagle dove down into a field of white mice, but instead of scattering, the white mice turned on and devoured the great red eagle.

Angrily Man lurched to his feet, fingers forked across his mouth:

"Tah-nick sah-ban!" Man said, *the vision is a lie.*

Little Rabbit, eyes closed, shook his head. "No, sit, Manuel Choke Breath. I have tasted the Wasichu medicine—in their tipis, along their stone trails, in their engines. They are as many as forever. As strong as the Shaker of Forests. We shall be devoured by the mice men."

"Your vision comes from your sickness, Little Rabbit—the One of Evil."

"*They* are the Evil One, Manuel Choke Breath. You must do as I have done, see into their faces. See the greed and lust and you will know. We cannot defeat them. Ever. You must tell the Four Nations. Pledge me this, Manuel Choke Breath. You will go back into the streets and see. Then you will return to tell the Four Nations."

Manuel didn't answer, and, eyes still closed, Little Rabbit struggled, sweating, up on his elbows. "Pledge, Manuel Choke Breath."

"You hurt yourself, Little Rabbit."

"Pledge!"

"I pledge."

Little Rabbit sighed, gasped and fell back, and Manuel went back out in the streets. But not to look at faces.

25

Never Trust a Red Nigger

Manuel first saw the soldier reflected alongside him in the gun-shop window, a trooper, the same as he'd fought on the plains, in blue, in a siege hat, a saber clanking along one leg. A broken shadow. But enough. Manuel followed the trooper all the way out to the Third Army Fort, a wooden stockade just outside town on a flat overlooking the Potomac. It was where the commissioner had taken us earlier, Manuel all the way back to town from the fort memorizing landmarks so as to find his way back, which is what most exasperates the savage about civilization, not being able to place himself by a rock, a butte, a clump of trees. It's what had worried Gray Owl on the train coming out, Gray Owl day after day studying mountains, canyons, hills, horizons, so he'd be able to find his way home. Only, it all went by so fast, Gray Owl said. Until he couldn't keep any more in his head and cut his stick, mumbling say-ha, say-ha, *too much, too much*, the same as in the commissioner's carriage, after a half hundred turnings down as many streets, Manuel had hung fire and given up.

For four days and nights Manuel tried to crack the fort. First, simply by walking in, the way the trooper had, and, failing that, circling all night for weaknesses, clocking the guards, feeling for loose seams to squeeze through or dry rot to go under, but the stocks were overlapped, the ground rock hard.

The second night, he tried to go over the top, when, halfway up the wall, the guard, not believing his eyes, spotted him and panicked, hollering they were being attacked by Indians. Firing. Burning the back of Man's neck. The fear of Indians such—especially after the Heilman massacre—that in thirty seconds the catwalks were alive with half-dressed troopers blaspheming down into the dark. The guard who'd shouted the warning later court-martialed for drunkenness.

The third night—the last two days having rained and still raining—Manuel tried to tunnel under the stocks, but though it was coming on the month of the Moon of the Falling Leaves, it was frozen six feet down.

Then, the evening of the fourth day, a wet, bedraggled detachment of cavalry, trailed by a dozen Pawnee scouts afoot, approached the main gate.

Manuel waited until they were opposite him—the guards huddled inside the blockhouse out of the rain—when he slipped in among the Pawnees.

(How can you figure a savage? For the better part of a half century they'd been death's-head enemies, the Pawnees and Kiowa, but for them to have let on about Manuel to the guards would have been a betrayal and to lose face.)

Six weeks Manuel holed up in that fort, and when he came out, he had the secret of their medicine. Or so he thought. I'm not sure he hadn't.

The next morning—except for a single hunk of jerky in his shirt, Manuel hadn't eaten in three days—he tracked his nose smack into the cookhouse to stand dumb before more food than he'd ever seen in one place at one time in his life. That breakfast enough to feed a tribe, man, squaw and pup, for a month. Mountains of food, a "big eat" marching into the chowhall in massed formations: planks of beef and pork, trenchers of eggs; stacks and platters of bread, muffins, flapjacks, biscuits; basins of potatoes; pots of porridge; tubs of butter; casks of milk; caldrons of coffee, while around him seethed an army of cooks, swampers, dishwashers, countless helpers. A fiesta.

In the confusion, Manuel, forgetting his hunger, backed against the wall, and for two hours, until breakfast was over, he stood pressed against it in wonder.

Next to him, a young recruit who'd seen him come in washed dishes.

"You hungry?" the young dishwasher asked.

Stanley Meeker was the dishwasher's name, I found out later, a boy, too soft for soldiering—even Manuel saw that—an orphan who, like a lot of others during those hard times, joined up for bunk and board.

Manuel nodded, yes, to Stanley, he was hungry.

"Out back is where the scouts eat. Come on, I'll show you," Stanley said when one of the cooks threw Manuel a half-cooked chunk of meat, Manuel a quarter through it before the young dishwasher could stop him. The meat rotten, Manuel starting to retch, everyone laughing.

Stanley said he was sure Manuel was going for the cook. (His not going for the cook some indication of just how much it meant to Manuel.) But not so the next day, when Manuel, fascinated by the first bar of soap he'd ever seen, was called over by one of the soldiers to smell the bubbles, bending down, getting his face shoved into the dirty water. Everyone too busy laughing to see Stanley holding Manuel off the soldier, and they became friends. Manuel as close anyway to Stanley as, I guess, he'd ever be to any Wasichu, learning Stanley, who was slow in man things, how to swing an ax, use a knife, care for his mount, handle a gun, set, shoot and even make bullets.

In exchange Stanley laid out the base for Manuel, who went over her port to privy. *Tame* Indians, as they were called then, treated like children and pretty much given the run of the place. Manuel into the barns, the commissary, lofts, work sheds, map rooms, the smithy, stalls, stockrooms, supply rooms, and above all —the one place they *did* keep an eye on him—the armory.

To anyone else, to Little Rabbit, all that Manuel had seen would have been evidence of the Wasichu's unassailable power; to Gray Owl, a sign of his impregnable medicine; even Sonofabitch would have had long thoughts. But Manuel wasn't interested in conclusions, only methods. In learning, not interpretation. So in the kitchens he'd help clean up; in the barns, stack hay; in the storerooms, pile boxes; in the smithy, work the bellows. They even let him march close-order drill so afterward he'd stack rifles. Most popular redskin on the base.

Manuel even became something of a celebrity when, one day, the sergeant, an old drillmaster learning a gang of recruits to ride without saddles, called on the lazy Indian—all Indians were lazy, Manuel only less so—to demonstrate bareback riding.

Sleepily Manuel looked over the horses, picked out a hunch-shouldered palomino, gently scratched its nose, blew softly into its ear, whispered something to it, and grabbing its mane, swung up onto its bare back. To sit.

It wasn't quite what the drill sergeant had a mind to, and he yelled at Manuel, continuing to sit, gently stroking the horse's neck, when, without a sign or sound from Man, the horse stepped out in a slow walk around the parade ground, Man stiff up over the horse. Then into a canter, easy and pretty, once more around the parade ground, then into a full lope. Man still stiff up over her the way the troopers learned to ride, reining up easily before the sergeant, a picture ride, but not what the sergeant wanted, and he yelled for Man to get down and he'd show them how, when, before their eyes, Stanley said, the strangest thing—Stanley couldn't say how or what except something in Man seemed to loosen and pour—Stanley's word, *pour* into the horse, so suddenly Man and the horse were one.

Again, the walk and canter, but fluid, Man's knees bent, thighs caressing the palomino's sides Indian style, so the horse seemed to lift over the ground. Exploding into a wild, careening gallop, Man cutting the horse from side to side like a buchara in the bush. Cutting and swerving, dodging and ducking, driving straight at the sergeant and the company of recruits, who started to break ranks. Scudding back off them across the field, when Man gave a WHOOP and the palomino erupted, sprinting the length of the parade ground, Man all over her. Under her neck, on her rump, bouncing from side to side, riding her flanks, crouching, flat along her spine, standing on her back. Dropping to one side so when he went by they couldn't see him, swinging back up on her, a devil, Stanley said, pounding across the parade ground, rearing back, jerking the palomino up before them in a wild, rump-dragging skid, vaulting over the horse's head to land lightly next to the sergeant, who, Stanley said, knew, along with everybody else, he'd been took by Man, who, looking in the beginning more like a trooper than a trooper, had given an exhibition of horsemanship (which was exactly what it was, Stanley said, an *exhibition*) that none of them would ever forget or equal, so that, knowing that that's what they'd be up against out there in the field, there wasn't a one of them, Stanley said, who wouldn't't've turned in his enlistment, if he could, right then and there. "It was," Stanley said, "—magnificent."

It wasn't until the sixth week that Manuel found what he was looking for, when, Stanley said, the whole base was called out one afternoon, this fella with long lemon hair and matching ruddle-handled revolvers standing up before them on the parade platform—by my guess, the general himself, Custer (Stanley didn't know his name)—the commander of the base and all the officers massed behind the lemon-haired fella, on a table in front of him a long object covered over with a purple velvet cloth.

"Gentlemen," lemon hair said, "I have mustered you out here today for a very special reason." He sounded, Stanley said, like a prophet or preacher. (Custer, I thought, for a fact.) "I have brought you here," lemon hair said, "to show you what, I believe, will revolutionize warfare," and lemon hair commenced to draw aside the purple cloth, a rifle underneath, not the single-shot long gun, but a neater, trimmer, shorter, square-barreled weapon without the big firelock.

Carefully, as though it might shatter, lemon hair lifted the gun from the table, holding it before him:

"Gentlemen, this is a repeating—I reiterate, a *repeating* rifle. Not a single-shot, not a muzzle-loader, but a *repeating* rifle!" and lemon hair raised the gun to his shoulder, cocked and rapid-fired the gun over the astonished heads of the troops until the gun was empty—seven times.

"Your next fieldpiece, gentlemen," lemon hair said, "the Spencer .56-caliber Seven Shot."

For a moment there was only a dumb silence, the shots still echoing across the parade ground. And the troopers broke into a wild cheering.

Stanley said Manuel's eyes were big as butter tubs.

After that, Stanley said, the Spencer Seven Shot was put on display in a locked glass case in the armory, Manuel going every day to look at it, hanging over the case, face pressed against the frame, tracing with his finger its outline on the glass as if to memorize it. Every day until, at closing time, they'd have to chase him out.

Then, one night a week later, Manuel stole the gun.

They caught him cold five steps out the armory door. In one hand the Spencer Seven Shot, the other bleeding where he'd smashed the glass with his fist. Two guards in front, one behind, and sprawled near the entrance the sentry he'd stabbed breaking in.

The guard closest yanked the Spencer out of Man's hands; the one behind jammed a muzzle-loader under his ear; the third one went over to look at the sentry, on his stomach, the knife under his ribs.

"He dead?"

The soldier bent down and felt the big artery at the sentry's neck and nodded, yes.

The soldier with the muzzle-loader under Man's ear pushed it hard against his head.

"From behind, he got him from behind."

"Who is it?"

Gently the soldier rolled the dead sentry over. "Shit!"

They all turned to look at Man, then back down at the body:

"That's how he got *by* him."

"That's *why* he got to him."

"*How* he got so close to him."

"Walked right up to him."

"His sidekick."

"Never trust a red nigger."

"I tol' him that, too; I said, 'Never—'" The voice trailed off.

They stood silent; then the soldier who'd rolled the corpse over to see who it was, rolled it back over on its stomach so they wouldn't have to look at Stanley Meeker's dead face.

26

A Question of Defense

Across from me the senator sat swung around from a great roll-top desk watching Gray Owl making medicine, Gray Owl running his fingers down over the printing of one of the senator's lawbooks, the senator glancing over now and again at his daughter at the high office windows, tugging angrily at the long curtains so that little daggers of dust knifed off into the sunlight; then the senator grunted and threw the newspapers into my lap as if I didn't know what was there.

They'd been full of it, the papers had, of Manuel's attempted theft of the new Spencer Seven Shot along with the betrayal and stabbing of his friend Stanley Meeker, "a martyr," the papers said, to "humanitarian principles," newsmen manufacturing Indian intrigue, conspiracy, plot and counterplot by the yard—the Pawnee scouts long since sent home as spies; the red man carrying his war butt up against the white man's hearth; a plan, the papers said, to infiltrate munitions plants; another to steal state secrets (which, of course, the Indians couldn't read, which was really what the Four had been doing all the while when talking to the President); many plains tribes now in the employ of foreign powers, notably the English and Italian: the English because of high tariffs; the Italian when, in a downtown hotel, Wormley House, a native of that country was found in bed with a Santee Sioux, her husband, also a Santee Sioux, dead in the bathtub. Most of it the backlash from the slaughtering of a pair of wagon trains and the wiping out of a small settlement west of the Wichitas.

The senator's eyes cut across to his daughter, then he swung back into the big roll-top, the upper half of him hidden.

The girl, hearing his chair scrape, whirled around to glare at him.

It was Honor had brought us together: Gray Owl along to lend credence, me because I'd been the only one to have seen Manuel since the stabbing, meeting with him in the old county jail off Judiciary Square, the room not much larger than a closet, a guard at the door, Manuel in striped pants and shirt with the number 76 on his back. Honor had arranged it. The senator wouldn't have anything to do with it.

I'd brought Manuel some fresh fruit, jerky and the pipe. He wouldn't touch the food. For a long while we sucked at the pipe, his black obsidian eyes unblinking, then—not that I'd doubted, but I had to hear it from him—I made the large, round sign, *why?*

He didn't answer but went on smoking; then, deliberately, he lay down the pipe and took off his shirt.

"Hey," the guard said, "hey, what're you doin'?"

Manuel commenced to tear his shirt, twice up the back and front, then each of the sleeves, ripping off all of the buttons, the collar and the number 76 off the back of his shirt, the guard jumping all around, "Hey, hey, cut that out. . . ." Then Manuel put on his shredded shirt and took off his pants. "You crazy? What's he doin'? You can't do that. That's government issue . . ." and, like the shirt, Manuel tore the pants, each leg twice, then poured the still-burning ashes from the pipe over his head.

Manuel had done for Stanley, all right. He was going into mourning for Stanley.

They marched out Manuel, shirt and pants flapping. I picked up the 76 and put it in my pocket.

From what I could make out, Honor expected Gray Owl and me to persuade the senator—*of what* I was never sure, because from the moment we'd come through the door, the senator had made it plain how he'd felt. Nobody, so far, saying much of anything.

I waited till the girl turned back to the window. "We can still defend him," I said.

The senator surfaced from the roll-top. "Oh, yes, we can defend him," the senator said with a quick smile, "but *I* can't afford it."

"Oh, Papa," Honor said into the curtains.

The senator pointed to the paper in my lap. "Read it . . . theft, coercion, premeditation, spying, sedition, treason, murder— Christ!"

"Attempted murder," Honor said.

"It doesn't much matter at this point," the senator said.

"The sentry's still alive," she said.

"All are federal crimes. Do you know what that means?"

The silence was like shouting.

I handed him back his newspaper. "To defend him, Senator," I said, "what would it take?"

"It's not now and never has been a question of defense. You know the feeling of the country."

"But we can do something, can't we?" the girl's voice came muffled from the curtains.

Careful, I said, "How much *would* it cost, Senator?"

"Don't be absurd," the senator said, back in the roll-top.

Honor turned away from the windows. "But he's still alive, Papa, the sentry."

"For how long?"

"That's why we should do something now."

"That's just why we can't."

"Oh, Papa!"

"What do you think they're waiting for?" With a pair of clippers, the senator snipped off the end of his cigar. "Jesus," the senator snorted, "the only man to befriend him."

Honor crossed to him. "Manuel said he didn't know it was his friend. It was night. It was dark. He couldn't see."

"Do you think it matters to anybody? He could see well enough to steal that Spencer Seven Shot. Honey, you don't know what you're talking about."

"We can't just leave him," she said.

"The way things are, he might just as well have wiped out an army. There were three witnesses." He lit the cigar.

I'd never been able to reckon the senator: Courageous, he'd lay out his life on principle the way he had in the baggage car; generous, he'd give money and time and influence on blind belief. But then there was also that other thing in him, the way he'd shot the trapper in the baggage car. Unfeeling as a bush hog. The same as he'd been at the party. Like now. It was that I was betting on.

"We could talk to 'em, Senator," I said, "those three witnesses."

He studied me over the roll-top.

"Most men," I said, "are—reasonable."

His eyes were gray-green.

"*If—*" I said, "approached right."

The gray-green eyes narrowed. "And how's that, Clay?"

"Well, Senator, I'm not sure, 'ceptin'—" I wasn't sure a-tall.

"You think you could make them listen?" he said.

I jumped in with both feet. "Yes, sir."

"Tell me."

"Senator, you know what a trooper makes a month?"

He sat up. "No," he said, "there'll be none of that."

From then on, all I had to go on was the difference between his sitting up and that *no*. Because for one cut second there I wasn't sure he hadn't thought about it.

"Please, Papa."

"It's a waste," he said, "no. . . ."

She slammed her purse down on the table.

"Of time and effort," he said, "and money!"

"Papa, we can't just abandon him."

"Honey, you got any idea at all what legal counsel alone could run to in a case like this, not even counting—"

"What?" I said.

"Don't be absurd."

"I'm not."

"I'm rich, Clay, but I didn't get that way throwing it away."

"Suppose we could raise it?" I said.

I caught him in mid-draw on his cigar. He coughed. He looked around. "*We?*"

For an instant, all you could hear was the swish of Gray Owl's turning the pages of the senator's lawbooks.

Like that time in the snake pit, I thought. All of us not looking, looking at Gray Owl. I went over to him.

"They will kill Manuel, Gray Owl," I said. "Unless we stop them."

He went on turning the pages.

"Gray Owl?"

Running his hand down over the law print.

"It is not like ban-ah phat-fut. We need others, many, many others to help—*turn* the law."

Gray Owl looked up from the book, away from me. "Law all same, all man. No turn law."

"Wasichu law is different than Sioux code. Sometimes, with much medicine from others, it can be—*moved*. But it takes much, much. You must help, Gray Owl. Will you help?"

He put down the book. "I pray."

"No, Gray Owl, that is not enough."

"I go."

He started for the door. I stepped in front of him.

"Gray Owl, we must have the yellow dirt, much, much yellow dirt to help Manuel Choke Breath."

He looked at me. Hard. So I couldn't hold it and looked away. Far off, I could hear the clanging of a fire engine.

Then the senator's words dropped into the room like pebbles in a still pond. "Ask—him," the senator said very deliberately, "where—they—mine—it."

Honor's head came up at her father, features slack as yesterday.

But, now, for the first time, I knew my ground. "Ah-ha na-hee-set, cudt man-tee?" I said.

No answer.

I took the book out of his hands. "Gray Owl, *they are going to hang Manuel Choke Breath*. Now, the yellow dirt, where do we seek it?"

I knew in general where it came from. But the Black Hills are also burial grounds. Hallowed. For anyone to lift Grandmother's flesh (the earth) was an abomination. To betray her, a desecration. To exploit her, to damn one's heart. Gray Owl also knew something else now: the yellow dirt had a power beyond his people's imagining. It could be their last defense. Also, to reveal it could loose the same flood as destroyed the Hupas, Yuroks, Washoes and a dozen other tribes in California during the gold rush of '49. And yet, to permit Manuel to hang. . . .

Gray Owl looked from me to the senator, whose cigar had gone out, to the girl, tense in the center of the room, back to me, then bowed his head. I had him.

Gray Owl started—or so it seemed to me the way he brought up his hand—to make the *yes* sign, when the girl said, "No!" She stood directly in front of me. "Not this way," she said, "no. You're not going to *use* them—or him. Any more."

The abruptness of it caught me with a loose bit. "You were the one brought us here, Miss Honor," I said, "—to your daddy."

"No."

"You heard your daddy; it'll cost—"

"No. No!"

"Then," I said, "just whatta you got in mind?"

"Can't you see what he's doing to you?" she said.

"Who?" I said.

"Him. To you. You think you're so clever with your questions and money and petty bribery. Can't you see—*you!*—you're the one's being used."

"Me?" I started to say. She made me feel heavy and dumb.

She nodded at the senator. "Him. Papa. Why do you think he insisted you stay with them? Why? To help them?"

It *was* what I was thinking.

"Papa knew something like this was going to happen. Couldn't help happening. Was bound to happen. And when it did, you'd be there—*for him!*" She turned on the senator. "Didn't you, Papa?"

The senator didn't back off from her as I had. He blew a plume of smoke like spitting.

"Like that dinner, Papa. You knew, *knew* they'd make fools of themselves. In front of all those people. All those important people. You knew, Papa! They weren't invited to help the poor heathen, were they? Were they!"

There was a knock at the door.

"I did what I could for your Indians," the senator said.

Again there was a knock. The senator nodded at me and I opened the door. A clerk entered.

The senator's calmness seemed to drive her. "You did it for you, Papa."

The clerk handed the senator a piece of paper and went out.

"The opportunity was theirs," the senator said.

"What opportunity? For whom?" The girl was beginning to shout.

"They misused it," the senator said.

"What did you expect them to do?"

"Exactly as they did. I also expected *you* to understand what the others understood."

"What, that you were exploiting them?"

"That there is no place for them."

"No, you were giving them an excuse, Papa. . . ."

The senator looked puzzled.

The girl swallowed. "To help you—" her voice so low now you had to strain to hear, "to help you *cheat* them, *steal* from them."

The senator smiled and that seemed to infuriate her.

"Like right now!" she burst out.

"Honor, this has nothing to do with you."

"And the yellow dirt—*their* yellow dirt?"

The senator glanced down at the piece of paper the clerk had brought him.

"Girl, you have no idea what you're talking about."

"Stop saying that!" Her eyes began to well. "Papa, they're children."

"Exactly." The senator seemed to relax. "Now you're beginning to grasp it. You don't let children play with the family silver." He paused. "Or matches."

"You don't take advantage of them either."

"They have to be watched," the senator said, "cared for."

"That's all we're asking," she half whispered.

"Yes, but you've already let them burn the house down." The senator handed his daughter the piece of paper the clerk had given him.

"All the more reason for you to help, Papa. . . ."

The senator pointed to the slip of paper in her hand.

"No excuses, Papa. . . ." She glanced down at the paper. "No more—" She went gray, and, still looking at the slip, she sat down in one of the large leather chairs.

The senator nodded at the slip in his daughter's hand. "Stanley Meeker just died."

"He just—"

"An hour ago," the senator said and swung back into the roll-top.

An hour ago, I thought, even as we'd been at each other, Stanley was dying, *had died*. I went to look out the window. The girl began to cry. I felt something in my right pocket and pulled it out.

Through her crying the girl said, "This makes it all just perfect, doesn't it, Papa?"

I looked down at my hand. It was the number off the back of Manuel's striped shirt—76.

"Now, Papa, you don't have to do anything. Now you can—"

We wouldn't have heard him at all or known if, when the door closed behind Gray Owl, the lock hadn't clicked.

···

27

Close as the Grave

Naked except for a loincloth, Gray Owl sat in a corner of the basement, eyes closed, head thrown back, lips moving soundlessly, praying, legs loosely crossed around a small block of wood along whose top lay a ceremonial knife.

Cross-legged, I sat directly in front of him.

The prayers went on for a long time. Finished, Gray Owl opened his eyes, looked at me, through me, then with great formality placed his left hand on the block where the knife had been, and with his right hand laid the blade in front of the knotted string just behind the first joint of the first finger of his left hand. Gray Owl's invocation of the gods. A sacramental offering. Self-immolation for his dying friend. For Little Rabbit was dying.

Gray Owl was asking Wakan Tanka to take His brother to His Great Heart, and for this act of love, Gray Owl made this atonement in pain.

Still looking through me, slowly Gray Owl pressed the knife down into his finger, the sweat starting around his eyes and mouth. The finger turning chalky but hardly bleeding. Slowly, slowly. Slowly to endure and so make himself and the offertory the worthier. Slowly. So watching, I felt the hollow hurting. I looked away. Then, like chopping cotton, the whole of him made a sharp downward movement. Sawing. The lineaments of his neck and face corded. Still looking through me. Expressionless. Then, though I hadn't heard it, I felt him sigh. His eyes refocused. It was done. I glanced down. The finger lay nail up in the dirt like one of the animal droppings, the amputated stump barely oozing.

Then, for a long while—to feel and endure—Gray Owl sat. And when the pain commenced to lessen, he held out his hand to me and I pulled the loose ends of the knotted string tight behind the stump to stop the bleeding. I then helped him on with his holy shirt, his medicine bag and eagle feathers, supporting him across the basement to where Sonofabitch, a Bible out in front of him as though he were reading, his new blue eye staring straight on, recited Comanche prayers over Little Rabbit, in his grave, eyes shut, as still as the morning star.

All that night they chanted and prayed, until the next morning, when, eyes still closed, Little Rabbit, the red roses of death fiery in his cheeks, commenced with great difficulty to make sign.

"Little Rabbit say he gonna be dead by Moon of First Frost in Tipi," Sonofabitch said, and I was sure he would be—if not before. But Sonofabitch said, no, that he would pray to the great Wasichu Christ to spare Little Rabbit. And Sonofabitch prayed. Every day. For hours. For weeks. Sonofabitch keeping Little Rabbit alive up to the Moon of the First Frost in the Tipi to the Moon of the Dark Red Calf to the Moon of the Snowblind, all the way up to the Moon of the Red Grass Appearing! And Gray Owl, too, was converted to the Christ Spirit, who could work this great wonder over Little Rabbit.

In that time, the senator twice got Manuel's trial date put back. But "no more," the senator said, because what with a small town in northeastern New Mexico and another in central Utah all but wiped out, a detachment of cavalry beaten by the Blade in the Panhandle and the Apaches setting the whole Southwest afire, Manuel had become what the senator called a *cause célèbre* in reverse, the army, the newspapers, the public, everyone calling for Manuel's neck, so "no more," the senator said, his opposition starting to turn it to account with the voters, though I knew if I could get Gray Owl to lay open—"Where do they mine the yellow, Gray Owl?"—I could cinch down on the senator till he forgot about himself, the voters or anything else, Man's trial less than a month off, Gray Owl close as the grave, though I never once let up on him: at the library, in the basement, the streets, so much with him and Sonofabitch I got to be a regular at the Salvation Army meetings, away from Buff so much that all that kept her with me was the buying of furnishings for the house I said I'd buy her. Still Gray Owl wouldn't tell me a thing.

In that time, Little Rabbit had dwindled away to a bag of rags, shaking to pieces from the coughing, his eyes like two great sink-holes in the snow, his head a skull, brainsick and wandering one whole week, during which I sneaked in a doctor, who took one look at him, said it was hopeless, and, to make him more comfortable, gave me a drug which I mixed in with the Rabbit's food so he wouldn't know. It helped for a while. He rested easier, the rattle in his throat not so harsh. But for only a while, and, one day, the little Arapaho asked Sonofabitch not to intercede for him any more with the Christ Spirit, and Sonofabitch stopped praying. A charity and a blessing. The little man had suffered so much for so long for so little. Uncomplaining, undemanding. The Rabbit as close to a saint, I thought, as the Plains people would ever produce.

He died the second week of the Moon When the Ponies Shed, praying and humming love songs to his bride. I stayed drunk four days, one for each of the powers of the four directions the Rabbit would have to traverse before entering his paradise. (I think I cared for that little man as much as for anyone on the face of this old earth.) The little Arapaho had been the center of our hoop. Our soul. It broke Gray Owl.

Now, what you got to understand about Gray Owl, Sonofabitch, Manuel and Little Rabbit is that when they set out for the land of the Wasichus, they didn't know any more than the Blade either what they'd find or were getting into, so when the Blade gave them that final blood oath as Brothers of the Body—to insure their courage—they were certain they'd all die together in some battle, which, as far as they could see, couldn't be no different than the plains wars, but, of course, what they found was fruit off another tree, so that now, for all *not* to have died together, worse, for one of them *not* to be at the funeral rites of another, was to damn all to the place of everlasting barrenness, and the morning after the night of Little Rabbit's death, Gray Owl unrolled an animal skin to show me where I could find the yellow dirt to make the money to get Manuel Choke Breath out of prison for Little Rabbit's funeral ceremonies. Except, like always, Manuel couldn't wait.

28

....

Die the Caged

The third week of the Moon When the Ponies Shed, a week after Little Rabbit's death, the Blade, too, was dead.

> *Oklahoma*
> *Boise City*
>
> Architect of the central plains uprising, Kiowa Chief Broken Blade was killed here today in a battle with Federal troops south of Boise City in the Oklahoma Panhandle.
>
> A stunning victory, trooper Captain Silas Henry estimated approximately forty-five braves to have been killed in the battle, the troopers losses very light . . .

the article going on to say that the Blade was "father of Manuel Choke Breath currently in a Federal prison in Washington charged with murder," about the only fact the Washington press had right, because, as I found out later, forty-five braves hadn't been killed but, rather, fourteen braves, twenty-five squaws and six children, which came to forty-five; the troopers losses light for a fact: they hadn't lost a man; nor was the Blade killed in battle, but in an ambush, Manuel knowing about his father's death a full week before the papers or anybody else, the guard, Mr. McCauley, said shaking his head in wonder, so I thought *long, long before that*, remembering the *yuwipi* ceremony, when Manuel had seen his father and cried. This was what he had seen.

Manuel had gone into a second mourning, Mr. McCauley said, from Stanley to his father—a full week before! And three days later Manuel made his first prison break.

They marched, surrounded by a twelve-foot-high brick wall, in a tight circle in the prison exercise yard. Once a week for an hour.

Coming on the Moon of Making Fat, it was cold, no snow but cold, cold, so all except Manuel marched dully, stamping frozen feet, heads turtled into shoulders, hugging themselves, blowing into cupped fists. The guard, Mr. McCauley, an old-timer I'd gotten to know from his bringing Manuel into the visitors' room, also cold and stamping, stood, fists jammed into pockets, rifle balanced in the bend of his elbow, out of the wind, in the cellway, when near the end of the hour, the kid stepped out of the circle— Manuel never anything but *the kid* to Mr. McCauley—no doubt Mr. McCauley said of the kid's having planned it that way, knowing how dozing and drag-assed from the cold they'd be toward the end of the hour.

He'd not thought anything at the time, Mr. McCauley said, except the kid wanted to go to the crapper, so, without taking his hands out of the pockets of his mackinaw, he'd tilted his rifle up to the kid, yes, to go to the crapper, when, ducking behind the others, the kid broke into a sprint across the compound.

With a start, Mr. McCauley had jerked his arms, catching his balled hands in pocket openings too narrow for balled hands, the rifle sliding out of the crook of his elbow onto the ground.

But he was never worried, Mr. McCauley said, because where could the kid go? Stir fever, Mr. McCauley said. It got to them all. Some sooner. Miss the second buttonhole one morning and over they went. So let 'em dance. They'd bounce back—and the kid, streaking toward the far end of the yard, made a running jump onto the top of a rain barrel, swung up onto a cell ledge, gathered himself, and made an insane leap out into space at the top of the brick wall.

Manuel caught the top of the wall with the tips of his fingers, scratching, digging his nails into the brick, feet, knees, thighs clawing for holds, unable to get grasp of enough to pull himself up. Hanging numbly.

After his first surprise, Mr. McCauley said, he got control, moving in under the kid, reaching up with the barrel of his gun to tap the bottom of the kid's feet.

"All right, son, it's all over," Mr. McCauley said. "Come on down." And for the third time in as many months, Manuel went into the hole.

An Indian can't understand prison. They have no prisons. Among a people without locks, keys or money, there are no thieves. Warriors stole from their enemies, yes, but these were deeds of valor. Of these a man could be proud.

Without lawyers, contracts or anything in print, men found it impossible to cheat one another. Without jails there could be no criminals.

A plains tribe has no caste system, no classes, no inherited leadership, no underdogs, no judges. Even the chiefs—a chief chief only as long as he was an able leader. And no power of punishment. Against the meanest member of his tribe, a chief dare not raise his hand.

And since there were no cuss words, men found it hard to insult one another. If a man did wrong, he wasn't punished but shamed into behaving. And if that didn't work, he was ridiculed, made fun of, jokes told about him, laughed at by the women.

The killing of a tribal brother the worst crime that could befall a tribe. The sacred bundles in the medicine lodge had to be purified. The whole tribe cleansed. The murderer's relatives offering to pay the victim's family with all they possessed. The murderer sometimes offering himself as a substitute provider and protector. Banned thereafter from all tribal activity for four years. Without the pipe. Outside the village. Unspoken to.

Prison to an Indian a cage. Caged things die. Or escape. Or die escaping.

And at first Manuel, like an animal, went wild. He wouldn't eat. He wouldn't drink. Prisoners refused to work or even live with him. When they wouldn't help him escape, he'd bully or beat them. Two who informed on him, he almost killed. The guards were afraid of him. Anything that could be made into a weapon was taken from him: his toilet bucket, toilet roller, the spring from his bunk, the bunk chain, eventually the bunk, all his clothes, even, when he tried to strangle a guard with the flapping strip of one of his pant legs, the tops off the faucets, and finally the pipes out of the walls. So, day after day, Manuel paced a stripped cell in nothing but a loincloth.

From the escape attempts, the fights and near killings—this even before he'd gone to trial—Manuel had piled up enough *bad time* so trying and sentencing him were rapidly becoming unnecessary.

They finally let us in to see him in a barred cell cut in half with a chicken-wire wall. Manuel still snake-eyed and salty in torn pants and shirt but with a new number on the back, refusing to tell us what happened, to answer questions or talk, even to Gray Owl or Sonofabitch.

He seemed stunned, numbed. Deadened, Honor said, crying at sight of him, not going with us on our last visit to see him.

"Domesticated," Mr. McCauley said, "housebroke. And just in time." The other inmates starting to talk execution, Mr. McCauley said. Manuel finally learning after all those weeks in the hole, Mr. McCauley said, that he wasn't going to bully, butt, gut or cut his way out.

And you could see it, the wrath humble in him, the rage gone out of Manuel's eye. But what Mr. McCauley didn't know was that Manuel had become a philosopher: the snake got what it wanted on its belly; the coyote played dead. And Manuel went on a hunger strike.

He'd gotten the notion when, upon first entering—like all wild things when first caged—he couldn't eat. Then, for a while, he hadn't eaten because he couldn't stand the food. And, lastly, because he'd wanted to die. The authorities all the while making a big fuss over him.

"Let 'im be," Mr. McCauley said he'd told them. "But the captain of the guard—" Mr. McCauley winked, "has an itch to be warden.

"The kid's the senator's client. Senators choose wardens. So down comes the captain bust-assin' into the hole."

(The only one able to get on with Manuel even a little—which probably saved Manuel's life—was Mr. McCauley, for which Mr. McCauley had been rewarded with a transfer down into the hole to look after Manuel. Mr. McCauley was a good old boy with a swagbelly hanging down over his belt so the top of him looked twice again that from his hips down. You could see Mr. McCauley didn't like the guarding business, but he wouldn't quit, he said, because he'd been at it so long and was getting on. But I didn't believe that. I think Mr. McCauley stuck it out of fear of who'd take his place—most guards then, with their guns and clubs, like wild dogs. It's probably why everyone in the place called Mr. McCauley *mister*.)

Mr. McCauley hitched his belt up under his belly. "For an hour the captain stood at the slit lookin' in at the kid, flat on his back in a corner of the cell.

" 'How long's the Indian been like this?' the captain says to me.

"Almost two weeks, I tell him.

" 'An' not a bite of food in all that time?'

"Nothin'.

" 'An' water?'

"Not for the last forty-eight hours.

" 'Christ,' he says an' goes back to the slit, 'he's dead.'

"I dunno, I say.

" 'Whatta you think?' he asks.

"You're the captain, I say.

"So he mulls it over some more, then says, 'Open the door.'

"Shit-o-day, I think, open the door!

" 'If he's dead,' says the captain, 'the senator'll have all our asses. An' our jobs! Open up.'

"So I open up, an' the captain goes in to look at the kid. I stand by the door in case.

"The kid looks dead, all right, an' the captain reaches across him to feel his pulse, when whammo! the kid yanks the captain down across him an' like that he's on top of the captain.

"I start into the cell, but shit-o-day, the kid's got a spoon handle from somewhere—honed like a hatpin—stuck in the captain's ear. If the captain makes a move, or I don't do what the kid says, he'll shove that spoon handle out the other side of the captain's head. An' yes siree, mister, that was it."

29

Nits Make Lice

What it all came down to, after nearly a year, was I was bust.

A stake I could have packed it all in with!

Lordy!

I looked at the wall clock. The senator was late.

I tied the silk tie under my chin, wondering where my buckskins were, and put on the top hat Buff insisted I wear and the coat with the fur around the collar, beaver—hell, a beaver I might have trapped—but what was the use. I took off the coat. The senator wouldn't be home. Or at his club. Or in his office. He never was when *I* called. So, more and more, I'd got to thinking about that afternoon in the senator's office with Gray Owl and what Honor had said about my being *used:*

Backtracking, remembering how from that first moment in the baggage car when the senator had taken the rock out of the tiny, old miner's hand, he hadn't once let us out of his sight; having us watched and followed; insisting I stay with them—"Stick with them, Clay"; sore when I'd moved into the Princess Hotel; forever afraid they'd track back to the plains before he'd found out; the way, Lordy, he'd shot that trapper in the baggage car—*not* for how they were cheating Manuel but for what Manuel knew, for what would happen to the rest of them if anything happened to Manuel; the way the senator had silenced the doctor about Little Rabbit's TB; righteous as the cross when I'd hinted at buying off Man's witnesses; the same as twice he'd got the trial put back; re-

fusing to lay out for Man's defense not because of what it'd cost
but because when their gold was gone they'd have to come to
him, knowing, as the girl said, they were bound to do just as
they'd done—because they'd need him; the same as all those
months the senator had stalled our meet with Sam the President
—to drain them—to make them need him; with me there all the
while, as the girl said, to screw down on them—"Ask them, Clay,
where's the mine,"—because I couldn't *not* ask, because, Lord
help me, broke, I needed him too.

I looked around the house. Buff's house. A quitclaim I could
have foraged from here on out. And suddenly that awful prairie
emptiness came down over me like river smoke—Buff: supple as
sable, pretty as ribbons. Buff. With me! A girl. An old fart with
enough years to be her—I remember the senator's dinner party
that night, the only dinner party he'd invited me to before or
since, his introducing me to her, and the way she'd hung on my
arm, her eyes well black and liquid on me all night and the next
day and the next, the little lunches and drives the senator took us
on, and, like heaving, my stomach rose up against my craw. She
was the senator's, too, wasn't she? Was she? Signed on to leach
till, like the others, I'd no choice but to ask, "Where's the mine,
Gray Owl?"

I got up and walked on my new—*her* new carpets; I set down
on my—*Buff's* new settee; I studied the fancily carved tables and
chairs and chests and something called a chifforobe; then I got up
and looked around the house, big enough for some plains nations,
with a cook, a maid, a gardener, Buff forever at sixes and sevens,
lamenting and wanting, so I thought of those snug nights before
the fire in the wickiup with the snow outside or the soft rattoo of
the rain on the hides, inside with Fleet Fawn, her up before
daybreak gathering brush and berries, all day skinning and scraping, mending and making, cooking over a chip fire in an earthen
pot, and all the time—though I know how, looking back, you big-
gen those things—all the time singing and humming. And still I
wanted the Wasichu! What a perverse thing is a man!

Then I walked through all fifteen rooms, somewhere along the
way beginning to tote the cost, seeing us backed up in the gorge,
the flies and heat, the swamper dying, the Frenchman with his
skull halved, smelling the dead mules and bodies, hearing the high

KI-YIing across the sand and the screaming of Pock Face and the others burning that night, Little Rabbit's dying and the Blade dead, and I decided this was one hand of the senator's I called, and again I put the coat on, when the doorbell rang. Buff, I thought. From hunting another, larger chifforobe. She had a key, but she liked the maid to open the door for her.

It was the senator and a young, sand-faced fella in a gun-gray suit.

The senator handed the maid his hat and coat, watching her hang them up before turning to me, smiling after the maid. "Very stylish."

I took them into the living room for a drink.

"Clay," the senator said walking around the room touching things, then turning to the young man, introducing us, "Mr. Vale."

We didn't shake hands, but, like strange dogs, wary, sniffing, sized one another up, the young man Vale smug with knowing what I only sensed.

"Lovely place you have here, Clay," the senator said, "lovely. Where's Buff?"

"Shopping."

He smiled a secret smile, glancing down, hitting one of the piano keys, the sound keening through the house like a lamentation.

I poured myself another drink.

"Mr. Vale here is a geologist," the senator said sipping his drink.

I must not have hidden how I felt, because the senator couldn't look at me neither.

"I assume, Clay," the senator said, "that by now you've pretty much figured it out for yourself?"

I drank my drink.

The senator nodded. "Good. Mr. Vale here will go with you to Gray Owl's diggings."

I didn't find out about Manuel until that night, Honor and the senator at dinner when I pushed by the butler.

They knew, looking at me, something was wrong. They didn't greet me or ask me to sit down.

"Manuel broke out of prison," I said.

Honor started up from the table, knocking over a glass of water. "When?"

"Just now."

"Where is he?"

"I don't know. They're lookin' fer him."

"Oh," she said, hollow, picking up the glass.

"He stabbed a guard named Mr. McCauley."

She made another "Oh," darted a look at her father and ran out.

The senator glanced after her, thought about it, then reached for a decanter on the table. "Something to drink, Clay?"

I shook my head, no.

"Look like you could use one."

"They got the whole city out, Senator."

"Something to eat?"

"He's armed, Senator."

"Might as well eat. Nothing anybody can do until they catch him."

"They're not out, Senator, to *catch* him."

"There's nothing to be done."

"They'll kill him."

"Sit down."

I stood and the senator went on eating. He finished his plate and a glass of wine, then held out the box. "Cigar?"

"Senator—"

"I want you out of here tomorrow, Clay."

"What!"

"In the morning."

"Hold on, Senator. . . ."

"As early as possible."

"I can't do that, sir, not now."

He got up from the table. "Especially—now!" He drew deep on the cigar. "You think I'm insensitive to what's happened, don't you, Clay?"

"I think we should help him," I said.

He studied me through the cigar smoke. "Your Indian," he

said, laying out the words as evenly as cards on a dead call, "is—
not—going—to come out of this—alive!"

I started to speak.

He held up a hand. "You said as much yourself, boy."

Someone, Honor I thought, was rustling about in the front of
the house.

"Clay, the moment—God forbid—Manuel is killed, Gray Owl
and the others stop needing us for the gold to defend Manuel or
for anything else."

So it was, I thought, pretty much as I'd thought it was.

The front door opened and slammed.

"That's why I want *you* out of here before *they* can stop *us*."

When I got home, Buff was waiting up for me with two young
army officers who stood back by the door watching Buff and the
captain of the guard from the prison, a large, handsome man, sitting across from one another, Buff smiling up at the captain pouring himself and her a drink, the captain grinning, leaning toward
her, handing her a drink, looking down the front of her robe, then
lounging back on what Buff called the *chaise longue*, the captain
of the guard more at home, Lordy, in my house than ever I was.

I'd come in a side door so as not to wake anyone, and they
hadn't seen me until the two young officers snapped to attention
when the captain of the guard stood up into the room, big, all
stomach and strut, the drink in one hand, shoving a cigar at me
with the other. Another Colonel Chivington, I thought. The captain as massive, too, as Chivington, the chest and shoulders of an
ox. So, suddenly, the way I could never stop it, she was there,
asleep, curled around her sister's two children, Fleet Fawn, her
breath so light you had to listen for it, Chivington up on the bluff
above Sand Creek with the 3rd Regiment and part of the 1st Volunteers, 750 men against 300 sleeping men, women and children.
"Kill an' scalp all," the colonel said. "Nits make lice." And they
swung the cannon into position.

Speckled Arms, coming out of her tipi at dawnlight and the
first to see them, shouted the alarm. Old Black Kettle dashed out
of his lodge to run up the American flag and a white flag because
weren't they at peace? So always I think of Fleet Fawn's terror,

awakening at the rifle and cannon fire sweeping the camp—I was away on a hunt—her awful scrambling for the kids; the camp instantly ablaze; the breathless, panicked running with the children; her ducking the charging, yelling soldiers, the plunging horses and slashing sabers; dodging through the smoke, the falling cinders and bodies; the frantic burrowing, hiding under the bank, the clinging to one another, breath-stopped and gagging, a hand over the little ones' mouths; listening now, hearing the guns and cannons and bugles, the horses screaming and the crackling of burning; underneath the roaring, the praying and dying, the weeping and moaning—a horror!—her seeing how, to protect the women and children, the braves made stands in the hollows and the little pockets along the creek banks; below her on the bluff, the forty squaws collected, sending out a six-year-old girl with a white flag, the girl shot, the squaws slaughtered—she must have seen all that.

Is that what had brought her out of hiding?—the babies hurled into the creek; pregnant squaws cut open; White Antelope's privates gouged out for a tobacco pouch; Spring Tree's breasts cut off for shot bags; the old woman Sweet Flower made to run through a burning tipi only to be shot coming out the other side; old Thunder Cloud, blind, walked off a cliff; a small boy, Tiny Pony, hidden by his mother, Blue Cloud, in the sand, decapitated, and on and on—back in Denver that's how they bragged on it—an orgy of butchery, is that what had brought her out? Or had the soldier (like one of the two young ones here) had the soldier stumbled over their burrow in the side of the cliff? Had he looked into her soft, doe eyes, had he seen the little ones' white faces before he killed them? Is that when she'd gone for him with the skinning knife? Killed outright, from the hole in her. One of the lucky ones. The slaughter going on until late afternoon, chasing and killing.

Of the 200 killed, 175 had been women and children. They also took two men, three women and four children captive, exhibiting them in cages in downtown Denver.

I wasn't there, I hadn't seen it, but night after night for months after I lived it, beginning to end, with me always somehow in one of those cages in Denver with Fleet Fawn's corpse.

Chiving— The captain of the guard from the prison poured

himself another drink, pointing his glass at me, looking at her, sitting back down, the only man, I thought, I'd ever known who could swagger sitting down, a spurred boot ajangle up on the shakedown. They hadn't an address for Manuel, the captain said, because Manuel hadn't known it (because, I thought, where Manuel lived the houses didn't have addresses), but since I'd been more or less their guardian, the captain said, I should know where Manuel lived, because that's the first place he'd head, wasn't it, back to the others?

Yes, I said, that's what Manuel would do, all right, go home.

"An' where's that?"

They'd find them all, I lied, east of town, in a camp on the outskirts, last I knew.

The captain nodded at me, at the same time looking down the front of Buff's robe, then smiled, saluted gallantly and toasted Buff with the last of his drink, thanking her for her hospitality and me for my information and turned to go.

"How's Mr. McCauley?" I called.

The captain stopped abruptly in the doorway.

"We'll git that Indian. Oh, we'll git the—" apologizing to Buff "—bastard." Then to me, "You tell the senator that. You tell him that!" the captain bellowed so I wondered if it wasn't the senator got shot.

That soldier who'd cut out White Antelope's privates for a tobacco pouch . . . I ran into him one night in a notch house east of Cotton. He was showing off the pouch to the girls.

I went across the street and lined up the sights of my buffalo gun with the doorknob, and when the soldier came out that's just where he got it.

30

God Not Man

"Dar-ha kay-too lah men sak-o-gren tadu-kay do-sad. . . ."

"Lo, though I walk through the valley of the shadow. . . ."

On one side of Little Rabbit danced Gray Owl, turning in place, chanting softly, a gourd rattle in either hand, a red string tied about the stump of the left forefinger he'd cut off for Little Rabbit to remind the gods of his offertory. Across from Gray Owl stood Sonofabitch, blue eye glinting, a crucifix about his neck, squinting out of his one good eye at a Bible held out in front of him, reciting the Twenty-third Psalm. The room throbbing. Unreal as Little Rabbit's corpse. Pulsing with the reflections of a half hundred candles encircling Little Rabbit's grave. Shadows reaching out from the ceiling and walls. Like wings. Misshapen. Beaked. Hovering. I seemed to hover, hanging in a cone of light, dark shimmering and luminous as night fish. Sleep waking. The room reeling, a haze of mists off the dawn river. The red roses forging the quick in Little Rabbit's dead cheeks, facing him west, the way of his soul, Little Rabbit now walking the deep, beaten Spirit path, coming to the great Oda-e-min (Heart Berry) strawberry, which stands in the path like a huge red rock and from which the Rabbit would take a handful to eat for strength on his way until he reached a swollen stream over which lie the dread Ko-go-gaup-o-gun, the *sinking bridge*, which, after crossing, turns into a great serpent, twisting and untwisting its folds across the water—Little Rabbit four days later entering the Spirit Land of his fathers.

May your journey be gentle, little Arapaho.

Over Little Rabbit's head rose a cross decorated with flowers, beads, strips of colored paper and cloth; at his feet stood a statue of the holy Virgin Mother Mary, also with flowers and beads, a cape over her shoulders, around her neck, Sonofabitch's feather boa. (All lifted from Lord knows where.) On Little Rabbit's chest lay a Sioux totem from Gray Owl. Alongside Little Rabbit in the grave were his gun, blanket, kettle, fire steel, flint, moccasins, a beaver trap and a rattrap. Little Rabbit had learned. He'd go on living in the good old way up there, but first ridding his Heaven of rodents with the white man's gadget.

To one side, next to the grave, lay the dead sacrificial carcass of the old broken-back from the department store, head to the east, tail to the west, for Little Rabbit to ride until, in the Spirit Land, he found something better.

Heathen or Christian, I thought, they sure weren't taking any chances with Little Rabbit's soul.

Gray Owl prayed. "We do not bemoan thee as if thou wast forever lost to us or that thy name be buried in oblivion. Thy soul yet lives, and though we be left behind, we shall one day join thee in the—"

The door burst open.

"Dah-kee!"

It was Manuel.

Seeing Little Rabbit, Manuel raised both hands up, then out, dropping his left hand over his heart, right hand to the side of his face in the sign of *apology* and *sorrow* and *honor* to the dead.

Blood caked in a gash over his right eye, the convict clothes little more than ribbons, the left sleeve gone at the shoulder, the right pant at the thigh, Manuel stood looking down into the grave.

Without once glancing at him, Gray Owl and Sonofabitch continued to pray.

Again Man made the sign of obeisance, then went directly to his weapons, slinging a quiver of arrows over one shoulder, crossing the bow over the other, sticking a knife and pistol in his belt.

I handed him his rifle. "Where will you go, Manuel Choke Breath?"

He pushed past me to the table, wolfing down leftovers, gorging, then choking and spitting up food from the starving, and for the first time he seemed to see around him.

He nodded at the cross. "Ha-mah nee sut?"

Sonofabitch held up the Bible. "Kah-da-haul!"

"Tak-ka-ha," said Gray Owl.

Manuel pointed to the candles and the statue. "What is this you do with Little Rabbit?"

Gray Owl shook one of the gourds. "We make the dirge of death."

Man fingered the beads on the cross. "What means this totem?"

"The sign of the most sacred holy," said Sonofabitch warily.

Man circled the holy Virgin Mother Mary. He ran a hand down over her breasts and stomach and between her legs.

Sonofabitch was shocked.

"This?" said Man.

"She is the Keeper of Life for the Most High."

Man lifted the crown of flowers from the Virgin Mary's head. "These are the Christ things?"

Sonofabitch nodded.

Viciously Man threw the crown of flowers across the room. "Why?" Man said.

Sonofabitch recoiled. "He brings benevolence to all."

Man lifted the beads over the Virgin's head. "And does not Wakan Tanka do this?" He threw the beads.

"The Christ is stronger."

Man threw the flowers. "Is it the stronger you would have or the more good?"

"He is love," Sonofabitch said.

Man stripped the colored paper off the Virgin like leaves off a branch. "Is this, then, why He thieves our land! Is this, then, why He slaughters our creatures, starves our children, diseases our girls —whores our women! Is this why He murders our people!"

Sonofabitch looked down into the open grave.

Gray Owl made the sigh for *unfair*. "The man is not the God, Manuel Choke Breath," Gray Owl said.

Man jerked the cape off the Virgin. "Does not the God teach the man, Gray Owl?"

"The man will not learn."

Man ripped the cape down the center. "We learn from Wakan Tanka. We do not as they do." He hurled the cape across the room. "So whose God is the more benevolent!"

"You blaspheme," said Sonofabitch.

"You forsake," said Manuel and made the wide, round sign at Sonofabitch, biting off the end, "Wasichu eye," apple Indian, *red outside, white inside.*

Sonofabitch didn't understand. He looked alarmed. "Would you not go up to the Heaven place, Manuel Choke Breath?"

"I would not!"

Gray Owl peered closely up at Manuel. "Why would you not, Manuel Choke Breath?" asked Gray Owl pointing the stump of the forefinger he'd cut off for Little Rabbit into Manuel's face, so Manuel, charged with the stump, knew he could not lie.

"Because in that place are only Christians," said Manuel and pulled the ends of the boa about the Virgin's neck, the ball of rage in him starting to unravel: "You dishonour—our brother!" and Manuel snatched the Bible out of Sonofabitch's hand, ripping out the pages, throwing the book across the room, kicking and stomping on the candles, uprooting the cross, and, holding it where the sacred feet had been nailed, swung it like a scythe, cutting the holy Virgin Mother Mary in half, when the front door opened, Man snatching up his rifle, cocking, whirling—

"No, Man!"

It was the girl Honor.

They stood facing one another, Man gasping, with the blood flushing his eyes, Honor's eyes filling with the basement, a shambles, nose crinkling at the smell, her hand still on the knob of the door half open behind her. A roach ran over her feet.

I pushed the door shut and climbed up to the grill window. At street level you could barely see out, but it was enough. The road roiling with blue legs. Soldiers. The legs uncertain, running about without purpose. I could hear them running now up the front steps. They hadn't yet found us.

"Like locusts out there, Man," I said.

Quiver and bow crisscrossing his chest, bowie and pistol in his pants top, rifle in one hand, Man snatched up yet another weapon, his spear, and started for the door.

Honor moved in front of him. "No, Manuel."

"She's right, Man," I said. "You ain't got a prayer out there."

"Manuel, if we, Clay and I go out first, talk to them, then you follow—unarmed . . ."

Man shook his head at her.

"It's yer only chanc't, Man. What they got out there, they must think they're fightin' the whole Kiowa nation."

"Please, Manuel," she said going up to him, laying the tips of her fingers along the back of his spear hand so, suddenly, I thought of what it had taken for her to come here, because it would start all over about her and Manuel, the rumors—how or where or by whom they'd got started I had no ken, but, then, nothing in this town is a secret for long, ever . . . nor should it have surprised me after that night in my hotel room: She'd come asking me to intercede with her father for Manuel, when out of some perversity which, other than that I had to be sure, which I already was, I'd held out the tiny, silver spur the Rabbit had found in the glade. She'd reached for it, then caught herself, her hand stretched out over it like a benediction, then she glanced at me, eyes wide as a fawn's in cover, so in that slit moment I saw—I'm not now sure, her pledge, her avowal? to what I can't rightly say— it was how she was looking at Man now—to him?—just that slit moment and then she'd taken the spur from me . . . maybe as an admission to let me know she knew I knew and it didn't matter because it was all nonsense anyway, I don't know. Anyway that's how she stood before him now, her hand on his. Bound.

"They got an army out there, boy," I said.

"For me, Manuel," she said, "please. Please?"

Again he made the *no* sign.

I knew he wouldn't.

From above I heard someone run down the front steps. "There's another way out, Man . . ." I said.

He looked through Honor over my head to the grill above with the blue legs running by, so I thought how, yes siree, ol' Clay's always got a way out: out of the barricade, out of the Blade's camp, out of Dodge, out of Pap's peonage, the senator's stalling and Sam's indifference, out of fires, floods and *this*. An instinct ingrained as breath. One with the primordial slime. A mountain man's catechism. Because a man without an *out* is a fool. So why'd I feel a Judas?

"If we could hold 'em, Man," I said, "till I got the senator. . . ."

About as much chance, I knew, getting the senator in time as a
worm in a spring-net.

"Oh, yes, yes," Honor cried. "Please, please, Manuel. . . ."

And again Man made the short, hard, slash across his belly, *no!*

I think if it hadn't been for the girl, I think maybe I could have
held him, and it would all maybe have been different.

Man looked from the blue legs at the grill down and around at
each of us—at me, at Sonofabitch, at Gray Owl and Honor, so in
that moment I knew what it was I'd felt all the way from Independence. Like now. Like my finding the senator. Fault. Because,
all along, they'd been given what didn't exist, *hope*. And I remembered the McMurtys, Tom and his wife, the girl and the little boy
back there in the Kiowa camp—waiting. *Hoping*.

Only, this time Man knew. He knew what was out there because he'd been there. He'd been fighting, running, hiding from it
for twenty-four hours now. Or was it twenty-four years? Or
twenty-four hundred years? You could hear them all around us.
Everywhere. But I think—I think Man mostly wanted to be rid of
her. Or maybe, studying each of us the way he had, that's when
he'd decided to go, because there wasn't a one, not a single one of
us by whom he hadn't been betrayed.

Mad Dog

As Manuel started out the back door, the soldier entered, firing. Honor made a sucking sound, the shot ripping off the top of her shoulder. Man slammed the door back onto the soldier, knocking him up against the wall, pinning him to the wall, smashing the door back and back again and again on him like crushing a bug, until the door began to shatter, when he rammed his spear through the flimsy center panel. The soldier made a noise like coughing. Man jerked the spear out of the man and ran up the steps to the back yard.

"No, Man," I shouted and followed. Three soldiers came over the back-yard fence.

The nearest fired the same time Man hurled his spear. The spear impaled the man to the fence, the man grunting, holding the shaft in him as though embracing it.

As Man dropped to the ground, the second and third soldiers fired, the shots plowing into the cow behind him, the old girl pitching forward to her knees as if at prayer. Man's shot knocked the second soldier back over the fence, and the third, seeing he was alone, turned to run.

"Man!"

He whirled; the mounted cavalryman, sword upraised, jumped the fence landing, horse and rider, on top of Man, who came up opposite the soldier's sword arm, cupping the soldier's left heel in both hands, jerking upward, unseating the rider, whose forward momentum sent him headlong sideways off the horse into the house and down the stairs, Man up on the horse's back before the soldier had cleared the buckhorn.

At the Indian smell the horse reared, sunfished and stumbled over the dead cow, righting itself against the house.

The house was at the end of a cul-de-sac, so the only way out was straight up the alley—factory and tenement walls on either side.

I looked over the fence. Lord! Soldiers all over the alley. On both sides. On the roofs, at the windows, on the ancient, falling-apart fire escapes. An impossible gantlet.

Man swung the horse, a big bay, still rearing and frightened, in a tight half circle to steady it. Then . . . more horses. A second cavalryman charging from the far end of the alley.

"No, Man, no!"

Man kicked the bay over the fence; and down the alley (barely wide enough for one) they came at one another, a mistake that at this moment probably saved Man's life, the soldiers hypnotized by what they were seeing, also now afraid to fire for fear of hitting one of their own, the two coming down the funnel of the alley at one another like a pair of runaway coal wagons.

"My God!" It was Honor, holding a potato sack to her bleeding shoulder. I pulled her down into a corner of the fence with me.

Whuuump!—the horses came together, hoofs clattering like pistol shots on the cobblestones, eye whites rolling, chest to chest, squealing and grunting, in a tangle of thrashing heads, shanks, rumps, so it was hard for Man or the cavalryman to get at one another, the cavalryman snapping off a shot that took off the right ear of the bay, already frightened, now terrified, the other, smaller horse, a piebald, no match for the bigger, heavier bay, snorting and rearing and pawing, the piebald backing and backing, slipping on the cobblestones, falling, Man riding the bay right over the top of them, and the soldiers opened fire.

Man's dash down the alley like that day on the parade ground, Man all over the horse, hanging from its side, under its neck, bouncing from flank to flank, a fish in a barrel, wheeling, dodging, darting, never letting them draw a bead on him.

Coming up from one side, he shot a soldier out of a window; swinging out from the other, he missed another with his knife;

then the horse jerked sideways, the hide all along one side twitching. The bay had been hit. Man reined it in, hugging the wall next to the factory so on that side he was partially protected from the overhang, so they had to shoot straight down at him. Then he yanked the bay to a halt. Jesus! They were pushing a wagon piled high with hay across the mouth of the alley. Man reined about, starting back—*into* the muzzles of a dozen guns now blocking off the way he'd come. He was trapped. Honor began to cry. Man wheeled the horse in a circle. Then he clutched at his side above the hip. He'd been hit! Then suddenly he kicked the horse forward, and, crouching, gathering his feet under him on the bay's back, he rode straight at a soldier reloading on one of the fire-escape balconies; at the last second standing, balancing on the horse's back, he threw himself over the railing into the soldier's arms, hitting the soldier in the chest, pulling the man down over him so the soldier took the full fire power across his shoulders and down his spine, a bullet knocking Man back through a window into the tenement.

In a corner of the tenement—bed, bath, kitchen, all in one room—a young mother, a pretty, dark woman, Mrs. Zamacona, huddled in a corner holding three small children to her.

Mrs. Zamacona said the bullet had creased Man's skull upward diagonally from his left eye across his forehead, the blood streaming down his face.

Momentarily dazed, Man lay on the floor, she said, gathering himself, then shook his head, picked himself up out of the window glass, staggered to the door and started out, when he heard shouts and footsteps coming up the stairs. He ducked back into the room, locked the door and pushed a bed in front of it.

For a long time, Mrs. Zamacona said, they rattled and shook the doorknob, Man, a hand up, warning her to silence. Then it became a pounding and a voice outside said, "Down here, Charlie, down here," and the pounding stopped.

The strange thing, Mrs. Zamacona said, was when Man came toward them—terrible, she said, savage and terrible, in one hand a knife, in the other a bow, blood running down his eye and over his face and chest, yet she wasn't afraid, she said, neither she nor the children. He didn't smile or say anything. It was his eyes, she said, seeing and not seeing through them to something else, soft,

so the children stopped crying, Manuel gently reaching out to lay
a hand on top of her head, softly pushing her and the children
down till they all lay flat on the floor, out of the line of fire.

Outside was like being at the core of a whirlpool, everyone silent, watching, waiting to suck or be sucked under, the only movement when a young soldier ran across the alley to the protection
of a doorway. Honor was shaking. I put my arm around her.

"Come on out, mad dog," someone shouted, and they began to
yell "mad dog, mad dog," which was what the papers called him
now (same as the plains troopers earlier)—little matter they'd
murdered his oldest brother, murdered his middle brother, murdered his father and poisoned his mother, "vengeance is yours,
saith the Lord," and Manuel Choke Breath, the carver, became
"mad dog," the berserker and butcher.

"He won't come out?" Honor said. It was more prayer than
question.

"He won't," I said.

"There he is," a soldier half whispered, raising his gun.

Unthinking, I spun, reaching, slapping at the gun, but the soldier was too far off. Pugh! Like slapping at flies over a dung
mound.

Man came through the window, the quiver of arrows over one
shoulder, a string around his middle. He stepped out on the balcony, exposed, an arrow fitted to his bow, blood lacing his face,
his chest and stomach, and from the wound above his hip, running down his thigh.

For one stopped second the bold daring of it froze the alley.

He stood hacked out against the sky, contemptuous, arrogant,
and as fair a target as a man could ask, yet not without his armor:
above his left elbow an armlet of the hoof and skin of a white-
tailed deer, making him swift to run, a spear of grass in the string
about his middle making him as slender and as hard to hit as a
spear of grass, in the browband, behind his head, a bat wing, for
the bat flies at night and is hard to see or catch, and though you
may throw things at him, you will not hit him, the bat sometimes
even flying down, pursuing after what has been thrown at him;
the thing you shoot at not really there, the real person high up
above—the bat.

Man began to make signs. "Come on, kill me! I am a chief; it will be a good thing for you if you kill me; if you do this, you can have many dances, for you have killed a chief," and he pointed to the sun; *I am like the sun.* A cry of defiance, ancient as the plains.

Honor gasped, "He's—" and stopped.

I didn't know, either, *how* he was. I did know *what* he was: you could see it plain the way he'd stripped naked the way they go into battle—he'd decided to die, a fighting brave, red under the yellow sun in the blue day with his own weapons.

32

The Dancer

In that moment they must have hated Manuel beyond telling, his contempt so complete a denial that their waiting became a savoring. Then, from the fire escape opposite him, a shot—out of the silence like a clap from the Thunder People—ricocheting off the metal steps above Man's head. It broke the spell. Then a fusillade. Furious. Wild. Man, enshrouded in lead—Lordy!—lifting his bow, as though on a casual hunt, to draw and release. A soldier, the one who'd first fired, howled, dropping his rifle into the alley, wrapping both arms around his chest as though he were cold, slumping to one knee, that arrow going clean through him to the wall behind, a good five feet.

For a moment it seemed to unnerve them. Most, I guessed, never having seen a man taken by the shaft. They stopped firing. But how fear a lone savage with a bow and arrow! Again they erupted.

Deliberately, calmly, as though shooting at a sprig of leaves someone had set up for him, Man drew and released, drew and released.

(It wasn't the rapidity of shot so much as the range of the new repeating rifle that frightened the Indian.)

(But here, within the narrowness of the alley, they saw precisely how deadly a campaigner the plains bowman could be.)

A shot slammed up from below against the grid where Man stood, Man whirling, snap-shooting, missing the boy in the door-

way, Man continuing in what looked like the same motion, transfix-
ing the soldier on the roof, standing, drawing a careful bead, the
soldier twisting, falling, the arrow in his groin, a look of great specu-
lation and wonder in his face, hitting belly down on the cobblestones, driving the arrow out through his rectum.

This time it unnerved them to the man, because this time the
fear was laying out there in the alley. And abruptly it got still.
Man with a full-drawn bow and looking. A second soldier on the
roof eased over the edge. To see after his fallen comrade, I think.
Man swung his bow up and the man ducked back.

Lord, Lord! A bare-assed savage with a gut string and a pine
bow holding off half a company of the Third Army! Which, of
course, was impossible. Then I heard a rumbling and saw it. The
hay wagon! Soldiers pushing it down the alley, using it as a mova-
ble shield, firing and ducking, ducking and firing. Man seemed to
study it; then, as it got closer, he stepped back through the
window.

Unsure now, the soldiers also stopped pushing the wagon. And
yet I knew—we all knew he'd step back out through that window.

Inside the tenement, they were back at the door, rattling and
pounding and shouting to open up, Man ignoring them, said Mrs.
Zamacona, still down on the floor with her children.

The first thing he did, she said, he ripped away a strip of cur-
tain and wrapped it around the head of an arrow; then he went
through the house till he found a bottle of whiskey, with which
he soaked the clothbound arrowhead. From the wood box he
shaved off a long splinter, lighted it in the stove and, sticking the
unlighted end between his teeth, stepped back out through the
window.

The soldiers began to push the wagon toward him.

It wasn't hard to tell what was coming. I couldn't stop it. I
didn't want to see it.

Honor was shaking all over.

"Come on, girl," I said standing, "I've got to git you looked
after."

"What's he doing, Clay?"

"Let's git; come on."

"What, Clay?"

The firing was furious like before but spaced, careful, more deadly.

Man glanced down once at the wagon, took the lighted sliver from between his teeth, lit the clothbound, whiskey-soaked arrowhead and shot the torch into the hay. WHOOSH! the wagon went up, soldiers scurrying from under and around her like roaches.

When Man stepped back into the room, Mrs. Zamacona said, the soldiers were just starting to break through the door. Man stood, she said, just inside the window, watching them, and when the first arm reached through the first opening, Man put an arrow through the wrist, nailing the man to the door, "the screaming awful," Mrs. Zamacona said, so it was hard now for the others to work around the pinned man. And still, Mrs. Zamacona said, Man waited and watched. He waited until the door was almost shattered through, soldiers poking their rifles around their moaning comrade, firing wildly into the room; then, when the smoke began to fill the room, Man stepped back out on the fire-escape balcony.

The wagon had smashed and overturned, spewing burning hay all over the alley, both the factory and tenement on fire, flame and smoke boiling up from below in great, gummy gray clouds— the cover for which Man had been waiting, and he started up the fire escape for the roof.

You couldn't see him at all now, the soldiers pouring volley after volley up into the smoke where they thought he should be, when someone shouted, "Look, look," and Man's shoulders and back loomed up through the smoke at the top of the ladder, ghostly, heaving headless up onto the roof.

Of the four soldiers waiting for him on the roof, two were dead from the blind volleys from below, the third, a mossback old campaigner, sat up cursing, holding his side, wounded in the same way the others had been killed, the fourth, the old mossback said, "buck yellow an' shakin', chokin' an' coughin' in the smoke so he didn't see the fuckin' Indian till too late. The Indian with the drop on the bastard an' all the time in the world to spill him. . . ."

The fourth soldier, according to the old mossback, had gone stone stiff before Man, who'd "missed the sonofabitch by a good yard," said the old mossback, who couldn't seem to decide who he hated more, "the prick-yellow soldier" or the "fuckin' Indian." It was Man's last arrow. The soldier dropping his gun, running for the roof exit, Man after him, when the door burst open, soldiers pouring onto the roof. Man ran back to the fire escape, it, too, now crawling with soldiers. Seeing him, the firing from below became a roar. The alley now an inferno. Man threw his bow down the fire escape on the soldiers. It was his last act of defiance.

The first soldiers on the roof were hesitant, wary, "shittin' their drawers," the wounded old mossback said, "fannin' out, keepin' low along the edges in the smoke, jump-firin' at gusts and ghosts. Like crows in a cornfield. Then they saw him, shucked off from the firin'; below, to the center of the roof, where the smoke had thinned out—naked as a jay-sparrow. An' unarmed." The old man snorted. "An' suddenly they're all lions."

Unhurried now, curious, relishing the moment, they commenced to close in. You could see, the old mossback said, they were going to kill him, but first, like corralling a wild hog, they wanted to get a look at him close up. Man backing away, looking over his shoulder. Across the building tops. At the factory roof across the street. Empty . . . -looking. Which was part of it too.

Man talking to himself the whole while, the old mossback said. Singing his death song, I thought.

Man backing and backing. Them tightening and drawing in. Calling. "Look smart." Daring him. Pushing and pushing. "Careful." Man circling. Giving way and giving. Herding him. Eyes wide, black wide. "Over there." Looking. "Over here." Again looking. "This way." Across to the empty roof. "Watch it." Watch the wild hog wheel. "Watch." Watch him circle and double back. See him looking and reckoning. "Soo-eee." Pull the drawstrings. Draw and cinch. "Stay close." No, no. Impossible. "Soo-soo." Tighter and tight. Wheeling and twisting. "There now, there." Still now, rooted now. Stark and quivering. A caught thing. Penned. "Shoo shoo sooow." And he lined up with it. They halted. "Run . . . HAWG!" And he bought it. Sprinting, Man sprinting. Catching the roof edge with his toes. Digging. Lifting. Jumping. Naked jumping. Jumping the way as a boy he played the arrow game. Broadjumping. Reaching for the factory roof and reaching. Hanging. Naked. Between the two buildings. Over the street. Over the caldron below.

Into the gun muzzles!

From behind the ledge fronting the factory rooftop toward which he'd jumped, a dozen riflemen. Hidden. Waiting. For this jump waiting. Rising up. Gleeful. Upjumping like crows. Into the dozen waiting muzzles. To stop the escaper. The murderer must not be murdered—executed. So he must escape—into the guns. He'd found it then—the Wasichu medicine. The roofroar. From the alley below. From the tenement behind. From the muzzles before. The Wasichu power. This the *find-out*. Found. This! The danceroar. Skykicking. Windclapping. Cloudjigging. Lead-dancing . . . the reel, tap, buck-an'-wing. Arms, legs, eyes, ears, broadjump toes, fingers, elbows flying. Off him pieces flying. Sun-swimming. Fire-drowning. Burning. Swimming man burning. Jerk and jiggle. Jounce the strings. Lead string, wampum strings. Now and forever. Arms flapping. Silly bird to fly without a beak or claws or wings.

Down-falling now. Gnarled dropping. Torn and mangled plunging. Plummeting. Through the white smoke, through the gray smoke and black into the yellow and orange flame and flame.

Head against the fence, Honor cried softly, weakly. End to end the alley burned. Firebells clanging all about us. The only way out, back through the tenement. I lifted her, the potato sack beginning to blood-crust against her shoulder, and turned to go, Sonofabitch and Gray Owl side by side behind us, the red flickering dancing across their faces, faces squinched up against the heat, Sonofabitch's blue marble eye wide, wide and smoking and spitting sparks, ablaze, like the Thunder God, glaring down into the roaring pyre.

"He's gone," I shouted over the fire.

Impassive, they stared.

"It's done," I yelled.

They didn't hear.

"Come on," I yelled, "let's git."

From somewhere in the factory came explosions.

"It's all goin'," I shouted.

From the fire hoses silver lizards arched out over the smoke and flame.

To get out we had to go back down through the basement. Already the house was starting to burn. But at the top of the stairs, the girl wriggled out of my arms.

"What're you doin'?"

She held out her wrist. "Look," she shouted.

"What?"

"It's not there."

"Let's git outa here."

"Manuel's bracelet; it's not on my wrist."

She started back.

I grabbed her. "You can't go back! It's gone. It's lost."

"No . . ." She tried to pull away. She began to cry.

I held her. "It's too late! It's too late."

She looked back, the tears glistening bloody from the fire down either side of her face like wounds.

I took one last look: The sun had set, so it was dark now, smoke and cinders blacking out everything but the tip of the Capitol dome east, all the sky to the west aflame.

Epilogue

Like a rich stand of wheat, the three columns positioned along
the eastern ridge: one from Fort Lyon, in southeastern Colorado,
under Braddock; another from Fort Bascom, in New Mexico,
under Harney; the third and main column, the 7th Cavalry, from
Camp Supply, under General George Custer, with eleven companies, five companies of infantry, a train of 450 wagons and the
19th Volunteers.

Strung out across from them along the opposite ridge, the Four
Tribes, led by Gray Owl.

Entering the camp, the first thing I'd seen was Manuel's totem.
Like I'd reckoned—like, I'm sure, Manuel had reckoned, a powerful part of the tribe's medicine now, one of the sacred holies, the
length of it, from the great buff holding up the world to the holy
White Cow Buffalo Woman, Light Hands, at the crown, decorated with sacred sage and sprinkled with the sanctified red
powder; Gray Owl, tall and stately, coughing Little Rabbit's
cough, the red roses in his cheeks, greeting my arrival with a
warmth I'd never known in him, heaping gifts and delicacies on
me out of all season or understanding, *until* that night in the
Council Lodge when, with everyone sitting around passing the
pipe, Gray Owl began to talk of Wasichuland.

He told about riding Eater-of-Fire (the train), about the water
that flowed straight up (fountains), about the fancy carriages and
rosy lamps, the horse-drawn streetcars and fire engines, about the

zoo with its striped ponies (zebras), and humped-backed deer (camels) and the long-necks (giraffes) and the two-tails (elephants), then about the crowds of Wasichus, more than the fires in Tunkashila's sky during deepest night—that's when I began to notice, first a brave then two elders slipping out. They didn't believe Gray Owl! and rather than call such a one liar or ridicule him, they'd quietly left . . . that's when I began to understand Gray Owl's welcome—relief at my arrival. Gray Owl had been through this before, but now with me to face them down, to back him up, they had to believe. *I was his proof!* And I began to snug in his harness, nodding vigorously at all he said, seeding the ground behind him all the way to the fence posts. More Wasichus, I said, than the drops of rain, than the stones of hail or flakes of snow, which only seemed to make it worse—the white man had bewitched Gray Owl—and Gray Owl stopped.

The commissioner had warned us against just this when we returned. He'd told us of Big White, Shahaka, a Mandan, the only one in his tribe with courage enough to live with the whites and who, coming home after three years to tell of the white man's wonders, was laughed at, ridiculed and all but jeered out of the tribe, the Mandans unable to imagine a greater or more numerous people than themselves. Like now with Gray Owl, they said the white man had put a spell on Shahaka and made a great liar out of him. It had happened to many, many, the commissioner said. It's what the commissioner had been trying to tell Sonofabitch about the blue, Wasichu eye. The Assiniboin Wi-jun-jon's lies about the whites were considered to be such bad medicine among his people, the commissioner said, that they blew out Wi-jun-jon's brains with a specially made bullet—the filed-down handle of an old iron pot, strong medicine for a strong liar. But what made it even worse for Gray Owl was that not only was he a great warrior, hunter and leader but a man of medicine, of the sacred power. For a medicine man to lie was a sin, great, great, against Wakan Tanka personally. Such a perpetration could destroy a tribe. (Could certainly destroy Gray Owl.) It was why up to now they'd been afraid to accuse Gray Owl.

For a week and a half Gray Owl was silent; then, one night, Cut Arm, a cousin of Cut Hand, on whose photograph Sonofabitch had made water back at the Indian Bureau, an old enemy, asked Gray Owl to tell more about the white man, in an attempt to make Gray Owl look foolish and perhaps devour himself, and, angered because he knew what Cut Arm was doing, Gray Owl went whole hog:

Gray Owl told of Mr. Barnum's *American Museum*, of the Great Highs (giants) and the Too Smalls (dwarfs), of the educated dogs and trained fleas, the Many Hands (jugglers), the Lost Voices (ventriloquists), the All Whites (albinos) and mechanical figures, and Lord, Lord, the more they showed their disbelief, the wilder Gray Owl's tales; he told of canoes bigger than this whole camp, with sails higher than the Standing People and about lodges that reached up and up all the way to the clouds—so many were the Wasichus they must live on top of one another—more guns than limbs on the trees of the great forest and bullets beyond counting, winding up with the full story of Sonofabitch's new blue eye that could look all ways opposite the other eye, up and down and sideways and even inside Sonofabitch's head so all the white showed.

For a moment after Gray Owl's recital there was only his coughing and the sound of the loose hides flapping outside. I kept silent. I couldn't help him, only make it worse. If they decided Gray Owl had become an evil man of medicine, whatever happened to him would happen to me. Gray Owl's friends squirmed uneasily. Gray Owl was surely possessed. Only Cut Arm, smug, looked about with contempt. Then, suddenly, Gray Owl threw back his head and laughed and laughed, slapping his thighs, pointing at Cut Arm, who, Gray Owl said through great bursts of coughing and laughter, had been taken in by all his forked stories and tall tales, and Gray Owl held up the forefinger he'd cut off for Little Rabbit for all to see—to show his sacrifice, his sincerity and truthfulness—and abruptly all were roaring at this fine joke played on Cut Arm, who stalked angrily out of the Council.

During it all, Gray Owl had glanced at me only once, near the end, the corners of his mouth pulled up with laughing, but sadly.

For all Cut Arm's goading of Gray Owl, it was a thing, I think, the Owl had to do. He'd had to tell them everything, whether they accepted it or not, whether they hung him from one of the Standing People or roasted him bare on a sapstick spit, because Braddock and Harney were out there on the east ridge waiting for

Custer to bring up and Gray Owl was the only one to tell them and they had to have that because the cost was going to be too high.

Still, if Gray Owl hadn't convinced them, he'd given them long thoughts on a short time, their laughing at Cut Arm loud but uncertain and as much their out as ours.

Every day of the two weeks we spent in Gray Owl's lodge the young geologist, Vale, had been at me to get moving, that boy, 'spite all his schooling or whatever I might say, unable to comprehend anything about Indian protocol: We were guests. We did homage through our presence, rendered honor in our gifts, and so acknowledged our indebtedness. Anything less was trifling with your hairline. Gray Owl in all that time never once mentioning Manuel nor the gold, though he knew. He'd seen our wagons and equipment and the men hanging around outside the camp. But whether it was because it was too painful to speak of or he needed me to back him up or was just too busy making ready for what was ahead, I couldn't say, his silence a tacit consent, and I sure wasn't about to push it. For the rest, the McMurtys were gone: Mrs. McMurty and Tom dead, the girl cast out mad, and the boy God knows. All around us preparations for Custer, praying and purifying, Gray Owl coughing Little Rabbit's cough more and more, the red roses brighter every day, but in full command. Gray Owl had had the vision, and Gray Owl made the medicine, stringing the braves out in long lines before the open crates, so, as they filed by, they picked up first a Spencer Seven Shot, a bandolier of shells, and lastly the King James version of the Bible.

Enough gold, I reckon you can get just about anything, weapons easiest of all the way this old earth turns. Oh, there was an investigation in Washington, all right, but not about where did all them Indians get all them new repeating rifles our own troops didn't even have, but where did the Salvation Army get all the money to supply all them plains nations with Bibles. A desecration of the good book, Congress said, giving it to all them heathens.

Course it didn't matter no one could read. Gray Owl had been convinced by Sonofabitch through Little Rabbit and shown by

Manuel Choke Breath, and that's how every last man jack of them went into battle against Custer, a Spencer Seven Shot in one hand, the King James version in the other. The Wasichu medicine.

When reports started filtering in of Custer's 7th just north of Antelope Hills, I'd gotten out—yes siree, ol' Clay's always got an out—by not more than a couple hours.

As the geologist, Vale, kept pointing out, to have been caught in the camp of the enemy with all that mining equipment, four wagons of it, would have scuttled the whole enterprise.

I reined up on the hill road overlooking the battleground and got down from the lead wagon. The others started to follow, but the geologist wouldn't let them. And he was right. Before this day was done—to be on the safe side—we'd need twenty miles between us and whoever won—or lost: Gray Owl not above changing his mind; Custer, out of spite, blistering us and calling it treason.

I climbed a rise and took out my binoculars, Vale worrying and worrying at me till I flared and said they could go on without me, I'd catch up later. But the geologist was afraid and sorer than I'd ever seen him, red-faced, swearing and calling me squawman. Later I saw him talking to one of the lumpers, who reminded me of Pock Face and who was ever after never more than a length off my hip, elbow crooked over his handgun, so it must have showed. Vale was afraid I'd pull out and join up with Gray Owl. It was where I belonged. For a fact. The guilt riding my insides like sand.

I glassed the field with the binoculars.

Lord, Lord!

A thousand men could die out there this day.

Mounted, head thrown back praying, Gray Owl sat out in front of them, coughing, arms outstretched forming a cross. In one hand Manuel's rifle, in the other Sonofabitch's Bible, around his neck Sam the President's medal. He had it all.

For a long while Gray Owl coughed and prayed; then, finished, he looked across the valley at Custer's 7th, back at his warriors, up along the ridge behind him at his wife and sons; then, slowly, Gray Owl brought the Spencer Seven Shot and the Bible together in front of him—the Wasichu power!—and gave a screech. The tip of Manuel's totem dipped, pointing into the valley, and down they came at one another, guidons flapping, wagons clanking metal on metal, horses snorting and screaming, men YIPping and KI-YIing, when, over it all, like the rat-a-tat of a flicker bird on bone bark, the goddamnedest shooting, and I swung my glass into the valley, where from out behind a stand of scrub they'd rolled this gun, round as a snubbing post, four feet maybe in length, with five or six barrels sticking out in front, a soldier cranking her, another feeding her a scarf of shells, that thing belching bullets like a one-man battalion—a Gatling Gun, I found out later they called it—so suddenly all Gray Owl's Seven Shot Spencers were as yesterday as the spear, and I thought of Manuel's taunt to his father: "You would put feathers on a dog!" Manuel right, that gun spouting lead like someone had pulled the bull hatch on a sluice lock, Gray Owl charging it, that gun flicker-birding across his chest neat as a whipcat stitch, Gray Owl jerked backwards as if he'd run out the length of his halter, slammed backwards, somersetting over his horse's rump—the first to fall—dead, the way he slithered along the ground, soggy and flattening out like a wet pelt.

I closed in on him with the glass. Gray Owl lay on his back, the Spencer Seven Shot still in one hand, on his chest the Bible, a hole in one corner, blood leaking out from under and around the hole down his chest, Sam the President's medal over his eyes.

So it was over before it began (when the leader, the vision man, dies, their medicine dies and they quit), Indians milling, trying to get away, riding back up the hill, crashing into one another, troopers whooping and chasing them, sabers flashing in the sun, that flicker bird scything Indians like wheat. The Blade's dream of a rout!

"Enough?" Vale called after a while, so I thought of going up in the wagon after him, whomping him, dwelling on going up in the wagon after him, whomping him—like a child—so as not to have to dwell on down there in the valley, going back to the wagon, the geologist scooting quick across the seat.

Custer was all over the field now, yellow curls bouncing behind as he rode, waving his arms and firing his ruddle-handled revolver.

At the top of the ridge, what was left had formed a scrimmage line behind a skein of rock so the women and children could get away. A slaughter.

"Wasting time," Vale said after a while, so I had to stop and think how I was wasting time and found I was weeping. I wiped my face and handed up the binoculars without looking at him.

Standing, staring out one last time into the blear of the valley, I thought, *all took* by the white man's—what-all I couldn't even name. Which is what you always got to do—blame!—yourself or them or somebody. Like that fella I'd killed outside that notch house in Cotton who'd carved out White Antelope's privates for a tobacco pouch because some savage had maybe carved out his sister's husband's whose brother was maybe right now out looking to perform the same surgery on me. Everyone sucked into it: Honor with the top of her shoulder blown off, Mr. McCauley with Manuel's spoon handle in him, Stanley Meeker dead, Mrs. Zamacona down on the tenement floor with her kids. It was the condition. Everyone was taking—us, them, the Plains People, the conquistadores, the Mexicans and Aztecs and Lord knows, back and back finally to the rocks and trees who'd maybe again wind up with it all, because, like in the sun dance, all a person really owns on this ol' earth is himself, man forever a thief.

I pulled back, wincing, the reins slapping down over my right shoulder. I looked up. The geologist Vale had thrown the reins down on me, not in anger, fear, a white spot on either cheek, so I thought of Manuel snatching the whip out of the streetcar conductor's hand.

I lifted the reins off my shoulder, half glancing into the valley. All gone, I thought, Gray Owl, Manuel, the McMurtys, Little Rabbit, all except Sonofabitch. *All except me.*

The big *find-out* . . . over.

And what had they found out?

There was no one left to say.

Or maybe Sonofabitch back there with his Nigra-Cheyenne, maybe Sonofabitch had seen and found out something with his new, blue eye. I thought then of Buff. Lord help an old fool.

I climbed up in the lead wagon with the geologist Vale. "Which way?" Vale asked looking down at a map spread across his knees. In front of us the road forked north, northeast.

Down in the valley Custer was regrouping for a second attack. He wanted them all. Twenty miles at least today, I thought, between us and Custer.

Vale ran his hand over the map.

The barricade thrown up along the top of the ridge for the women and children to escape behind was beginning to crumble.

"Well?" Vale said.

He was dead right, the senator. Along with their land, the antelope, the beaver and buffalo, in two, three years it would all be gone. We'd have taken it all from them.

Vale held out the map to me.

The cries of the women and children echoed across the gorge. "Ee-eee-yi, ee-eee-yi . . ." so I thought, one time, one time! just once would the Indian give what he got, measure for measure? Just once? When, oh, Lord!

I jabbed at the map. "Here, we'll go here," I said.

"Why, that's over—" Vale calculated under his breath. "A third longer."

And twice as hard, I thought, Vale's eyes wide and wild on me, so I had to explain how this was one rope you didn't shake out, that through the mountains, making it as gnarled and knotted as a storm of snakes to follow, that was our one hope—if Custer decided he wanted us—of keeping him off us. We'd go all the way to the Little Big Horn.

The sounds from the valley floated up tinny and muffled, Lord, like children at a picnic.

A massacre.

Vale dropped the reins across my knees. "The senator's an impatient man," he said.

Yes, I thought, they were all impatient men, the senator, the geologist Vale, Gray Owl down there, the Blade, even Little Rabbit, and me, Face on Water.

I gathered up the lines. No one wanted to wait. But the gold in Gray Owl's diggings, now there was something would wait.

Heat lightning stuttered across the horizon. I clucked to the horses. The Thunder Persons were calling.